THE BROTH

SULLY

alternate edition

PENELOPE BLACK

SULLY ALTERNATE EDITION

THE BROTHERHOOD
BOOK 3

PENELOPE BLACK

for Rachel.
I'll never forget your kindness and encouragement.

PLAYLIST

"Maps" by Yeah Yeah Yeahs
"Train in Vain" by The Clash
"MakeDamnSure" by Taking Back Sunday
"The Scientist" by Emily James
"Don't Cry For Me" by Cobi
"Rebellion (Lies)" by Arcade Fire
"Hateful" by The Clash
"Punk Rock Princess" by Something Corporate
"River" by Bishop Briggs
"Guys My Age" by Hey Violet
"Gooey" by The Glass Animals
"Desire - Slowed" by Hucci
"I Should Live in Salt" by Ásgeir
"Transantlanticism" by Death Cab for Cutie
"Y Control" by Yeah Yeah Yeahs
"There Is A Light That Never Goes Out" by The Smiths
"Ready to Start" by Arcade Fire
"Do You Realize?" by The Flaming lips

"We Are Free" by The Mowgli's
"Cosmic Love" by Florence + The Machine

1

SULLY

"KISS ME, James, and tell me you love me."

The sun shines down on us as we stroll through Central Park. The trees form a sort of tunnel overhead, providing shade from the unforgiving summer sun.

I stop walking and tug on our interlaced fingers to bring her closer. The teasing smirk on her face taunts me, and like the enchantress she is, she lures me in with a quirk of her lips.

I can't deny her—I don't *want* to.

I unlace our fingers and curve an arm around her lower back. A nearby bird whistles a light melody, and a soft breeze carries the sweet scent of nearby peonies. I slide my other hand along the curve of her neck and into her hair at her nape.

She winds her arms around me and tugs me closer. She's addictive, my princess, and the shriveled-up organ that should be a heart throbs at her affection.

It's only ever beat for her. And after her betrayal and absence, it's all but ceased to exist.

"You know I love you, princess," I say against her perfect,

plump lips. Her bottom lip is just the slightest bit bigger than her top lip, and I can't resist pulling it into my mouth with my teeth.

Alaina pulls away to press her promise against my lips. "And I love you. Always."

Adrenaline flies through my veins at those simple words delivered with ease from those perfect lips. I used to think love was for fools, and then she crashed into my life, and everything I thought was bullshit was true.

Unfortunately, she left just as spectacularly, and I came full circle. I was the fool then.

Urgency pounds at my temple, demanding I make it so she can never leave me again. I won't survive a second time.

"This could be our life, you know. Walking through Central Park, holding hands, and bringing home our favorite pizza."

"And don't forget sneaking off behind that patch of bushes over there, bro."

I press my hand into Alaina's lower back on instinct. Once I realize it's just my brother, I relax. She twists her head around, and Wolf strolls toward her. When he's close enough, he snags an arm out and curls it around her neck, bringing her face to his for a kiss that's just a little too lewd for midday in the park.

"Where the hell did you come from, Wolf?"

He separates from our girl to lift an eyebrow at me and smirk. "I've always been here."

"Me too," Rush says from behind me.

My chest feels tight, and my gaze flies around us in alarm, kick-starting my adrenaline. *Why didn't I know they were with us?* I could've sworn it was just Lainey and me.

"Fuck, I need some sleep or something. I'm losin' it." I run a hand down my face as Rush leans in to greet Alaina with a kiss.

She turns to look at me, familiar mischief twinkling in her eyes.

"Wouldn't that be nice? All of us together, all the time."

I stare at my girl, the way her Ramones tank top flutters in the hot breeze. When I stare into her soulful eyes, I forget all the awful shit in my life. All the bad shit that still waits for me. I know deep in my gut that she's the only good thing in my life.

"Aye. I think that'd be nice, Lainey." I brush my lips along her jaw with each word.

Her fingers curl into my shirt, and she releases this little noise of contentment.

"Then why do you torture me, James? Why do you always leave me?"

I pull my head back, brows furrowed. Her smile fades with the sunshine. Midday rapidly turns to dusk, and sorrow replaces her playfulness.

"C'mon, Sully."

I whip my head around to look at my brothers. My chest squeezes again, and my thoughts stutter. "When did you get over there?" I ask Rush.

My brother just stares at me, his gray eyes darkening until they're pitch-black. When he doesn't answer me, I refocus on Alaina.

"Princess? What do you mean?"

Her beautiful whiskey-colored eyes fill with tears as she takes a step away from me, her fingers trailing down my arm.

"Come back to me, James." She takes another step back, and her fingertips just barely touch my own.

I take a step toward her, confusion furrowing my brow. I reach out for her, but there's an invisible force holding me back.

"Alaina! Wait. Come back. I'm right here."

I push against the invisible wall, panic tightening every muscle in my body and fear wrapping around my heart. She's walking away from me—no, that's not right. It looks like someone is dragging her! There, someone in a dark hoodie and dark jeans has her upper arms in a tight grip, and he's pulling her

3

away. His features are unclear, almost like he's somehow being blurred.

Alaina's eyes widen with fear, and she screams my name. Rage erupts in my gut, burning hot and fast.

"Get your fucking hands off her, motherfucker, or it'll be the last thing you ever do!" I pound my fists against the wall, putting every ounce of strength I have behind each swing.

And still. It's not enough.

I watch as someone drags the only girl I ever loved—fuck it, the girl I *still* love—away while some fucked-up invisible barrier traps me in some kind of purgatory hell.

"Alaina! I'm coming for you!" The words are ripped from my throat, born out of desperation and sealed with determination. I'm not sure how the fuck I'm going to get out of here, but I will.

Something jerks my shoulder, hard and to the right. I spin around, expecting to see the blurred-out guy, but there's no one there. The same thing happens on my other side, and I whirl to the left. No one.

I lift my hands to drag them through my hair, but something's holding them against my side, squeezing me tight. I try to thrash my way out of this hold, but it's strong. My breath stutters in my chest as the pressure increases until my vision dims.

And then I don't feel or see anything. I'm trapped in an endless black, alone.

I'm always alone.

Abandoned by those who claim to love me.

I succumb to the darkness, letting it roll over me.

"THE FUCK'S THIS?"

"Jack?" I hear my voice, but it doesn't quite sound like me.

Maybe if I were underwater. I can't shake the feeling of trepidation, and I can't quite remember where I am.

With effort, I pry my eyelids open, each of them weighing heavy, and darkness greets me. I raise my arm—or at least, I try to, but something holds it down.

"Settle now, boyo," Jack says before I feel two pats to my right shoulder.

"Alaina." Her name leaves me on a rasp, and fear sends my pulse flying. "Fuck. I need—I need to go. She's unprotected." I grunt and try to sit up, pain searing my left shoulder and chest. Black spots dot my already dark vision, and I break out in a sweat.

"Aye. We'll send someone to fetch our songbird," Jack says as he catches me by my less-painful shoulder.

I pant through the pain. "No. I don't trust anyone. Call Rush."

"Rush and Wolf are a little busy, man. I'll go get your girl."

I turn to look at Matteo, and with every single ounce of strength I can muster, I reach up and curl my fingers around his shirt. "If a single hair on her head is broken, I'm going to dismember you personally." The words come out through clenched teeth.

"You hear that, O'Malley? A knife in his shoulder, and he still manages to threaten me," Matteo says with a chuckle.

"Aye. He'll be alright. You go fetch us our girl, Rossi."

Matteo glances at my clenched fist with a raised brow before he looks behind me to where I'm assuming Jack stands. Jack pats my shoulder twice, and I reluctantly uncurl my fingers and meet Matteo's gaze.

"Bring my girl back, yeah?"

My jovial associate I've come to think of as a friend—or friendly—is uncharacteristically serious when he holds my gaze. "I'll get her. You have my word."

"She's at Blue Lotus Diner." I exhale and let my weight fall back to the table I'm lying on and stare at the ceiling. Out of the corner of my eye, I see Matteo turn and walk away.

"You just relax, boyo. We'll get our girl, and you'll be patched up good as new. Doc's already on his way."

"Call my brothers. And, Jack, don't trust anyone," I say through gritted teeth. "And what the fuck happened?"

"We were hoping you'd be able to tell us that, boyo."

Images of the dream I just had superimpose over my memories from this morning, and I'm having a hard time separating reality from fantasy.

Black spots crowd my vision, and I try to hold on to consciousness with both hands, at least until my brothers get here, but fate has another plan, and darkness swaddles me in its icy embrace.

I throw up a prayer to a god I don't believe in to keep my girl safe and surrender to the encroaching darkness.

2

ALAINA

I STEP over a fallen piece of drywall with wires sticking out and jump over a pipe, landing on the first stair. The building rumbles, and I feel the vibrations underneath my sneakers as I race up the staircase. Halfway up, I pause with my hand on the railing, knuckles white with tension.

The hair on the back of my neck stands up, and goosebumps zip down my spine. I turn my head first left, then right, looking for something. I'm not sure what it is, but something doesn't feel right.

What a fucking joke that thought is. *None* of this is *right*. But this feels different. Like the moment you're at the top of a roller-coaster, and it feels like the whole world holds its breath as you gaze across the horizon. Your heart slams against your ribs, and you feel invincible in your fear because you know you're going to be okay. It's a game—it's for fun.

This moment feels a little like that, except there's no reassurance that everything will be okay.

It doesn't feel like a harmless game, and I'm not having fun. I look around one more time, sweeping the area with my gaze and dismissing all the wreckage while looking for the cause of my unease. But this time, my fear doesn't feel invincible. It feels fragile.

Satisfied I don't see anything yet, I jog up the staircase, doing my best to dodge the fallen debris and missing stairs. It's when I get to the second-floor landing that it happens. That thing that's been pricking at my nerves the whole time.

There's a moment of quiet before a boom splits the air. The floor shakes, and the walls tremble, and I lose my footing. My back hits the wall with a thud, and I groan as something pierces my shoulder.

The noise reverberates, and I grit my teeth while I press on my ears to find relief. I stare, wide-eyed, as part of the exterior wall collapses in a heap of broken concrete and twisted metal. Wires flail and sparks flicker in the thick air. Dust and debris blanket the air, and I know my time has just decreased dramatically.

Panting, I wrench myself away from the wall, my shoulder screaming. I use my hands for leverage and push off the floor to stand up. Eyeing the sparks lighting up the space, I spin on my heel and jog toward the next staircase, keeping my left arm close to my torso.

I'm halfway up the staircase when it starts to sway. Dread fills my veins as I lift my head and look up toward the third-floor landing.

Or where the landing should be.

The staircase is moving. The stationary, built-in staircase is fucking swaying like a rope bridge on a playground.

My heartbeat thunders in my ears, loud enough that I almost miss the explosion.

I look over my shoulder and see a fire directly underneath the swaying wires and sparks.

"Oh fuck."

With fear hot on my heels, I race up the last staircase and jump over the foot of space that should connect the stairs and the landing.

I don't know how the hell I'm going to get Mom and me back down, but that's a problem for later. My shoulder pulses in time with my heartbeat, and I feel something warm slide down my arm. I don't look; instead, I focus on where I step. There are more broken pieces and parts here, and a quick glance up tells me why.

Sunshine and humid air pour in from the huge hole in the ceiling. I skirt around a busted pipe leaking brown liquid and jog toward the room we were just in. Two of the walls have now come down, so I see my mom before I'm inside the room.

"Mom!"

Heartache holds me immobile for a moment, eyes blinking rapidly, trying to clear the vision in front of me.

My adrenaline spikes, and I run toward her. I burst through the doorway, uncaring of where Liam is, my sole focus on my mother.

My mother, who's lying on the dirty floor with her blood-stained hands pressed to her gut.

Tears fill my eyes, swift and violent.

"Mom! Mom! It's me. I'm here. Oh, god, Mom." My words end on a choked sob as I land on my knees next to her. My hands flutter above her stomach for a moment before I whip off my tank top, panic and adrenaline overriding the pain from my injury. I ball it up and press it against her wound. "What should I —I don't know what to do. Tell me what to do!"

Mom tilts her head toward me as she lifts one of her bloody hands to my cheek. I grasp her wrist and hold her to me, leaning into her palm.

"My girl. My sweet girl. I never understood how someone so good, so pure came from me. But now, now I understand."

Mom's eyes glisten, a small smile on her face. "You were my salvation, Lainey. The only good thing I've ever done. And I didn't do right by you all these years, I know that. I did what I thought Aidan would want."

"Shh, Mom. It doesn't matter, okay? But we have to go now. We can't stay here."

She coughs, this horrible wet sound that stops my heart for a moment. Fear coats my skin, sticky and thick.

Her eyes shine as she looks at me, her smile growing wider. "No. You have to leave without me. I won't make it."

"Stop—just no. I'm not leaving without you."

As if fate herself is agreeing with my mother, the building trembles again.

Mom slips her hand from underneath mine and moves my tank top aside. Blood flows freely from her stomach, and nausea climbs up my throat. She holds my hand, her grip tight despite her blood-slicked fingers.

"Remember what I said in the car, okay? I love you."

I bite my lip to hold in the sob as I feel her lifeblood spilling from her and coating my knees.

"I love you too, Mom."

"My sweet girl. I need you to do one more thing, okay?"

I nod several times, my gaze darting between her eyes. "Anything."

"Find Auntie Sloan and tell her it's time."

"I-I don't understand."

"She'll know. Just tell her. It's important." Mom brings my hand to her mouth and places a single kiss on my palm before she curls my fingers over it.

Something inside me fractures then. How cruel is this world where the only affection I can remember my mom freely giving is while she's bleeding out in the middle of some rundown, crumbling building?

I squeeze my fingers into my palm hard enough to feel the bite of my nails into my skin.

I curl my torso over her, tears dripping from my eyes to land on her chest. Her chest that's rising and falling slowly—too slowly.

I nod frantically. "Of course. I'll find her right away."

Mom exhales. It's an awful sort of sound, wet and foreboding.

Cold sweat breaks out all over my body, and I feel paralyzed with fear. I can't get her down three flights and out into safety by myself. I need help.

I need someone to help me!

Her gaze darts over my shoulder, and a small smile curls up the corners of her lips.

My shoulders tense, but a quick glance over my shoulder settles my fear that Liam or anyone else is behind me.

"Oh, Aidan. I've missed you," she whispers, still staring over my shoulder. Goosebumps skitter across my spine and my sinuses burn.

"Mom? Mom, look at me."

She looks at me then, a single tear sliding down her temple and a smile on her face, her eyes sparkling. "Your father's here now. He's come to take me home, but it's not your time, Lainey. So, you need to leave."

"Wh-what?" I whip my head behind me. No one is there.

"It's not your time, Lainey. But it is mine, and I'm ready. Find Auntie Sloane." Another tear slides down her face, but her smile never leaves her lips.

The floor rumbles and a crash sounds in the hallway, stealing my attention from my mother for a single moment. When I look back, my mother's gaze is still upon me.

But there's no life shining from behind her hazel eyes.

There's no life inside her at all.

I stand up in one violent motion. My breaths come fast and heavy, my adrenaline all but tapped out. I scrape my fingers through my hair as I spin around, taking in my surroundings.

The fire from the first floor crawls along the entire side of the building, visible through the broken walls. Wreckage from the building lies all around me, intermingled with the broken dreams of a girl who just wanted to be loved.

They stole that from me. From her.

I tilt my head back, clenched fists, and muscles taut. And I scream.

I scream out the injustice of it all. I mourn over what was and what could have been. I lament my heartbreak over my official orphanhood.

I expel my grief into the summer sun until the only thing left is rage.

Muscles trembling and tears rolling down my cheeks, I make a promise to myself that I will have my vengeance.

And I will wreak havoc on everyone who had a hand in the destruction of the girl I used to be.

I was remade in the cabin in the woods. And I've been forged in this fire. And like a phoenix, I will rise anew.

3

WOLF

I CROSS the threshold with my brother, and heatwaves greet us. Not enough to make the space impassable, but enough that I know we need an alternate exit.

The fire to the right of us is manageable for now, but fires are unpredictable, and it could race across this space in two minutes flat.

We pause, shoulder to shoulder, both of us scanning the area for our girl. I look for her shock of red hair in the smoky air that's filling up the space. I glance at Rush just as he turns his head to look at me, both of us able to communicate without words what our next step is.

A perk of growing up and spending most of our waking hours together, I guess.

With the fire to the right of us, we head toward the staircase, wading through all the pieces of the broken building littering the floor. It's not until my foot is on the first stair that I notice it.

"Oh, fuck. Look." I tip my head toward the top of the staircase. The one that's not fully attached to the second-floor landing.

"Goddamnit," Rush grits through clenched teeth.

I blow out a breath and take the steps two at a time. My brother is hot on my heels, and we both jump over the broken and missing stairs. When we get to the stair third from the top, I look over my shoulder at him.

"It'll be just like that *Indiana Jones* movie."

"I'm more worried about how we're going to get down. Now jump, asshole. I don't like the way the floor is swaying," Rush says as he looks around.

I focus on the staircase—or lack thereof—in front of me and run the last three steps before leaping across the gap and landing on the floating platform.

I hear Rush land right behind me, but I keep my momentum going and jog up the second flight of stairs. We reach the third-floor landing when the building groans, and part of the roof crumbles, landing with a deafening thump.

We cover our heads out of instinct, and it takes me a moment to realize that my ears are ringing.

Yet, somehow through that, I still hear it.

A sound filled with such sorrow and grief that the world pauses to listen. And for a single moment, my heart seizes in fear. But when my soul aches, I know it's Red. She's the one pouring her grief into the atmosphere.

I don't know what it means, only that the alternative is much, much worse.

Rush and I run down the hallway, glancing through the half-collapsed walls, searching for our missing piece. We follow the sound of her anguish and find her in the middle of a room.

Head tipped back and fists clenched, hair wild and whipping around her in the breeze, blood coating her hands, clothes, and legs.

Raw and vulnerable, like she's shedding her exterior to let everyone see the tangled mess of pain she is on the inside.

She's never looked more beautiful.

I get to her a second before Rush does. I reach out to snag her hand, and she doesn't even startle. Red opens her eyes and looks right at me when I tug her into me.

As if someone pulled a plug on a drain, she deflates against my chest, all the fight leaving her in an instant. Rush steps in close behind her, effectively holding her up.

I slide my free hand into her hair and hold her against my chest as she curls her fingers around the fabric of my tee.

My gaze goes over Red's shoulder to the body next to her. Lana lies on the ground next to Red, eyes open and chest still. Fuck.

"As much as I want to stay like this forever, we gotta go, baby girl. We can't stay in here," I murmur into her hair, flicking my gaze around the open space.

I feel vulnerable as fuck, and I can't tell if it's because the whole goddamn building is threatening to collapse, or because the fuck that led my girl here is still lurking somewhere, or because my girl is fragile right now and my fierce desire to protect her is overwhelming on the best of days.

As if the universe is listening, the building rumbles again. Not big enough for me really to start losing my shit, but enough that I know we need to leave now. While we still can.

Urgency slams against my ribs, and I reluctantly push away from my girl. Her eyes are wide and bloodshot, but she's still here. She hasn't gone into shock yet.

"Okay, Wolf. But I'm not leaving her." Red nods to Lana.

I know I'm not some expert on parent stuff, but this whole situation leaves a bad taste in my mouth—rancid and sour. I don't know what the hell really happened between them, but we don't have time for a Q and A right now.

I nod a few times and step back. Red spins to hug Rush, and after a moment, he pulls away to take off his dark gray tee and pull it over Red's head. He whispers something to her as he helps her put her arms in the sleeves, but it's too low for me to hear. Bending at my knees, I scoop up Lana—my would-be step-mother and maybe even my one-day mother-in-law.

Her body is still warm, but her blood is starting to coagulate. It's cool against my tee, and I'm reminded again why I usually prefer black. Easier to conceal bloodstains.

I'm not sure if I'll ever get used to the feeling of carrying around a dead body—not that I make it too much of a habit. There's a reason people use the term dead weight. It's accurate as fuck. Stiff enough so she's hard to maneuver and heavy enough that I can't carry her easily.

"I think I saw a back staircase at the end of the hall," Rush says. I follow behind him and Red, adjusting my hold on Lana, so she's now in bridal-style.

For as familiar as I am with death and dead bodies, I'm not sure anything could've prepared me for the feeling of carrying the body of my girl's ma—estranged or not.

Old feelings of abandonment and rejection threaten to climb up my throat, but I shove those fuckers down where they belong. Red's an orphan now, but she doesn't need parents to have a family.

We're her fucking family now.

A tornado of emotions swirls around, and I can't pin down a single one. I'm trying to conjure feelings of sorrow for the woman in my arms, but from what I've seen and learned, I'm not sure she deserves it.

With my eyes on Red in front of me, I realize that's not my call to make. My throat tightens, and I realize with a jolt that I'm not used to this foreign feeling creeping up my throat. *Worry.*

I'm fucking terrified for Red.

Not only because some creepy fuck is after her, but she just watched her ma die not too long after she realized her da was dead. And I'm fucking worried about what that's going to do to my girl's emotional state.

Rush leads us to a stairwell at the back of the building—the side not already collapsed. This high up, the hot breeze swirls around us, sending heat from the fire and dust from the broken concrete into the air. The effect creates a mini-tornado, and I pray to whatever god is listening that it doesn't turn into an actual fire tornado. I saw that shit on a video once, and it was horrifying.

We make it to the second-floor landing before we encounter a problem.

"Fuck." Rush rakes his hand through his hair.

Three steps are blown out, leaving a substantial hole in the staircase. And unlike the situation with the other staircase, jumping down in the middle of this staircase is a lot harder than jumping above with a landing.

"Well, shit. Rush, hold Lana. I'll jump first."

"Don't be ridiculous," Rush says over his shoulder. "I'll go first. Then Alaina. Then you'll hand Lana to us, and then you'll jump."

"We're wasting time." Red looks between us, her fingers tapping an irregular rhythm against her thigh.

Rush looks from her to me as he climbs the few stairs until he's at the far edge of the landing. Red and I move to the side, so Rush has a clear path. He runs down the stairs and leaps over the hole. The toe of his sneaker misses the edge of the stair by a hair, and he pitches to the side, the metal railing catching him in the ribs and shoulder. His hands reach out and grip the railing, stopping him from falling.

"Jesus, Dec!" Red yells. Her hands shoot out into the air as if she's trying to help him.

"I'm fine. I'm fine." Rush waves a hand in the air as he takes huge gulps of air and spins around to face us. "C'mon, baby, your turn. I'll catch you, okay?"

Red backs up to the top of the stairs, biting her lip the whole way. Before she moves, she looks at me. "You sure you're okay with Mom?"

"I'm fine, Red. Now jump, and let Rush catch you, okay?"

She nods and backs up another few steps, so she's standing on the far edge of the landing like Rush did. The building groans and I hear what sounds like another wall collapsing, sending tremors along the wall I'm leaning on. Sweat beads on my brow and I bring up my shoulder to wipe it off.

Red runs down the stairs and leaps over the hole, landing perfectly in Rush's arms. He's braced against the railing, one foot on the stair below him for balance.

"Good girl." Rush kisses the top of her hair before he lets her go.

I bite my lip as I think about the logistics. The missing stairs are simply too big to toss Lana over—there's no guarantee gravity won't work against us and take her down to the floor below.

So, I do the only thing I can think of on limited time. I back up to the landing and readjust the hold I have on her, so she's over my shoulder. It's not the most dignified, but I don't have the option of being picky. And I think Red'll forgive me.

I run down the stairs and launch myself over the gap, catching Red's gasp and Rush's curse as I land on the stair below them. I can't slow my momentum enough, and I'm not trying to break my ankle, so I ride it out and run the rest of the way until the landing.

"What the fuck, Wolf? You could've gotten seriously hurt."

"Ah, but I didn't. Let's move. I've got a bad feeling about this." I continue down the stairs to the first floor landing, Red and Rush hot on my heels.

We make it to the first-floor without incident unless you count the shaking floors, walls crumbling, and growing fire an incident. Urgency pushes at me, and it only increases when I hear the ear-piercing sirens so close. They must be in front now.

I spy an emergency exit next to the stairwell, and I kick the door open before I stride outside. A gust of hot air greets me, and even if it feels like I'm breathing in hell, it's fresher than the smoky dust shit from inside. I adjust my hold on Lana, so I'm carrying her bridal-style again, doing my best to ignore the way her blood has soaked the left shoulder of my shirt.

I inhale as I walk away from the building, looking over my shoulder to make sure Red is behind me. Rush quickly takes the lead, and Red moves next to me, none of us speaking.

"Oh my god—Maddie!" Red stops, her mouth falling open.

"She was out front when we came. She's fine. C'mon, little bird, we can't stay here," Rush says as he places a hand on her lower back, nudging her to move. He leads us around the side of the building that's not on fire. Still, we all give the building a wide berth as we walk around it in the narrow space between this building and another abandoned factory.

I eye the factory to the right of us and then look to the warehouse we just left, apprehension skittering along my spine.

"Let's pick up the pace, yeah? I don't like how close these walls are." I raise my voice. The sirens are nearly deafening from right here.

Rush looks above, and I can tell from the tension in his shoulders that he just realized what I did. If the exterior wall comes down in pieces, the likelihood of either getting trapped or crushed is high.

"Aye. I can hear voices up ahead."

"How can you hear anything over the sirens?" Red clamps her hands over her ears as she keeps pace with Rush.

Finally, we clear the building and walk into the street. A dozen firefighters and cops greet us.

A pair of EMTs run toward us with twin looks of concern on their faces. "Jesus. We didn't think anyone was in there! Are you guys okay?"

Behind us, firefighters shout directions to one another, and someone shuts off the siren, but they leave the lights on. Blue and red lights flash across Red's face, but her gaze never strays from mine.

"Where's Sully?" she asks, turning her head from side to side. "And Maddie."

"Sir, I need to take her now," the female EMT says as she walks in front of my face, blocking my view of Red.

Anxiety gnaws on my nerves and crawls underneath my skin. I shift to the side to keep Red in my line of sight. I know my brother is around, and he'll protect her—I *know* that—but I can't stop the feeling from swelling inside my chest, making it hard to breathe.

The EMT moves so her face is right in front of mine again. "Sir, she needs medical attention."

"She's already gone," I murmur, craning my neck around the EMT's face, so Red stays in my line of sight. Some of the anxiety calms when I see Rush within an arm's reach, but I know I won't be able to take a breath until she's within *my* reach.

"Sir, please. I really need to examine her. There's . . . a lot of blood."

I refocus on the EMT, giving her my full attention. Whatever she sees on my face has her taking a half step backward. Can she feel the fear and worry and rage warring inside me? I haven't even begun to process the shit that just happened—and I haven't forgotten that Red went in guns blazing without us either.

She's going to give me premature grays, and that's saying something considering my line of work.

I let the EMT and her partner take Lana from my arms, never taking my eyes off of Red as she talks to another EMT. "Wait here, kid. I'll be back to check you out."

A cop walks into my line of sight, chest puffed out and eyes narrowed. "Wanna tell me what you were doing in that building, son?"

I glare at him. "I'm not your son." The words are low.

The cop steps closer to me, close enough for me to read the shiny badge. The scent of body odor and stale coffee wafts off him in waves as the sun beats down on us. "What did you just say to me?"

His pathetic attempt at intimidation only irritates me. I relax my stance, letting my hands drop to my side and ignoring the way my blood-soaked shirt sticks to my skin. I glare at him like the obstacle he is. "I said I'm not your fucking son. And I don't have time for this. Now, if you'll excuse me."

I move to step around him, already searching for Red and Rush, when I feel a hand clamp down on my bicep.

"Now, son—"

I whirl around in an instant, twisting the hand attached to my bicep and yanking his wrist toward the sky. He lets go of my arm, shrieking his displeasure.

I lean in, so our faces are inches apart. "Tell Captain McCarthy the Brotherhood thanks him for his service." I watch in perverse satisfaction as the color drains from his pudgy face. "And don't put your fucking hands on me again."

He nods, his head bobbing in small, frantic movements. "Of course, sir. My apologies. Please tell Mr. Fitzgerald I'm sorry for the inconvenience, and you can come back to the station to give your statement later."

"Sure thing, I'll tell my da all about it at the dinner table tonight." I raise a brow and smirk. I'd never run to Da about something as small as this. I can handle this minor inconvenience

25

just fine, but he doesn't know that. And if I really felt like fucking with him, I'd namedrop myself. Then he'd really shit his pants.

But I don't have time for that today. I let go of his wrist with a shove and storm around him. I'm so busy looking to the left in between the vehicles and people milling around for my girl that I don't see the female EMT until she steps right in front of me.

I expel a sigh, frustrated that there are so many fucking obstacles between my girl and me. I'm sure there's some fucking existential bullshit reason behind it, but I'm too keyed up to look into it.

The EMT raises her brow and presses her lips together in a thin line. "Your girl won't be impressed with your macho bullshit if you pass out and smash your pretty-boy face on the concrete. So let's just get you checked-out, 'kay?"

I didn't notice her Boston accent until now, but I'm oddly amused that she called me out like that. "Fine," I say with a shrug. "Lead the way."

4

ALAINA

I LACE my fingers with Rush's as an EMT ushers us to an ambulance. I let her look me over, but I decline her recommendation of going to the hospital. She reset my dislocated shoulder and cleaned up my scrapes and cuts, applying butterfly bandages to the worst of them.

She's an older woman, probably closer to my mom's age than mine. Her dark-brown hair is pulled back into a tight ponytail at the nape of her neck, and her gaze is as inquisitive as it is kind. I turn my head to look through the chaos for Wolf. And Sully.

Where's Sully?

My mind circles around and around, unable to land on one specific thing. I feel like I'm adrift at sea, trading one hell for another. I get moments of respite, but then another wave—another cataclysmic problem—crashes into me, and it's sink or swim.

I've never been a very good swimmer, but lucky for me, I'm a fast learner.

I hear the EMT ask me questions, but I can't bring myself to give her more than one-word answers. The events of the last hour play on repeat in my mind's eye. I imagine how differently it could've played out, and my mind wanders at the possibility.

She cleans some wounds along my face that I don't remember getting, and the sting pulls me from my musings.

"What's your name?"

She pauses for a moment before she answers, "Meg."

"Do you believe in the butterfly effect, Meg?" My words are low, but I don't worry about her not hearing me with her face so close to mine.

I see Rush tense out of the corner of my eye, and Meg pauses for a moment. She crumples the gauze and antiseptic wipes in her hand as she meets my gaze.

"That idea that one small thing can ultimately cause one big thing? Sure."

I wet my lips and nod. "Yes. And the thought that one small thing can snowball into a chain of events that result in something larger. Something catastrophic."

She holds my gaze, her eyes softening the longer she looks at me. "I don't know what happened in there, but I very much doubt that anything you did caused this."

I glance to the side of Meg, to the half-collapsed building on fire. I didn't think that anything I did caused this. In fact, I was thinking that I've let myself become a passenger in my own life.

I've fooled myself into believing this is the life I wanted. A life where I was begging for affection from my mother. A life where I wondered where the hell my father went. A life where the most spontaneous thing I did was try the Thursday lunch special at my favorite diner.

But I wasn't happy. Not really.

I was content at best. Waiting, always waiting for something. I never knew what I was waiting for, but I think I found it outside a train station in Boston.

Or, I should say that I found the first piece of it outside that train station. Then I found another inside a pool and another inside a cabin in the woods and another inside a safe house.

I found pieces of myself.

Pieces that I didn't realize I'd lost, parts of myself that I'd either been burying or denying myself the opportunity to explore.

Clarity settles on my shoulders, and I feel a sense of peace at the idea of discovering myself.

I refocus back on Meg in front of me, meeting her gaze. "No, I didn't cause this. But I am going to end it."

Rush steps up next to me, placing his hand behind my back. "She good?"

Meg steps back and tosses the garbage in a bag with a nod. "If you feel dizzy or experience any other pain, go to the hospital right away. Your shoulder will be sore for a few days, but you'll be alright."

I hop off the back of the ambulance and impulsively hug Meg. "Thank you."

She hesitates before placing a hand on my back, patting it a few times. Meg pulls away first, her brow wrinkled as she gives me another once-over. "Take care of yourself, kid."

I nod as I let Rush guide me toward another ambulance that's partially concealed behind a fire engine. Wolf's broad back is the first thing I see, and I quicken my steps. Rush's hand never leaves my back as he keeps pace with me.

"Conor!" I shout his name at the same time he turns around. He unfolds his arms from across his broad chest and extends them out to catch me. I jump straight into him and bury my face in his neck, inhaling his familiar sandalwood scent.

One arm curls around my waist, and the other goes underneath my butt. He crushes me to his chest as I wrap my arms around his neck and my legs around his hips.

"How's our girl?" Wolf's voice rumbles against me.

I feel Rush's heat against my back before I feel his fingertips trailing down my spine. Goosebumps chase his touch, but I don't move my face from Wolf's neck. I don't think I can right now. I need a few minutes to process what happened and what I know will have to happen next. Everything has changed.

"She'll be alright, dislocated shoulder. How's the cousin?"

My head snaps up at the mention of Maddie. I look over Wolf's shoulder into the back of the ambulance. I see her familiar red hair, but an EMT and another man block my view of anything else.

"Oh my god—Maddie!"

At the sound of my voice, I see her head peek out from behind the EMT. Her emerald-green eyes widen when her gaze collides with mine, and I watch her mouth drop.

"Lainey!" she yells as she jerks to the side.

I wiggle in Wolf's arms as he spins around, so he's facing the ambulance. I tap the side of his neck twice, and he releases his hold on me. His hands linger on me as I slide down his body until my feet touch the ground.

I move around Wolf at the same time Maddie slides off the back end of the ambulance. Worry settles like lead in my stomach, and I scan her from head to toe, looking for injuries. We're two steps away when an arm comes out and blocks Maddie from taking another step.

I follow the arm up to see a face I wasn't expecting, a frown forming on my face before I even realize it. "Matteo? What are you doing here? I thought you were with Sully? Oh my god, where the hell is Sully?"

He ignores me, his gaze firmly on my cousin. "Take it easy, Mads. You just got your head smashed open."

I watch in fascination as Maddie reaches up and curls her fingers around Matteo's hand, bringing it to her mouth. She

32

places a kiss against his fingers as she glances at him from under her lashes.

"I'm fine, Matteo."

My head spins as I attempt to process what my eyes are having a hard time believing. Before I can even begin to formulate one of the ten questions on the tip of my tongue, Rush growls from behind me. He honest to god growls like some sort of caged beast.

"What the fuck are you doing here, Rossi?" Rush moves around me, and in two steps, he's in Matteo's face. "You have something to do with this?"

A vein in Matteo's forehead throbs as he stares right at Rush. "Fuck you, man."

"No, fuck *you*." Rush grabs two handfuls of Matteo's shirt and slams him against the door of the ambulance.

The EMT spares a single glance at them before he finishes cleaning a cut on Maddie's hand.

Violence shimmers in the air, and I can't tell if it's radiating from the men in front of me or the decimated building behind me.

My heart slams against my ribs as I reach Maddie's side and look her over. Two butterfly bandages sit on the gash on her hairline. A bruise blooms underneath her right eye, but otherwise, she seems okay. *Seems* being the operative word. "Are you really okay?"

"I should be asking you the same thing. What the hell were you thinking going into that building like that?" Maddie's voice cracks at the end, and her eyes pool with tears. "I thought you were going to die. And I'd never forgive you for it."

She blinks several times, sending twin tears rolling down her cheek.

Out of the corner of my eye, I see Rush and Matteo engaged

in a heated conversation. I trust him to figure out what's going on and Matteo's involvement.

I have to clear my throat before I can speak. "I'm sorry, Maddie. I just . . . had to. It feels like everything is changing, and I'm not even sure who the hell I am anymore." My lip trembles as I blink to stop tears from spilling over. I sniff and look to the side to expel a breath.

She nods. "Alright, Lainey. You're going to tell me what's going on though, right? I know you've been keeping stuff from me." She looks pointedly at Rush and Wolf.

"I promise." I glance at Rush, who still has Matteo pushed against the door. Their exchange is mostly growls and raging testosterone, and they're talking too low for me to hear. "So, Matteo, huh?"

Pink flushes her cheeks as the EMT finishes applying a bandage on her hand. She shrugs a shoulder but doesn't say anything.

"I thought that was over years ago."

"It was," she says as she glances at the man in question. "But then we ran into each other and reconnected."

"Alright. If you get dizzy or feel nauseated, have someone bring you in, okay? Otherwise, you'll be fine. The wound on your head is more bark than bite."

Maddie tilts her head to the side. "Alright. Thank you."

"Head wounds bleed a lot," I interject.

The EMT nods his head as he takes off his blue latex gloves and tosses them into the garbage can.

Once he steps away from her, she stands up, and I throw my arms around her. She hugs me back with a ferocity that's born from spending your life with your cousin and best friend.

"We have a lot to talk about," she whispers. "Should we break that up, or?" Her words trail off, and I lift my gaze to watch the scene in front of me.

Matteo brushes Rush's hands from his shirt with a snarl. "Fuck off, Fitzgerald. I'm here as a favor to your brother and *her*." He cuts his gaze to my cousin before he looks back at Rush.

"Aye? And where is my brother then?"

"In the backroom of O'Malley's with a knife in his shoulder."

Matteo delivers his words with such nonchalance that I'm positive is intentional, purposely antagonizing Rush. And he gets his wish. Rush explodes, shoving Matteo against the door again with a hand to his throat.

"You better start fucking talking. Now."

Wolf grabs Rush by his other arm. "C'mon, man. Sully trusts him. Back off a little and let him speak."

I exhale a deep breath as I step away from Maddie and head toward Rush and Wolf. A sense of calm blankets me. It feels tight over my skin, like that too-small long-sleeve leotard I had to squeeze in two years ago for a dance class. It's both confining and comforting.

I square my shoulders and place a hand on Rush's back. His muscles flex under my palm, and Wolf shifts, so he's a few inches closer to me, his arm just barely grazing mine.

I meet Matteo's gaze. Poorly concealed fury shines from his dark-brown eyes, but I remember when he was a scrawny kid hanging around outside our door stealing glimpses of Maddie.

Okay, so maybe he wasn't ever a scrawny kid, but I do remember him at a time when he wasn't as imposing. I mentally conjure that image, and it helps ground me.

"Where's Sully?"

"I already told lover boy one and two here that he's at O'Malley's."

I nod, still partially concealed by Rush's body. "Tell me more. Please."

Matteo looks from me to Rush and then back to me with a raised brow.

"Let him go, Dec." My voice is low, meant only for his ears. Rush's shoulders tense for a moment before he releases his hold on Matteo's shirt and pushes off of him. He takes a step back, settling in next to me. I don't have to look to feel Wolf step up on the other side of me.

A tingle of pride skates over me. I try to imagine how we look right now to an outsider. My dark kings flank me on either side, the three of us covered in dirt, dust, and dried blood. We look like we just walked out of a battle, and in a way, we did. It's a good thing Wolf is so fond of black—all of them, really.

I tilt my head as I take in Matteo. Dark jeans, black sneakers, a black tee. Maybe there's some sort of badass dress code? I bite my lip as I wonder if I'll need to change my wardrobe as I start this next chapter of my life.

I chuckle and shake my head, the sound quiet in the chaos of the scene behind us. Nah. I'll be taking my revenge in band tees and twirly skirts with a smile on my face.

Maddie wedges herself in between Rush and me. She looks at me with a raised brow. "You okay? You were laughing."

I purse my lips as I glance at her. "Fine. Just thought of something funny." Her other brow rises to match the first, and her eyes narrow, but I don't have time to convince her I'm fine. I look back at Matteo and tilt my head, waiting.

Matteo leans against the door and blows out a breath. It's then I see the dried blood on his neck. My eyes narrow as I look at his shirt with a critical eye.

"Is that blood?" I point to his shirt.

"Fuck. Okay. Sully and I were supposed to meet. I knew he was dropping you off at a nearby restaurant, but then when he never showed and didn't answer my calls, I thought he got caught up in you. I left him a voicemail telling him how I felt about his brushoff and bailed. I was a few blocks away when I got the call that the corner store had been torched."

"From who? Who called you?" Rush asks, his gaze scanning Matteo's face.

"What corner store?" I ask at the same time as Rush talks.

"My uncle's guys called—they're good guys." He shifts his gaze to me. "And the corner store is under their protection."

That doesn't really clear anything up for me, but I nod anyway.

"Then what?" Wolf asks, widening his stance.

"Then the other reports trickled in minutes after that. My guys called with reports of another three locations were lit up like the fucking Fourth of July—a cafe, a restaurant, and a bodega." Matteo sighs.

My brow furrows when Rush and Wolf curse under their breath at the same time. I look between the three men and ask, "What does that have to do with anything?"

Matteo looks at me. "I put two and two together and realized that this was a coordinated attack. Two locations are a coincidence, but four are a declaration of war. I've known Sully a long time, and the guy always shows when he says he will."

"So you went looking for him." My heart jumpstarts in my chest, and I absently rub it. I knew something was wrong—more wrong than the obvious chaos behind me.

Matteo nods. "I retraced my steps, starting with our meeting spot. Then O'Malley's. Then all the restaurants in between. And that's when I got your call." Matteo nods to Rush. "So I went to his last known location and found him bleeding in an alleyway, two coffees spilled and a knife in his shoulder."

"Two coffees?"

"They left the knife?"

"Where exactly?"

Three of us talk at the same time. Maddie's the only one who doesn't voice anything. Urgency thumps inside my body, urging me to move. To do *something*.

Matteo runs his hand over his face before scratching his jaw. The stubble rubs against his five o'clock shadow, and I notice my cousin can't keep her eyes off the movement. "Yeah. I had to throw him over my shoulder to get him out of there. I'm feeling a little paranoid, so I brought him to O'Malley's instead of the hospital."

"You left him there unprotected?" Wolf practically yells when Matteo pauses.

I watch the muscle in Matteo's jaw clench as he stares at Wolf. "I left him with Jack. He has some on-call doctor at his beck and call. And Sully ordered me to find his girl." Matteo's glare swings to me. "He didn't say anything about who jumped him. Just made me promise to find his girl."

"That doesn't explain how you got here—how you found us." Wolf folds his arms across his chest, head tilted to the side.

"I called him," Maddie says from next to me. She steps forward, so she's standing next to Matteo and looks at Wolf. "When you went into the building, I thought you were going to die. And I was scared. For you. For me. For everything. I didn't know what to do." She looks at me. "So I called him."

"And exactly how do you two know each other?" Rush asks with narrowed eyes.

I'm not sure if the light is playing tricks on me. The surrounding air is getting smokier by the minute, and it almost looks like she's blushing. I cock my head to the side and wrack my brain. I'm having a hard time piecing these things together. It's right in front of my face, but . . .

I snap my fingers as it hits me. "So he's the one you've been meeting!"

Maddie shrugs a shoulder, her teeth worrying her bottom lip and her gaze flicking to the side.

I cock my head as I look at her with new recognition. That's not quite all of it.

Matteo turns to face Maddie, crowding her against the back of the ambulance and leaning down, so his face is level with hers. "You been meeting other guys on me, baby girl?"

"Oh shit," I murmur. Maddie meets my gaze, and I know she sees the confusion and apology there because she shakes her head a little.

Maddie looks back at Matteo. "You're telling me you aren't seeing other girls, hmm? I know how it is—I remember." Her sugary-sweet tone belies the ice in her words and the fire shooting from her gaze.

"No, Madison, you don't know what the fuck you're talking about. Who is he?" Matteo demands, his voice pitched low but not low enough that we can't hear him.

So I do what any best friend who's worried about her maybe-sorta third boyfriend would do, and I step forward. "Can we get back on track, please? Matteo, where is Sully right now?"

My obvious distraction works because he takes a step back, but not before he grips her at the back of the neck and places a hard kiss against her lips. "This conversation isn't over."

Maddie's eyes darken, and I realize that we have much more to discuss than I originally thought.

"I told you. He's at O'Malley's, in his upstairs apartment."

I reach out and squeeze his arm. "Thank you." Matteo nods, and I glance between him and Maddie. "You need a ride?"

"No," she says, keeping her gaze on me. "Matteo's bringing me home."

I nod and give her a quick hug before walking to Wolf's car and climbing into it.

5

ALAINA

WE PULL into the small parking lot behind O'Malley's. It only has enough spaces for four cars, but since a lot of people in the city don't own cars, we luck out.

Wolf pulls into one of the three open spaces, and before he even shuts off the engine, I throw open the back door. I'm out of the car in a flash and practically jogging down the alley toward O'Malley's back door.

I don't give myself the opportunity to think about the last time I was in this alley—even if I don't remember all the specifics. I heard enough from Wolf to know that this is where the red-eyed demon—where *Liam*—took me.

Just the thought of him and his red eyes is enough to send a shiver down my spine. I shove all of that down, way down deep, to unpack another day. Right now, I have more important things to think about.

Like my ex-boyfriend turned maybe boyfriend who's lying in some bullshit employee room while some backwoods doctor fixes him instead of taking him to a proper hospital.

Fear leaves a sour taste on the back of my tongue, and no

matter how much I try, I can't get rid of it. Luckily, anger is taking center stage right now, distracting me from my real emotion—fear.

And I am fucking furious. With everything and just about everyone. I know it's irrational, and it's a terrible coping mechanism, but I can't seem to stop.

It's easier to get angry than to let myself fall into the pit of emotional quicksand I'm hovering over.

I whip open the backdoor, hard enough that it slams against the brick wall behind it. I feel Rush right behind me, and I already know Wolf is right next to him without even looking.

I stalk down the hallway toward the little hallway with a staircase. It leads to Jack's office above the bar, though I've never actually seen it. We walk through the hallways and the employee's only doors as I absently wonder if I should be concerned that I have such a deep connection with these men.

It seems sudden. And alarmingly deep.

Maybe most importantly, it feels *right*.

These men feel more like mine than anything else ever has.

And I won't let anyone take them from me. Not ever.

With that thought etching itself into my soul, I stalk the last few steps to Jack's office door. I push open the door hard enough that it hits the wall behind it and bounces back toward me. Like I knew he would be, Rush is there. He throws his hand out, and those tattooed fingers I fantasize about wrap around the edge of the door and hold it still, stopping its momentum.

I pause just inside the room, stunned at the sight. It's less of an office and more of a living room with a desk shoved against one wall. But that's not what captures my attention, it's the scene on the other side of the room.

Jack stands at one end of a long rectangular white table, sleeves rolled up and hands bloody and busy as they move around. Some guy I've never seen before stands to the side of the table on the far side of the room, giving me an unobstructed view of the first love of my life.

A gasp leaves my lips before I can stop it. Even though Matteo told me Sully was hurt, it didn't prepare me for this. Sully's laid out on the table, skin pale and sweat coating his brow. His eyes are closed, and a half-empty bottle of Jameson sits underneath his fingers on the floor.

"Jack?" My voice comes out high-pitched, and I clear my throat.

"C'mon, kid. Get over here and help Doc out," Jack says without taking his eyes off of Sully, voice gruff, shoulders tight.

I'm moving before he even finishes talking, Rush and Wolf at either side of me.

"I guess the Rossi kid found ya then, yeah?" Jack asks as he wipes away blood from the wound on Sully's shoulder.

Fuck. Why is there so much blood? Is that normal? My thoughts spin around and around, unable to focus on one thing.

"Something like that. Someone better start talking." Rush folds his arms across his chest, his voice taking on that deep, commanding tone that usually scares everyone shitless.

"I dunno, boyo. Rossi brought him in, and I called Doc here. I didn't want to bring him to the hospital, seeing as I don't know what happened. Said he was jumped before he passed out, that's all I know." Jack glances between Rush and Wolf.

Wolf drags a chair from the other side of the room and deposits it right next to the table by Sully's head. With a gentle hand on my back, he nudges me to the chair. I take the hint and all but collapse in it.

Wolf nods and starts to pace right behind me. Two steps to the right, two steps to the left. "I'm going to check-in with Diesel."

"Call Matteo, yeah? Make sure Maddie's okay," Rush says, eyes on Doc's hands as he works on Sully.

43

"Thank you, Dec," I whisper as I lean over and press a kiss to his shoulder.

"Of course, birdie," he murmurs with a kiss to the top of my head. He turns back to the doctor, and his posture gets rigid, and his voice gets hard once more. "Talk to me, Doc. Explain what you're doing."

The doctor, however, seems to be immune to Rush's dominance.

"I'm a little busy, kid. I've got my hand inside your brother here, looking for any problems, and I don't have time for your posturing bullshit. So pack it away, yeah?"

"The fuck you say to me?" Rush uncrosses his arms and steps forward.

The doctor sighs and looks at Rush. I glance between the doctor's hand holding Sully's wound and his gaze and Rush's gaze. My heart pounds, and the violence that I felt from outside the building starts to swell.

"I don't have time to hold your hand. Not if you want me to save him—"

Rush moves so he's flush against the table. "I'm going to fucking gut you and string you up in the middle of the five points with crows as your companions just to make a fucking point—"

Something inside me snaps during Rush's tirade.

I'm sure if I look back on it, I could better figure it out, but all I know is that it feels like this doctor is threatening Sully.

And I won't allow it.

In one quick movement, I stand up, turn around, and grab the gun from Wolf's shoulder holster on one of his passes. Spinning around, I wedge myself between Rush and the table, enough to get his attention for a split second. That's all I need though. I look at the doctor, gun casually gripped in my hand and laid flat on the table. Everyone stops moving, and the noises of the city filtering in from two floors down is the only sound.

Good. I have their attention.

"Fix him now." After a pause, I add, "Please."

Wolf whistles as he slaps Rush's shoulder and brings him back a step. "We'll just wait until after he's fixed Sully to kill him, yeah, brother? Unless our girl here does it first."

I glance over my shoulder to see Rush glare at the doctor with murder in his eyes. Hell, if he doesn't fix Sully, I just might make good on my threat. Wolf stares at me with lust in his eyes, and the hunger sends a shiver down my spine.

I turn around and hold the doctor's gaze for a moment before he nods and gets back to work. I tuck my hair behind my ear as I set the gun down on the table next to me and lean over Sully. I place a kiss on each one of his closed eyes, his inky black lashes dark. I sweep his dark-blond hair off of his forehead, the long strands stuck to his sweaty skin.

The doctor's hands are a flurry of movement in front of me, and Jack's assisting. I pivot to block them out and focus my attention on the man lying unconscious in front of me.

Maddie always talks about the power of intention, and while I don't necessarily think it's the only thing at play, I think it can't hurt.

And I'd do anything—pray to anyone—to make sure he comes back to me.

So I close my eyes and rest my forehead against his, still running my fingers through his hair.

"Come back to me, James. I need you. They need you. There's so much I have to say to you still and we—"

"Ahh, there. Nothing vital was hit, but I had to be sure."

Lifting my head, I glance over my shoulder to see the doctor with a triumphant grin on his face.

"He'll be okay, then?" I don't miss the small tremble in Wolf's voice.

"He'll be alright," the doctor agrees with a nod. "I'll stitch

45

him up, and you'll need to watch for infection. I'll leave you with some pain meds and antibiotics, but it wasn't as bad as I thought it'd be. I'd say he'll be good as new in no time. Until then, rest and recuperation."

Wolf's shoulders sink as he exhales, but Rush doesn't budge from his perch on the wall facing us. His narrow-eyed glare hasn't left the doctor for a second.

"Where'd you go again, Doc?"

The hair on the back of my neck stands up at the controlled malice in Rush's tone. I don't understand what the real question is, but I know it's not a simple inquiry about his vacation habits.

"Hmm?" The doctor doesn't look up from his precise stitches on Sully's shoulder.

Rush pushes off the wall with his shoulders and crosses the small room to stand next to me. The old floorboards creak as Wolf shifts his weight closer to us.

"I thought you were going on an extended vacation, Doc? When did you get back?"

I feel it then, the change. Suspicion sparks in the air, and without much thought, I hunch over Sully's upper body, shielding his head from whatever's brewing between the doctor and Rush.

Doc doesn't lift his attention from placing the last stitch. "We just got back."

"Is that right?"

Doc cuts the excess thread, and Jack wipes the edges of the stitched-up wound. He applies a layer of thin ointment to the wound and then places a thick gauze bandage over the entire area, securing it to Sully's skin with medical tape.

Doc strips off his blue latex gloves and levels Rush with a tired sigh. "Look, Rush, I don't want any part of . . . whatever this is, okay? I came because Jack called me. And because I've known you boys since you were in diapers."

"Aye, you have. Which is why I'm wondering why you went on vacation suddenly a couple weeks ago. Strange that it happened when I needed you." The tone of Rush's voice says he's leveling Doc with an accusation despite his seemingly harmless words. Rush idly straightens some bandage wrappers on the edge of the table. His forced nonchalance doesn't fool anyone in the room.

Jack finishes cleaning Sully up, and the doctor balls up his gloves and tosses them in the garbage can behind him. I'm trying to curb the impulse to drag Sully out from between them, but it's hard. My nerves are fried, and I can't tell if my instincts are too because right now, the urge to flee from this *doctor* who literally just saved Sully is riding me hard.

There are too many questions without answers and too many unknowns and variables. The worst part might be that I don't even know what I don't know.

I'm adrift at sea, clinging to a life raft made of three men. I know the sharks are coming closer, they can smell my blood in the water, but I have no idea what else lies in the darkened belly of the sea. She's indifferent on the best of days, and she's unforgiving and cruel on the worst.

I know one thing to be true—I'd be lost without Sully, Rush, and Wolf. I would've been ripped apart weeks ago if it wasn't for them.

I want to think that they'd be lost without me, but I can't be sure. Maybe momentarily, they'd be crushed. But as I look at them exuding power and confidence, I don't think they'd be without company for long. So what ties four people together—especially one who doesn't always want to be tied together?

I'm not sure that I have the answer yet, but I'm willing to find out. And that has to be worth something, right?

"You better hope you bet on the right side, Doc. I can't guarantee mercy when this is all done." Rush delivers the threat with such little emotion. Once again, I'm thankful to have him in my corner.

And a little buzzed from the power and dominance rolling off of him. He's such an alpha male—they all are. And there's something so alluring about that. It calls to my inner woman. The one that's just now being discovered, venturing out of this carefully constructed shell I've been living in for my entire life.

Doc sighs and looks at me. I hold his gaze for a moment before I glance at Rush. I feel like I'm missing something, but I'm not in the right frame of mind to dissect the threats behind the glares the boys are sending his way.

"This the girl then?"

"What girl?" Wolf steps into me and folds his arms across his chest, his thigh and leg pressing against my side as he partially blocks Doc's view of me.

"Cormac mentioned you boys were getting a stepsister—"

"Nah. He was mistaken. She's not our stepsister." Wolf tips his head back and cocks it to the side. From this angle, I see his profile backlit by the streetlights shining in the open windows. His jaw looks sharp, his shoulders broad and the usually playful air is nowhere to be found.

"You'd do well to forget you ever saw a girl here tonight, yeah, Doc?"

I run my fingertips down Sully's face and peek around Wolf's body to see what Doc's response is. I'm not disappointed when he nods and picks up his navy blue bag. I don't even remember him having a bag, but I suppose I was preoccupied when we came in.

"Jack," Doc says with a nod.

"Until next time, Doc." Jack follows the doctor across the room and sees him out.

6

ALAINA

"WE CAN'T MOVE HIM. Not yet." I wet my lips and prepare to make my case why we have to stay here for a while.

Wolf settles his big palm on the back of my neck with a sigh. His fingertips run back and forth over the sensitive skin on the side of my neck.

"Aye. We'll stay here for a few hours. Jack won't mind, will ya?"

The floorboards creak as Jack re-enters the room. "Nah. My songbird is dead on her feet. Mind telling me what happened?"

"It's a long story." My voice is soft as I continue to run my fingers over Sully's face, memorizing the shape and cataloging the differences from two years ago.

"I've got time, kid."

"I'm tired, Jack," I say on a sigh.

"That's alright. I'll tell you a story then. You just relax and watch over our boyo, yeah?"

I nod, and Wolf's hand leaves me for a moment before he bends down to brush his lips across my cheek. "I'm going to grab us some food. Rush'll stay here with you, okay, baby?"

I turn my face and catch his lips with my own. "Okay. Be careful," I whisper against his mouth.

"C'mon, boyo. I've got a spare bedroom up here with a bed. Let's get your brother in there, yeah?"

I step back and watch as Rush and Jack pick Sully up and move him down the hall and into the first doorway. I hover behind them, ready to dive in and help, but the hallway is narrow. As it is, the three of them can barely fit on an angle.

I look around the room as they maneuver Sully on the twin-sized bed in the middle of the wall. A big bay window with a seated windowsill takes up most of the outer wall, and the noise from the street filters up, quiet enough to remind me of a white noise machine.

There isn't much in this room, just a bed, a floor lamp, and a dresser in the corner.

Jack smooths his beard with one hand as he stands in the doorway. "I'll give you guys a few minutes, yeah? You come find me for that story, Alaina. I think it's time you hear it."

"Okay. We'll be there in a few minutes," I say as I pull a thin blanket over him and try to adjust the pillow underneath Sully's head.

Jack nods before stepping out of the room.

Rush leans against the windowsill again, one leg bent at the knee and the other firmly on the ground. The thick curtains are open, but the blinds are closed. Rush flicks one blind up and peeks out the window from the side. The afternoon light shines off the surrounding buildings, casting shadows on the floor of the room.

"Relax, baby. We'll be heading home soon."

I worry my bottom lip, adrenaline fading and making me realize how frazzled I am. "Maybe we should just go now. I bet Sully would be fine. Don't you think?"

I look at the man in question. He's currently sprawled out on a quilted blanket in the center of the bed. If I ignored the dried blood on his pants and the glaringly bright white bandage taped to his shoulder, it looks like he's just taking a nap.

But I do know better. And I don't know if I'll ever get the image of him lying still on the white table, some random doctor I've never met bent over him, blood everywhere out of my head.

I fiddle with the thin blanket covering him, readjusting it, so it rests right up to his shoulder but not covering his wound. I realize that the blanket likely doesn't do much, but it helps settle this restless energy inside me. The waxy pallor of his skin haunts my waking thoughts, and I have a feeling I'll be seeing it in my nightmares for weeks to come.

He removes his finger and lets the blinds slide back into place as he turns to look at me. "Come here, birdie."

I look up at the sound of his voice. It holds that deep, commanding quality that I crave.

The light from the outside slants across his face, leaving half his face in complete shadow.

My heartbeat picks up at the sight of him. His chestnut-brown hair hangs over his forehead in a messy style that has nothing to do with seduction and everything to do with our unusual circumstances today. Still, it has the same effect on me.

I take slow, measured steps toward him, trailing my fingertips along the blanket covering Sully as I walk. Rush waits by the window, shifting his weight, so he's sitting on the window seat, spreading his legs further apart.

I step into him, wrap my arm around his neck, and give him my weight. He tugs me closer with a hand around my back.

And I exhale.

For the first time in . . . I'm not sure how long . . . I feel like I can breathe a little.

"Should I be alarmed by how quickly I'm becoming attached to you? To all of you?" It's a thought that I can't get out of my head. I mumble the words into his neck as I bury my face in one of my favorite spots.

He slides his palm up my back until it rests on the back of my neck. I feel his words rumbling in his chest before I really pay attention to what he's saying.

"There are very few people in the world fortunate enough to meet their soul mates. Even fewer are those who meet while they're this young. I think it's a gift. You're a gift, birdie. To me. And to my brothers. And I'll raze the world to keep you. You know that, don't you?"

I pull back from his neck to stare into his eyes the color of the sea. A myriad of emotions greets me. The dark blue and charcoal flecks swirl around, but the thing that takes my breath away is the honesty and devotion shining in his eyes.

"I love you, Declan Fitzgerald," I murmur as I lean in and press my lips to his.

He closes his eyes on a deep exhale, a small smile tipping the corners of his lips up.

"I love you too, Alaina Murphy Fitzgerald," he whispers against my lips.

It takes a second for me to pull back, but I do with a raised brow.

He shrugs a shoulder and slides his hand to wrap around the front of my throat gently. The move sends a shot of lust through my veins, and I press closer to him.

"You have too many last names right now, what's one more? And you'll be a Fitzgerald soon enough." He brushes his thumb back and forth over the sensitive skin on my neck.

My skin tingles as giddiness clouds my head, a smile spreading across my face almost involuntarily. "I'm nineteen, Rush. I'm not getting married now," I tease. I don't even bring up the fact that Sully and I have yet to work our shit out.

He doesn't respond with words. Instead, he tips his head

forward and seals his lips against mine. Our tongues tangle in a dance that feels a lot like a promise, and I tighten my arms around his neck to bring myself even closer to him.

I'm lost in his kiss when a loud screech splits the air, and I jump a foot in the air. I press a hand to my racing heartbeat and yell, "Oh my god!"

"Sorry, Alaina. Didn't mean to startle you," Jack calls from somewhere in the house.

I step back from Rush and will my heart to slow down. "I guess we should hear what Jack has to say now. Raincheck?" I bite my lip as I give Rush an obvious once-over.

He lets his hand slide down my body as he stands up. "Aye, baby. You can count on it."

I lace our fingers together as we walk across the room. Stopping by the bed, I glance at Sully to make sure he's not paler or sweatier than before. I lean over and place a kiss next to his mouth. "I'll be right back, okay? You rest now."

We hear the screeching noise again, and we follow it to the front room where Jack is dragging three chairs by one another.

The big, bearded man sits in the chair with a groan and looks at us. "You believe in fate?"

I shrug a shoulder and sit down in the chair across from him. Rush stares at the last two chairs for a moment before walking toward the window again.

"I never used to. I didn't disbelieve it, but I didn't put much stock into it either. When I was younger, I prospected for the Brotherhood. I was a kid who didn't know his thumb from his asshole, and I thought I was a little badass. My cousin hooked me up with the Brotherhood, introduced me to some guys, and before long, I was running around town with them. I didn't have much responsibility. I just hung around them, went with them on collections, that sorta thing."

Jack pauses, and it's long enough that it captures my attention. When my gaze meets his, he blows out a breath.

"One night, I was with my cousin and a couple of other guys. We were collecting from a line of places—protection money and that sorta thing. Well, one particular shop owner didn't want the Brotherhood's protection anymore, and he let us know by pointing a shotgun in our faces. I don't know if I ever knew real fear until that moment." Jack runs his hand down his beard. "It's still a little blurry, but somehow someone moved, and the shop owner got trigger-happy. He fired several times before one of the guys could wrestle it away from him. He knocked the guy out with the butt of the gun, and it was only then that I realized my cousin had been shot. And so had I. I was fourteen."

"Jesus. I'm so sorry, Jack."

"It's alright, Alaina. It's a long time ago now." He clears his throat. "The guy who wrestled the gun away ended up forcing me out of the Brotherhood. I was livid. I wanted revenge. It took a few years for me to realize that he was doing me a favor. If I had stayed, I'm sure I would've died long ago, probably in the half-hatched plan of vengeance I was working on at the time."

My head tilts to the side as I try to reconcile the man I've known for the last two years and the picture he's painting. It sort of explains how he knows the guys, but it's still such a strange coincidence.

Jack looks out the window for a moment before he looks at back me, his face carefully blank. "It was Aidan."

I can feel my brows bunching on my forehead as a flush of heat prickles along my skin. "Who was?"

"The guy who saved me. Who checked in with me every month for the rest of his life. It was Aidan. Your father."

"I'm sorry—what? What did you just say?" I turn to face Jack fully. "You knew my father?"

"Aye," Jack says, mouth thin and eyes pinched.

"Wh . . . Why? Why didn't you ever tell me?" My head feels foggy, like I'm dreaming, and my fingers start tingling like they've fallen asleep. I turn around in my seat to face Rush, subconsciously seeking him out for clarity. His face is closed off, but I see the muscle in his jaw twitch. He gives me a tiny shake of his head. So this is news to him too. That's oddly comforting.

"I didn't realize it at first. You look so different from the last photo I saw of you. You were a wee girl, seven or so in the last photo he showed me. Your top front teeth were missing, and you had your hair in pigtails. And then he missed a month, which wasn't that uncommon. Sometimes, his, uh, job took him on extended trips—"

"Eight." My voice comes out as a croak, and I clear my throat. "I was, uh, eight in that photo. I remember he always carried it on him. And I know now that he worked for the Brotherhood, so you can speak freely."

Jack rubs his beard between his thumb and index finger as he assesses me. He glances behind me to Rush, and I peek over my shoulder.

He sits on the oversized windowsill, fingers splayed to hold open the cheap blinds. He reminds me of one of those gargoyles on old gothic buildings. Tall and menacing, his posture alone warns people of what they might face should they breach the walls. Forever watching and protecting.

Warmth unfurls inside my chest the longer I watch him. He flicks a glance in our direction once but otherwise doesn't move.

"Are we still in danger?"

"We're always in danger, Alaina. I've almost lost one brother today. I'm not about to lose another one," he replies without looking at me. His words aren't harsh or unkind, but they send a ripple of fear through me.

"Maybe you should go after him."

Rush turns his head and looks from me to Jack and back to

me again. His face is as cold as always, but I notice a twitch in the corner of his right eye that I've never seen before. "No."

I open my mouth to argue when the door opens. In an instant, Jack and Rush are on their feet. Rush crosses the room in a second flat and stands in front of me, gun outstretched in his hand.

"Whoa, whoa, whoa. It's me. Put down the guns, yeah?" Wolf says from right inside the doorway.

Rush holsters his gun right away and strides toward Wolf to grab the bags of food. From the smell of it, it seems Wolf went to the fried chicken place a few blocks over—one of my favorites.

Wolf meets my gaze with a sly wink, and the vice grip of panic around my heart loosens a little.

"Let's take this to the kitchen. I need a drink for the rest of this conversation." Jack leaves the room and walks down the hallway.

"What conversation? What did I miss?" Wolf asks as he places a hand on the back of my chair and brushes his lips across my forehead.

I tip my head back, and he places a kiss on my lips without me having to ask. A girl could get used to this kind of attentiveness.

"Jack was part of the Brotherhood. And he knew my dad."

Wolf's gaze bounces between my eyes, but his face doesn't change too much. Either he has a great poker face, or he knew one of those two things. I'm betting it's a combination of both, honestly. There's no way they didn't know Jack was at least affiliated with the Brotherhood. Otherwise, why would they have come here—or let Sully be brought here?

"That's an interesting twist I didn't expect." When I don't say anything, Wolf asks, "How's our boy?"

Relief sits on my shoulders, fluffy and soft, but the fear that has been eating away at me still weighs heavy in my stomach.

"He's okay, I think. We should stay here for just a little longer, until we can move him more safely. I don't want him to get hurt worse."

"Okay, Red. We'll stay here and eat and hear what the old man has to say—"

"I heard that, boyo," Jack yells from somewhere deeper in the apartment. He doesn't sound all that mad about it though.

"Good. It means your hearing hasn't gone yet," Wolf yells with a grin on his face.

"Let's go eat, birdie." Rush places a hand along my shoulders from behind.

"But what about Sully? We can't just leave him in there unprotected." The thought of someone walking in here and harming him while I'm eating and tripping down memory lane shreds the light weight of relief and replaces it with anxiety. It drapes around my shoulders, hanging low and weighing me down.

"We have some of our guys posted at all exits—inside and out—as well as the two doors between the bar and here. Plus, all the doors are locked. We'll be alright to eat for a little bit, Red."

7

ALAINA

WOLF LACES his fingers with mine as we follow behind Rush down the narrow hallway. With my free hand, I reach out and snag the fabric of his shirt and curl my fingers around the soft material. I feel a little more grounded when I'm physically touching them like this. It makes me feel like I'm really here, that I'm not in some strange fever dream that's going to end brutally for me.

The floorboards groan under our weight, and I look around as we walk past the open doorway to the room Sully's in, two closed doors, a small bathroom, and into a living room and kitchen.

The walls are empty of decoration, not even old wallpaper—just beige paint. This whole apartment seems like it's confused. The architecture seems original, all tall ceilings and domed arches between rooms. The hardwood floor looks like the real thing—that original stuff they used back at the beginning of the twentieth century, and not the cheap laminate stuff they use nowadays. The furnishings are more modern. All clean lines and dark accents.

The furniture is minimal, and it seems more random. It's hard to tell since the only furniture in the front room Jack uses as a backup office is a white table, some random chairs and folding chairs, a couple of dusty floor lamps, and the window treatments.

My confusion grows as we enter the kitchen, and it looks like it belongs in the nineties. The cabinets are that golden oak color that all the homes had in that decade. It's large enough to have an island with two stools and a small built-in four-top table in the corner. The appliances look practically brand-new, though.

"What is this place?" I ask as I follow Rush to the small table in the corner. He pulls out a chair and places it against the wall before sitting down. He reaches over and palms the seat of the second chair and drags it next to his before he taps it twice.

I oblige his request and drag Wolf along with me. Jack leans against the island and faces us with his big arms folded across his chest. Letting go of Wolf's hand, I settle into my chair. With a huff, he drags another chair from around the table and slides it next to mine. I feel a little stuffed in between the two, but it's a feeling I'm learning to enjoy. I suspect one day I'll crave it.

"It's my apartment."

I raise a brow and look around pointedly. "It doesn't look like anyone lives here."

"Aye, I don't. But it's mine all the same. I own this one and the two above it."

With a start, I realize that I'm used to Jack being open and inviting. His current expression is hard to read, but not enough that I don't pick up on his unease.

"What are you not telling me?"

Jack huffs and rolls his eyes. "A man's entitled to his secrets."

I nod before he even finishes speaking. "Sure, sure. But secrets are part of the reason we're in this mess."

"Aye, they are." His voice is low, and he rubs his hand down his beard.

"How long, Jack? How long have you known who I was?"

His gaze snaps to mine and softens almost instantly. "The second or third time I saw you. It's your eyes, Alaina. You've got Aidan's eyes."

"The Gallagher eyes, I'm told." Rush and Wolf stiffen at my musing, and I remember that there really are so many secrets. I look at each of them as I say, "Once Sully's better, we need to have a serious chat, the four of us."

Rush slides his hand through my hair to grip the back of my neck lightly. "Aye, we do. Don't think we forgot about your little stunt today."

"Both of them," Wolf adds as he palms my thigh with one hand and opens the greasy paper bag with the other.

It's easy to ignore the way my clothes still stick to my skin in places when the alluring aroma of fried chicken wafts into the air.

"Did you know Golden Chicken was a favorite of mine?" I ask as I open the container he put in the middle of the table.

Wolf just looks at me with that stupid hot smirk on his face before giving his brother a weighted glance. Rush just shrugs a shoulder as he reaches for some food, unrepentant.

"We might have to have a conversation about your stalking, Dec," I murmur, holding back the smile threatening to cross my face.

"Not stalking, baby, just staying informed." His words are low, but I don't miss the wry twist of his lips.

I focus on the food in front of me and dig in. I can't remember the last time I ate. Did I even eat anything at the diner? We were waiting for Maddie, so . . . My thoughts take a dangerous turn as I recall the reason we're sitting here right now.

I finish my food and wipe my greasy fingers before I look right at Wolf.

"I . . . I don't regret it, so if that's what you're looking for, you won't find it. I'd do it a thousand times over to save Maddie."

Wolf nods, easily picking up our earlier conversation. "I know. But we still need to have a conversation about it." Wolf's voice is right next to my ear, but I can feel Rush's penetrating gaze on my face.

"And address your punishment."

Wolf's curious fingers dancing along my thigh distract me enough that it takes a minute to hear what Rush said. When it filters through my brain, I whip my head to Rush.

"Punishment?" A shot of lust infiltrates my confusion as I envision a different type of punishment.

"Aye, birdie. When you're with us, sometimes following orders is the only thing that stands in between you and death. And you disobeyed them. You put yourself in danger."

"*Twice.*" Wolf's voice is soft against the skin underneath my ear. "And we can't let that go unpunished. Not even for you, baby girl."

My heart beats harder against my ribcage, and my head starts to fog up, feeling lightweight. My eyes are locked on Rush, but every inch of my body is acutely aware of both of them—the way Wolf curves his body around mine and the way his breath feels sliding along my skin.

Rush shifts his hold on me so his hand curves around the side of my neck, his thumb gently brushing across my pulse point. He stares, fixated, at the spot his thumb caresses for a moment. I don't tear my gaze off of him, dazzled and dazed by the way his pupils dilate with each passing second. "We're a family, and we rely on the trust we have for one another. Without it, we're as good as dead. You understand, yeah?"

I nod as I bite my lip.

"Give me your words, baby."

"I understand, Rush." The words leave my lips on a sigh,

anticipation building in my veins. My skin feels tight, and I strain to bridge the gap between our mouths when I hear a throat clearing.

From the obnoxious sound, I hazard a guess that it's not the first time Jack's cleared his throat. My cheeks flush in embarrassment. "Uh, sorry, Jack. I—I don't know what came over me . . ."

"I don't think we got to that part yet, Red."

I cut Wolf a glare, but his stupid, handsome face is doing that cocky smirk thing that makes me forget why I'm annoyed with him. And I figure since I'm already treading the awkward waters with Jack, I might as well make it worth it. I lean into Wolf and tip my face close enough to barely brush my lips across his.

It has the desired effect, and in less than a second, he surges into me, deepening our kiss.

"Alright, alright. Break it up, kids," Jack grumbles from his perch against the island.

After a moment, I take my time pulling away from Wolf and opening my eyes. My lips part at the look on his face.

His espresso-colored eyes promise dark fantasies that his cheeky grin attempts to cover up or hide. He stares at me for a moment longer before he pulls back and slouches into his chair, spreading his legs wide in that stupid hot way men sit.

"Ah yes, where were we again? Oh, right. The punishment." Wolf waggles his eyebrows and grins over my head at Rush.

"That's enough of that, boyo. I've known the girlie since she was a child. I don't need to see all of that. And don't think I missed the way you possessive assholes circle her like buzzards."

I run my hands down my legs to give myself something to do while I cool down. I don't know what the hell has gotten into me. First Rush in the other room and now Wolf in the kitchen? I shake my head a little and blow out a breath. Time to think of something else. "Right. About that. So you knew me as a baby, then?"

Jack reaches behind him for his cocktail. The ice clinks against the glass as he brings it to his lips for a sip. "Aye. He brought you around a few times when you were little. Aidan Gallagher was a good man and one of the best friends I've ever had."

"Then why don't I remember you? Why didn't you come around?" I ask with a tilt of my head. Before the question is even out of my mouth, I straighten in my seat. "My mom."

Jack nods. "Aye. I never met your ma, but Aidan loved her, and that was good enough for me. They had a . . . complicated relationship."

"Complicated how?" Rush asks.

"Your da loved you, and he loved her, and he loved the Brotherhood. At least up until the end, then things got murky. But your ma? She didn't love anything more than she loved your da. At least that's the way Aidan told it."

I look at the table in front of me, follow the swirls of the grain with my eyes as I mull over Jack's words. He delivered them with such tender care, it's almost worse.

I wonder if I'll ever be at a place in my life where I can say without shame or sadness that yes, my mother didn't care for my company. And that's putting it mildly. Intellectually, I understand some people weren't meant for motherhood, and that's okay. But it's different when it's *your mom* who falls into that category.

It's ridiculous to feel shame and unworthy from a dead man's words about a now-dead woman's feelings from almost twenty years ago, but I do. It chokes me, flushing my cheeks and sending heat radiating through my body.

But words can hold power, regardless of who wields them. And if the speaker isn't a stranger, but a friend? A loved one? A *parent*? It takes a cutting remark and sharpens it for maximum impact.

Wolf laces our fingers together, and I wonder if he's recalling the brief interactions he witnessed between my mother and me. How stilted and cold they were. I try to envision that first night from his perspective. He brought me to his house, so I wasn't entirely a surprise. But I imagine the dinner was. Watching any interaction between the two of us paints a particular photo. Most people put on a front when they're in front of *mixed company*, but not Lana McElroy. She didn't bend for anyone.

Or she hadn't.

"Is it possible to miss the idea you had of someone more than you miss them?" My words are soft, and only the hum of the refrigerator fills the silence. "My mom is com—was. My mom *was* complicated. And I think—I think I always loved her. But I think I might've loved the idea of her, ya know?"

Wolf twirls a lock of my hair between his fingers, drawing my attention to him. "I understand, Red. Sometimes life gives you these things that you think you need, and it's up to you to decide if you really need them. And I . . . I don't think you needed your mom. Not really."

I nod as flashes of my mother's dead body materialize in front of my eyes. The way her eyes stared into the sky, lifeless and yet somehow still full of pain.

I turn to look at Jack. "Do you believe in heaven?" If my question startled him, he doesn't show it.

He takes a large swallow of his liquor—whiskey, if I had to guess. "I think—I think the world will be a darker, crueler place when you're gone, songbird."

A wry smirk tips up the corner of my mouth. "You trying to sweet-talk me instead of answering, old man?"

He clutches his chest with mock horror. "Not you too? What's this? I'm hardly an old man."

I lift a shoulder in a shrug. "Feels like a good enough nickname." I pause and really look at him. "Thank you, Jack. For being there for me—and for my cousins."

"Aye. Once upon a time, I made a promise to Aidan that I'd look out for you should anything happen to him."

"When's the last time you spoke to him?" Rush's voice comes from right next to my ear, and I can't stop my shoulders from jumping. He's been so quiet, I wasn't sure he was going to chime in at all.

"It's been years since I talked to Aidan, longer since we saw each other."

"When, Jack?" Rush's intensity takes me by surprise, and suddenly, there's tension in the small room.

Jack scratches his beard with his middle finger. "Ah, probably ten years or so since we spoke. He called me on his way out of town for a job, but that wasn't out of the ordinary. He often called to check-in when he was on his way somewhere."

"You mean when he was on his way to kill someone."

Jack startles, and his glass slips from his hand, but his quick reflexes catch it just before it falls too far. Whiskey sloshes over the side of the glass with the movement, but Jack doesn't flinch when it splashes against his hand.

I hold his gaze, a challenge written in my arched brow and tight shoulders.

"Well, I wouldn't put it quite like that. But, aye, he was a hitman."

I nod a few times as I worry my bottom lip, looking around the room without really seeing anything. "How many people did he kill? Were they . . . I don't know, bad? Or were they good people?" I meet Jack's gaze. "Did my father have the blood of innocent people on his hands?"

Jack shakes his head, the movement slow and measured. His gaze is soft as he holds mine. "He didn't always share that information with me, but the little bit he did, they weren't good people, Alaina. He was known as the Traveling Salesman. He traveled around like salesmen used to do years ago, only he wasn't selling vacuums."

Huh. The Traveling Salesman. It's such a random and seemingly innocent nickname to have. Marrying this idea I have of my dad, who got down on the floor and played with my barbies with me with the guy who was literally paid to kill people, is proving to be difficult.

It's a startling reminder that we don't really know our parents. At least not when we're kids.

And I won't ever be able to know them. Now—now all I get is diluted memories from people who knew them decades ago. It's easy to let melancholy sink in at my morose thoughts, but strangely, I feel fine—okay, even. Some part of me recognizes that I'm still in shock, but I think underneath that, there's a well of emotion.

My dad used to tell me that there's no easy way to do something. That the only way to get to the other side of something is to follow the steps, stay on course.

You just have to do it. Of course, that was about my dance recital, and I was eight. But the same principle can be applied to anything—to everything, really.

There's no easy way to fix the damage the relationship I had with my mother caused—especially if she's not here—except to dig deep and start doing the work.

I'm just not exactly sure where to start.

8

ALAINA

SEVERAL PHONES VIBRATE, interrupting the quiet of the kitchen. Rush slides his hand away from the back of my neck at the same time Wolf shifts his weight to the side. They both pull their phones out of their pockets.

I'm still musing about my parents, so I'm slow to pick up on the change in the air. It's not until the hair on the back of my neck stands up that I snap out of my thoughts and look between Wolf and Rush.

"What's wrong?"

They exchange a glance between themselves before they look at me. I get up from the chair and lean my butt against the table so I can see both of them at the same time.

"It's Da. He just heard about Lana."

I nod a few times and bite the corner of my lip. "Where is he anyway? I thought they both were supposed to be home." I look upward, trying to wrack my brain if Mom said anything in the Uber ride. "I can't remember if my mom said why she was here and he wasn't."

Rush hits the button on the side of his phone to turn it off. "We still need to talk about all those . . . things your mother told you, yeah? But Da didn't say anything about where he's been. Just asked if we knew where you were. Apparently some cops showed up at Summer Knoll to notify you and ask you some questions."

My shoulders drop, heavy with exhaustion. "Is that where we're going then—back to Boston?"

Wolf nods, his expression thoughtful. "Eventually. We have a place here in the city for situations like this."

"Situations where you get stabbed in some alleyway and have to get stitched up by some backroom doctor?" I arch a brow at him.

Wolf's playboy smirk makes an appearance, and as much as his smugness gets on my nerves, that lethal smirk he sends my way is much, much worse. "Sometimes it's a bar fight that leaves us too bloody and tired to drive back home."

My eyebrows hit my hairline. "A bar fight?"

Wolf crosses his arms across his chest, his biceps flexing with the movement. My eyes zero in on them, and if you would've asked me six months ago if I thought the idea of a bar fight was attractive, I would've laughed in your face. But I can't deny the way my pulse picks up at the idea of Wolf sweaty and swinging punches, all those muscles coiling and releasing. My chest rises and falls faster at the thought.

"What an interesting response, little bird." Rush's voice is close to my ear, and I tilt my head to the side. Surprise skates across my nerves at his proximity. I don't remember hearing him step closer to me.

"And what response is that, brother?" Wolf doesn't step closer to me, but I watch in amazement as every muscle pulls taut.

Rush skims his fingers from right under my ear, down the slope of my neck and shoulder, and down my arm. Goosebumps trail his fingers and I shiver in response.

"Such a responsive little thing, aren't you?" Rush's breath caresses the shell of my ear, each word from his lips elicits another wave of goosebumps.

"Jesus fucking Christ. Do I need to throw water on you three? Your brother's in the other room with a hole in his shoulder, and you three are panting after each other in my kitchen like a bunch of alley cats." Jack's harsh words cut the bubble of lust I was in.

I startle, my cheeks heating and my shoulders tightening with embarrassment. I definitely forgot that he was even here. And he's right. What the hell was I thinking starting something with them in Jack's apartment—and with Sully laid up, no less.

Rush doesn't miss the flush in my face and stiffens, his hand wrapped around my wrist. A glance at Wolf, and I see he's in the same position. Eyes hard, jaw clenched, menace rolling off of them both in waves.

Fuck.

I hold my free hand up, palm out. "Okay, okay. You're right. Sorry, Jack."

Jack runs a hand down his face and into his beard. "Aye, songbird." He pins me with a fatherly sort of look, all concern and hesitation like he doesn't want to say something, but he will anyway. "And just what the hell is going on here, anyway? I thought I saw you with Wolf on your birthday." His eyes narrow on the two men next to me.

Ah, there it is—the thing he didn't want to wade into, but for some reason, he felt like he had to. I decide I don't need to make it easy on him, so I shrug. "I was."

Jack purses his lips and leans against the island behind him. "And what about all those nights with Rush then? What were those?"

"What the fuck do you mean all those nights with Rush?" Wolf pushes to stand up straight, dropping his hands to his side. His posture is tight, and his chest rises and falls with deep breaths. He reminds me of some sort of beast, one wrong move away from snapping.

I lick my lips and look from Jack to Wolf. I refocus on Jack. "Those were—"

"None of your fucking business. In fact, none of this is any of your business, O'Malley," Rush says as he stands up too. His tone is firm and threatens violence.

"Ah, it's O'Malley now, boyo, yeah? Huh. I would've thought you would've told your brothers about your weekly visits to the pub to see our songbird." The smile on Jack's face is cruel and calculated. It's a look I've never seen on him before—and never about me, indirect or otherwise.

"What the fuck is he talking about, Rush?" Wolf takes a step closer to us, his hands clenching and unclenching at his sides.

I push to my feet and stand between them, hands touching each of their chests. "Let's just all relax. It's been a . . . really, really long day. Let's—"

"Not now, Red. I wanna hear what my brother has to say," Wolf says through gritted teeth.

I bristle at his dismissal, and it's enough to fan the flames of my rage. I thought I had it buried from earlier, but I guess I need to do a better job of controlling it.

"Yeah, boyo, tell your brother how you came into my pub every week to listen to her sing." Jack's smug smile grates on my nerves. Instead of defusing the situation, he's throwing gasoline on it.

"You've been with her for the last year?" Wolf tilts his head, his eyebrows bunched together.

My stomach roils, and the icy fingers of dread tiptoe up my spine. I open my mouth to explain the situation or, at the very least, defuse it, but before I can get a single word out, Rush steps out from behind me. And in one smooth movement, he pulls his gun from his shoulder holster and steps in front of Jack, gun tapping against his leg.

"Somethin' you wanna say, old man? Or did you forget who you were talking to?" Rush tilts his head to the side, the move more menacing than curious. "Because it seems like you're trying to create a problem between my brother and me. And you know what they call me, right?"

I take a step to the right, closer to Wolf. I want to see the expressions on their faces. I'm not sure which way this is going to play out, but I hope, for everyone's sake, that it doesn't end in bloodshed. I don't know if I can take any more today.

Jack's jaw is clenched and his stare is cold as he looks at Rush. "Aye. You're the fixer. You fix the Brotherhood's problems."

"Aye, I do. I like you, O'Malley, I always have. And I don't want you to become a problem, yeah?"

No one says anything for a moment, and I hold my breath in anticipation. I'm tempted to wade in. Despite the little bomb he just dropped on us, Jack's always been there for me. For years.

Whether he realizes it or not, I'm handing over control to him. I'm trusting Rush not to do anything irreversible. And for a girl like me, that's a big ask.

Jack sighs and breaks his stare-off with Rush, looking to the side for a moment. "I just don't want anything to happen to her. And you boys are trouble, always have been. The two of you—"

"Three."

All four of our heads whip to the doorway at the sound. Sully leans against the doorframe, his face pale and his dirty-blond hair disheveled. He's still one of the most beautiful men I've ever laid eyes on. My heart leaps into my throat at the sight of him.

"If you're going to insult us, might as well include me too, yeah, Jack? After all, if it weren't for me, she never would've stepped foot inside O'Malley's." Sully pins me with his ocean-blue-eyed stare. "Ain't that right, princess?"

I stare, transfixed at the first man I ever loved—aside from my father, of course. Tears well in my eyes, and I blink quickly, sending one trailing down my cheek.

"Oh fuck. What the fuck did you do to her?" Sully growls the words through clenched teeth.

I swipe the tear away and quicken my steps until I'm right in front of him. "I'm fine. Just relieved to see you awake." I scan him from head to toe. I'm not sure what I'm looking for, but I can't stop myself. "How are you feeling? You should be lying down still."

"I'm fine, Lainey." His voice, so soft and low, meant only for my ears, pierces my heart in the most welcome of ways.

I roll onto the balls of my feet, stopping myself from touching him, even though everything inside begs me to run my hands over him and make sure he's whole—as whole as he can be. I meet his gaze, and suddenly, I'm overcome with emotion. It's slow, like the tide in the mornings until it's all I can see and feel.

"James." There's more emotion packed into that one word than I've ever felt before. "I'm so glad you're okay." My voice catches on the last word, and I have to clear my throat a couple of times.

"I don't want any trouble with the Fitzgeralds—or the Brotherhood. I'm just looking out for Aidan's girl."

I'm too busy looking over Sully to watch the confrontation behind me. Besides, I trust them—well, I'm learning to trust them. Might as well start today.

"See, that's the thing, O'Malley, she's not your concern anymore," Rush all but growls out.

"Aidan was my best friend. I made a promise to him, and she was my responsibility."

"Guess it wasn't too much of a sense of responsibility if you didn't even find her for eight years." Wolf's tone is overly conversational, and it's enough to steal my attention. I glance at him, unsurprised when I see his sly smirk. Contempt dances in his gaze as he stares at Jack.

Jack shifts his weight to the other foot and affects a bored look. "When I found her, I made it—her—my responsibility."

"Let me clear that up for you then, O'Malley. You're absolved of any sort of responsibility when it comes to Alaina. That honor belongs to us now, and anyone who interferes will end up with an extended stay at our carriage house in Summer Knoll."

I don't know what the hell the carriage house is or what exactly is happening, but I know a threat when I hear it. Turning around, something inside me tightens, and if I was unsure before, this confirms my suspicions that something has changed. Or maybe I've always been this way, but it's been buried under so many layers of superficial shit that I didn't realize it was there.

Rush isn't in Jack's face, and the gun still lays casually at his side, but perhaps that only adds to his powerful, commanding presence.

"Watch it, boyo. You don't want to start a war with me." Jack's voice is measured and delivered in such a matter-of-fact tone.

The corner of Rush's mouth tips up, and his eyes twinkle with malice. "Take your own advice, old man."

Jack's always been kind to me, but there's something about how Rush took command of the situation that works for me.

It really fucking works for me.

Wolf claps his hands twice, startling me enough that I jump. "Alright. As fun and . . . enlightening . . . as this has been, time to go. Sully, get your shit, brother."

Sully's eyebrows manage to crawl into his hairline even when his eyes glass over in pain. "Okay." He drags the word out and makes a show of looking around and patting his pockets. He slides his hand inside the pocket of his jeans, pulls his phone out, and waves it around. "Ready."

"Red." I startle and look over at Wolf. He's standing right next to me, face lowered and eye soft. "Let's go, baby girl."

I let myself get lost in his expressive eyes for a moment, knowing he'll always be there to catch me. Impulsively, I push up on my toes and lean into Wolf, bridging the few inches between us. I brush my lips across his, a soft touch that I let linger for a moment. "I'm ready, Wolf." The words echo one of the first things I said to him, and I watch as a shiver rolls over Wolf.

"Don't push me, old man. I'm not fucking around when it comes to her. Feel me?"

Jack rolls his eyes. "Aye, I *feel* you, boyo. Now, get the fuck outta my house." He turns to look at me, giving Rush his back. "Songbird, you come see me soon, yeah?"

"Let's go," Rush growls out as he storms out of the kitchen. His footsteps get quieter until I hear the front door open and close with a bang.

I land back on my feet again and look over my shoulder. "Alright, old man." I lace my fingers with Wolf's and let him lead us out of the kitchen.

"Aye. And Alaina? Sorry about your mom, kid."

I pause in the doorway of the kitchen and look over my shoulder at Jack. A sense of foreboding washes over me and dread fills my gut.

Why does this feel like the last time I'll see him? A scary thought, for sure, but with the way my life is changing, I'm not so sure that I shouldn't trust these little instincts.

I untangle my hand from Wolf's and spin around. In three steps, I reach Jack and wrap my arms around his neck. "Thank you, Jack. For everything."

He returns my embrace and squeezes me once before he lets me go and steps back. "Be safe, songbird."

I nod and walk backward until I reach the doorway. With one final look at Jack, I turn around and join my place in between Wolf and Sully.

9

ALAINA

ABOUT TEN MINUTES into the ride, Sully nods off and jerks himself awake, grimacing in pain. After the third time and some cajoling, I get him to agree to lay his head down on my lap for the rest of the way. He's lying on his back, his large frame almost comical in this position in the backseat with me. I take the time to study his features, the lines and curves of his face. My fingers twitch with the need to trace everything. The dark smudge of lashes against his cheek. The way his hair waves across his forehead. The absence of his scowl and the smoothness of his brow. There's no way he'd let me be so close to him if he were awake.

I sigh, a quiet, wistful sort of noise as I cave and brush the hair from his forehead, letting my fingertips rest a little longer against his scalp. When we were younger, I used to run my nails through his hair and massage his scalp. I swear he used to purr every time I did it.

A smile ghosts over my mouth at the memory. Too soon, it's wiped away and replaced with the memory of him screaming at me in the hallway of Summer Knoll, declaring that he never wanted to see me again.

I had hoped that it was some sort of lash-out, a knee-jerk reaction to seeing me after so long. I haven't forgotten what he did, and I know we need to talk about it.

The last day has taught me that leaving things unsaid is never a good idea. And that some things are worth fighting for. I decided a while ago that Sully's worth fighting for, but the events of the last few hours only reaffirms that for me.

An hour later, the car slows as we approach a gray high-rise apartment building. From this angle, it looks like an entire side is floor-to-ceiling windows. I run my fingers through Sully's hair as we pull into the attached underground parking garage. Though the apartment isn't all that far from O'Malley's, traffic to get here —anywhere in NYC—is difficult on a good day and near impossible on a bad.

And because luck wasn't entirely on my side tonight, the roads were packed. Part of me doesn't mind since I got my unobstructed view of Sully for so long.

"Should he be sleeping so much?"

I flick my gaze to Wolf as he drives us around the parking garage at five miles per hour. He holds my gaze for a moment before returning his eyes to the road.

"Sleep's the best thing for him. We'll carry him upstairs to his room, and he'll be fine. Doc said he'll make a full recovery, remember, Red?" Wolf pulls his SUV into a spot.

Right in front of us is a sign bolted against the concrete wall claiming this spot for a Fitzgerald resident. I look to my left and see four more spots just like it.

It takes all three of us to maneuver Sully out of the car. Once he's outside the car and leaning against Wolf, he cracks his lids and looks between the three of us. Rush throws Sully's other arm over his shoulder and together, they help him to the bank of elevators ahead. I follow behind them and step into the elevator.

"Which floor?" I ask as I turn around to face the glowing white buttons on the right side.

"Here, stick this key in and press P, Red," Wolf says as he digs into his pocket to pull out a small silver keycard.

My eyebrows lift as I scan the buttons. P is at the top, though I shouldn't be surprised. The penthouse is usually at the top of a building, and if Summer Knoll is anything to go by, their apartment will be massive. I secretly hope that it leans more toward their taste from the cabin at Golden Oak—and that it has the same feel.

After a relatively quick elevator ride, the reflective black doors open, and I step into the long hallway. There's a door on either side, so I step to the side and wait for the guys to lead the way.

They turn right, Sully half-walking, half-sleeping between the two of them. Rush holds his thumb to an electronic pad outside the door. A green light flashes before it beeps and shines green. A click sounds, and the door opens.

"That's some high-tech security," I mumble.

"Think of it as a step above Summer Knoll, but a step below Golden Oak. We've worked hard over the years to create safe pockets of space in this city and others for situations just like this," Wolf calls over his shoulder.

The two of them walk-carry Sully to the left, up a few steps, and down a hallway to what I'm assuming are bedrooms.

I don't follow, too caught up staring at the space around me and taking everything in. In front of me, two low-profile gray couches face one another with a square black coffee table in between them. The floors are dark, almost charcoal in color, broken up by a large woven black-and-gray rug underneath the couches.

To the right of me is the kitchen. It's decorated in blacks, chrome, and pale grays and outfitted with what looks like brand-new black appliances and white cabinetry.

It feels like them to me, and yet, it doesn't. I don't spy any personal touches here like I did at Golden Oak—and even those were sparse.

I look around the open-concept space, my gaze snagging on the view of the city from up here. Colorful lights twinkle in the distance, and I cross the room to the windows for a better view. I was right, the wall is floor-to-ceiling windows. Actually, it looks like this whole side of the apartment might be floor-to-ceiling windows.

I bet they don't even need an alarm clock with the way the sun fills the rooms at dawn.

New York City greets me from beyond the thick glass. She's bustling and bright, and if I strain my ears, I can hear the low hum of the city below. But maybe that's my imagination.

Leaning my forehead on the glass, I let the sight blur until all I can focus on is the slow way my breath moves in and out. My exhales fog up the glass in front of me, but still, I don't move.

I just need a moment.

I just need a second to breathe and pretend that I didn't just watch my mother die. That I didn't then watch some guy stitch up my first love in the apartment above a pub. That I didn't get whisked away to a penthouse like I'm in some romantic comedy.

Right now, it feels like my life is more of a tragedy—I hope to god or any higher power listening that it doesn't end up like a Shakespearean tragedy.

So, I just need a moment to get my shit together. Because everything has changed.

I've changed.

And I'm not sure how to process. I've spent my entire life being this one person, and then—then all of a sudden, I'm this whole other person.

I was ready to hurt that man today. Like really hurt him. And the fact that I don't regret it is what scares me the most.

I feel Wolf before I see or hear him.

"Isn't it strange?" I murmur, keeping my eyes closed.

Wolf slides his strong, warm palm up my spine to rest at the base of my neck. "What's that, baby girl?"

I roll my forehead across the glass and open my eyes. Eyes the color of rich dark chocolate greet me, warm and inviting. "This. Us." I pause. "Life."

Wolf steps into me, not quite pressing his body against mine, but close enough for me to feel the heat of it. Something inside me settles at his proximity.

His tongue swipes across his lip as he stares at me. "Strange is one way to describe it. But I also might use enchanting, mesmerizing ... fateful."

The corners of my lips tip up and I turn around to face him. He doesn't step back, if anything, he steps further into me, pressing my back against the cool glass.

"Are you trying to charm me, Conor?" I ask with a grin.

Wolf presses his palms to the glass just next to my head and leans in. His shoulders flex in the most distracting way, and from this angle, he looks impossibly huge. I don't miss the twinkle in his eye as he aligns our mouths.

"Depends. Is it working?"

A laugh slips it past my lips, and I shake my head with a smile. "So cocky."

His own smile stretches across his handsome face as he presses his lips against mine. "You love it." His pouty lips caress mine with every syllable.

My breath hitches at the realization that we've never said these words before. Not to each other, not really. On speakerphone when my world just got rocked, and I was on the way to rescue my cousin like I'm the superhero in some movie feels almost like it didn't count. So this, right now, this could be my chance for a proper exchange.

I tip my head back, separating our lips and meeting his playful gaze. "I do. Love you, I mean."

I watch in wonder as the words leave my lips and infiltrate his consciousness. It takes precious seconds, but the transformation is beautiful. It's something I don't think I'll ever forget, not for as long as I live. I mentally pocket the memory up and tuck it inside my soul for safekeeping.

Wolf inhales, and it's like his body expands further. His pupils dilate and his muscles flex. He practically vibrates with energy as he holds himself tight. With a measured slowness, he brings his hands to either side of my neck, threading his fingers into the hair at the nape of my neck. I hold on to his wrists to ground myself as my heart beats wildly. Leaning down so our foreheads touch, he skims his nose along mine before placing gentle, soft kisses on each corner of my mouth.

"I've been waiting my whole life to hear someone say those words to me and mean them. And I—I don't deserve you, baby girl, but I'll spend the rest of my life worshipping you."

"So what you're saying is that you love me too?" I tease with a tilt of my head.

"So fucking much." The words are barely out of his mouth before he surges forward to capture my lips in a bruising kiss.

He tilts my head to the perfect angle to deepen our kiss as we affirm the mutual declaration with our mouths. I snake my arm around his neck and pull him flush against me.

His groan is music to my ears, and I hitch my leg up. Without missing a beat—or breaking from the kiss—Wolf palms underneath my thigh, holding me to him. I feel his cock harden, and my lust spikes further.

"Alaina."

Wolf pulls back at the sound of his brother's voice, his nose grazing mine. My eyes flutter open at the movement. Our chests rise in tandem, and I wonder how much further we would've gone had Rush not called my name.

"Impeccable timing, as always, brother," Wolf says without taking his gaze off of me. He uses his grip on my neck to tip my head back further, the back resting against the window behind me. He places soft kisses along my jawline and down my neck as I stare at Rush over his shoulder.

A month ago, I would've said Rush's face was unreadable, his gaze undecipherable. But now—today—I can see the lines of tension in his frame, the tightness around his eyes, and the elevated rising and falling of his chest. To the untrained eye, he might seem angry, but I know better now.

He's not angry. Jealous, maybe. Turned on, definitely.

He's far enough away that I can't see the color of his eyes, but I'd bet my life that they're dark like the sky before a storm.

"Sully's calling for you, Alaina." Rush holds himself still as he delivers the message.

Wolf lifts his head from my neck with one last kiss beneath my ear. "We're not finished, baby girl, not by a long shot."

A shiver of arousal courses through me at his whispered vow. "Promise?"

"Aye, you have my word on that," he growls out before sealing his words with a kiss that has my toes curling in my shoes. Almost as soon as it begins, he pulls back and takes two quick steps backward, letting go of me. He tips his head to the hallway. "I'll find you later."

I look at him for a moment, willing my heart to slow down, before I do something silly like jump him. Or Rush.

Or maybe both.

The only thing that settles my raging hormones is the knowledge that I'm tapped. I'm close to crashing, and when I cross that line with both of them, I don't want to be on a time limit.

I nod as I push off the window, my eyes find and hold Rush's gaze. When I'm close enough to touch him, I run my fingertips across the broad expanse of his chest. "I want you to come find me too, okay?"

Rush traps my hand right above his heart, and I wonder how long he was standing there before he spoke up. I search his gaze, but he's locked everything down tight. "I will. Right after we call Da."

I pause, one foot on the step to look at him. "Should I be there for this phone call? I'm assuming it'll be about my mother." I raise a brow and tilt my head. Then a sobering thought hits me, and my jaw drops. "Oh god, I have to call my cousins. I can't believe I—"

"Your cousins are fine. They're safe, and they're expecting your call tomorrow. You let me and Wolf worry about our da, yeah? We'll take care of you."

I bite my lip and look at him before glancing at Wolf. He's sitting on one of the low-profile gray couches, his arms stretched across the back on either side of him. He meets my gaze and tips his head toward the hallway with a reassuring smile. I look back at Rush. "Only if you're sure . . . I could use a shower, too."

Rush lifts my hand from his chest to his lips. He places chaste kisses along each knuckle as he says, "I'm sure. And please, help yourself to anything you need. This is your home as much as ours."

Something warm unfurls in my chest at the word home rolling off his lips and the sincere look in his eyes. My lips part and I nod, two small movements that have my hair swishing across my back.

I slip my hand from his, and he lets me, turning to watch me walk across the living room toward the hallway.

"And Alaina?" I pause and look over my shoulder at the mouth of the hallway. "Welcome home."

10

ALAINA

HOME.

I think about those four letters as I walk down the hallway, glancing at the artwork on the walls on either side of me. Black and white portraits of people I've never seen before and the occasional oil painting.

My feet slow as I see an eight-by-ten photograph framed. It's black and white, but even if it weren't, I'd recognize the three faces smiling back at me anywhere. There they are. The three people who are quickly becoming everything to me.

My home.

The realization is startling. I gasp, my heart thumping double-time. In the span of twenty-four hours, I lost my mother —and arguably, my father. The people that children are taught represent their home. My eyes well at the phantom heartache that pulses inside my chest. I'd tried for so long to get my mother to be my home—my safe place.

And she never was.

There's a certain amount of peace that settles inside my soul, knowing she tried, at least. And in the end, she tried to protect me. That has to count for something, right?

But she was never my home.

By a strange twist of fate, I think I found my home in the same day. Here, with these Fitzgerald boys. Though boys doesn't really fit them, but in my mind, that's what they are. Sometimes they're more like predators in the wild, fighting and snarling at anyone who threatens them. Other times, they embody the gods I often think of them as, staking their claim on the land and its people.

And I don't mean this apartment is home, though it's a gorgeous place from what I saw. I mean *with them*. I think . . . I think I might go anywhere with them.

I peek in the first open doorway and see Sully sprawled out on an extra-wide California King-sized bed.

"Lainey? That you?" Sully's voice is groggy, and his eyes are half-open.

I cross the room to his bed, pulling the bottle of pain medicine out of my pocket and shaking it. "I'm here with pain meds." Sully groans and throws an arm over his eyes.

I tap two out into my palm and grab the water bottle from the nightstand, handing both of them over to him.

Sully cracks an eye open from underneath his arm before he shuffles to lean on his elbow. He swallows the pills with a swig of water and flops back onto the bed. "Thanks, princess." His voice is soft, and his chest rises and falls in a slow, deep rhythm.

I spend another minute just watching him before I grab the teal throw blanket at the foot of the bed and cover him up.

As much as I want to snoop around, the idea of scrubbing the day off of me is more appealing. And knowing the Fitzgerald boys like I do, I can only imagine how extravagant their bathrooms are.

My skin crawls as memories of the day flash before my eyes like a strobe light. I don't even know how many hours I've been awake, and logically, I know it hasn't been anything crazy. But everything I've gone through makes it feel like it's been days since I slept.

And it feels like years since I felt the comfort and safety of *home*.

I walk into the en suite bathroom and give myself a moment to pick my jaw up off the floor. I just knew that they'd have something extravagant in here. I'm not sure if it's something unique to one of them or all of them, but one of these days, I'm really going to take advantage of their spacious, luxurious showers.

I leave the main lights off, flipping the switch for the soft spotlight above the shower. Stripping off my clothes one by one, I don't look too closely at them. Instead, I toss them into the garbage can in the corner.

Déjà vu hits me like a slap in the face, and I stagger backward a step. My gaze swings to the tank top hanging out of the garbage can—and the rusty-brown-colored stain on the side.

Blood.

I'm not even sure whose blood it is at this point. I feel my eyes glaze over as I go through the motions of showering. I don't even get to appreciate the three showerheads or the temperature-controlled panel or the speaker system.

It takes three times before I feel like the blood isn't on me any longer.

The hot water soothes my aching muscles and my bruised heart. I know I'm a long way from . . . processing everything, but I don't want to unpack that just yet.

After I'm done, I towel-dry my hair and wrap another towel around my body, avoiding my reflection in the mirror. Everything kind of aches, and I don't know if I have the mental energy to inspect all my physical wounds and tend to my emotional ones tonight.

I peek into the darkened bedroom, straining to hear any noise over the exhaust fan whirring above me. Satisfied that Sully's fine, I pull on the clothes laid out on the countertop.

I shimmy the black boxer briefs up over my hips, rolling them at the waistband a few times, and pull the white cotton tee over my head. The material is soft against my sensitive skin, smelling of clean citrus. I pull the collar up to my nose and inhale—*Rush*.

Of course he would've snuck in here and left me his clothes to change into. I don't think the man knows how not to plan.

I towel-dry my hair again before braiding it in a loose braid over my shoulder.

After putting the towels over the rack next to the shower, I hit the switch. The room plunges into darkness, and I take a moment to let my eyes adjust.

A chill runs over my body as I walk toward the bed, the air conditioning set low in here. Sully's still passed out on his bed, but instead of being on his back in the middle, he's scooted over to one side, half-turned over and underneath the blankets.

He might wake up and need something in the middle of the night, I reason with myself. Or he might get an infection, and by the time one of us discovers him, it could be too late.

I bite my lip as I stand next to the bed, my fingers itching to push back his unruly hair curling on his forehead.

"Get in bed, birdie."

I jump, turning around so fast my head spins. Rush reclines in a chair in the corner of the room right next to the windows that run from the floor to the ceiling. I hadn't even noticed it there until now, partially concealed in the shadows of the night.

I press a palm to my thundering heart. "Jesus, Rush. You scared me."

He leans forward, pressing his forearms to his knees, hands steepled in front of his lips. "Sorry, baby. If I didn't intervene, you'd be standing there all night debating on whether or not to slide into bed with Sully, yeah?"

I huff, warmth coloring my cheeks. "I mean, I would've made up my mind eventually. Besides, I was just about to get in." A wry smile tips up the corners of his pouty lips. I cross my arms and lift my chin. "I was."

"Alright." His eyes look dark from this angle, but I swear I see a twinkle in them.

"I was just . . . you know, unsure of the sleeping arrangements. And I, uh, didn't think he should be left alone tonight."

Rush stares at me for a moment before he stands up and crosses the room in three long strides. Standing next to him in his clothes, barefoot, and wet hair, I feel oddly protected.

He traces a finger along my collar bones, dipping his fingertips underneath the collar of his shirt. "I already told you not to worry about that kind of thing. If you're happy, we're happy."

"But Sully—"

"Is an asshole who needs to get his shit together. Don't worry about Sully, yeah? He's just afraid to admit it to himself. Besides, near-death experiences are known to change a man."

I look to the side, my jaw clenching. "I'm not going to force myself on anyone, Dec. Especially when he's vulnerable."

His quiet chuckle soothes something aching in my soul. He turns my face back to his with a finger on my jaw. "Oh, baby, you're not forcing anyone, I promise you that. Just get some sleep now, yeah? We'll talk in the morning."

I turn my face and place a kiss on the inside of his wrist. "And where will you be?"

Rush leans down and brushes his lips over my forehead. "I'll be right here, little bird."

"And Wolf?"

"He's making a few calls, then he'll be in here, too."

I nod, and Rush steps back to give me room to climb into Sully's massive bed. I scoot under the blankets, settling in and letting sleep take me in its clutches.

11

ALAINA

MY BODY IS heavy with exhaustion when I open my eyes. The hazy light of the city filters through the blinds, enough to make out Rush's sleeping form in the same chair he was sitting in earlier. His legs are propped up on an ottoman pushed against the chair.

I lift up to my elbow and see Wolf sprawled out on the floor, right next to my side of the bed. He's shirtless with an arm thrown over his eyes, the blanket pulled down to his waist. I watch his bare tattooed chest rise and fall with a small smile on my face.

Warmth unfurls in my chest. I like that they slept in here, watching out for me—and Sully. It feels right to have all of us in one room.

I lay my head back on the pillow and look out at the twinkling lights. Their apartment is higher up than my dorm room, and the city looks different from this angle—almost like Christmas lights, twinkling and sparkling. The wide window treatments hang to the side of the large window and the blinds are open, letting the night sky shine into the room. The moon is high in the sky, but only the smallest sliver is dark. I couldn't have been sleeping for long.

A full moon is on the horizon, and given the way my life has played out recently, I'm a little fearful of what that means. I scan the sky, looking for any familiar constellations. Grief pierces my heart when I see Ursa Minor.

It's my father's favorite constellation.

It was. It *was* my father's favorite. Isn't it strange that something ceases to be if that someone is no longer here? It was my father's favorite. I wonder what his favorite is now that he's among the stars. My lips tip up on one side as I imagine my mother and father dancing among the stars. Amusement flutters over me as I envision my father twirling her around. She always did smile the most around him.

A warm hand slides across my abdomen, startling me from my thoughts. A second later, I feel the warmth of Sully's body pressed along the back of mine.

"What are you thinking about at"—he leans over me to look at the clock on the nightstand next to me—"two o'clock in the morning?" His voice, raspy and deep from disuse, leisurely slides over me to settle on my soul.

I shift to my back and turn my head to face him. "Do you believe in soul mates?"

"That's a heavy topic to think about at this time of night."

"I know," I murmur with a nod. I let the quietness of the night settle between us. It's not unpleasant, but it does feel weighted. Sully and I have done this dance for what feels like ages. "Are you feeling okay? Do you need anything?" I search his eyes for any tightness or pinch of pain. He shouldn't need any more pain meds for three hours.

"I'm fine. Nothing that won't heal." He sweeps a loose lock of hair across my forehead, his fingertips trailing down my neck and lingering on my collarbones. "I'm glad you're here. I had . . . some sort of nightmare about you."

I reach out and place my palm on his heart, his steady heartbeat reassuring me. "What happened?"

His gaze focuses on his fingers tracing my skin. "When I was in the alley, after I was stabbed, I had some sort of . . . fever dream or something. We were happy, you and I. We were in Central Park, and you were marveling at the flowers blooming."

He's quiet for a moment, and the image of us walking through Central Park hand in hand flashes before my eyes. "That sounds lovely." My voice is low and hushed, a small smile tipping up my lips.

He looks me in the eye. "It was. Until you were taken from me. Someone came and took you from right in front of me, and I . . . I couldn't get to you in time."

I encircle his wrist with my other hand, holding him to me. "It wasn't real, James. I'm right here."

His thumb brushes back and forth over my collar bones, eliciting goosebumps. "I know, but it felt so real, Lainey."

I nod and wait a moment. "I was so worried about you. So, so worried." I inch closer, so we're face to face, our noses inches apart, and slide my palm to his cheek.

"I know, princess." He brings my hand up to his mouth and places a kiss on each knuckle.

"We have a lot to talk about."

"Mm-hmm. We will. Tonight, let's just"—he sighs—"let's just pretend, yeah? Let's just pretend that nothing else exists outside this bed, this room. And tomorrow—tomorrow, we'll figure everything out."

"Everything? Even about us?"

He stares at me for a moment, his lips pressing together in a slight grimace. "I—I've missed you, Lainey. So goddamn much my bones hurt. I feel like I've been missing you my entire life."

A tear rolls down my cheek. "Jam—"

He places a finger against my lips. "Not tonight, princess. Tonight, we're pretending, remember?"

"But I don't want to pretend. I just want you." There's a hitch in my voice, and my words are hushed, but I feel more emotion packed in those four words than I would've thought possible.

"Do you though? Because you have Wolf. And Rush. I'm not so sure there's room for me in that heart of yours." He places a big palm against my heart, and if in response, my heartbeat kicks up a notch.

"There's always room for you, James. Always. When I'm old and gray and dancing among the stars, there will always be a reserved spot on my dance card with your name on it, James Fitzgerald."

The corner of his lips quirks up. "Dance card?"

My mouth mimics his, and a smirk dances across my lips. I quirk a brow. "That's all that you got from that?"

"Well, I'm just curious, is all. Have you been reading that historical romance you used to love so much?" He waggles his eyebrows and smirks.

I move to touch his shoulder playfully, but he snags my wrist in his hand. "Maybe I want all of your dances. Then what?"

My smile falls at his abrupt, serious tone. "Sully, I—" I cut myself off and swallow roughly. I look between both of his eyes for a moment before I scoot even closer to him. "I want us to be open with each other, and I don't want to lose you, but I can't promise you that."

He nods once and looks over my shoulder out at the sprawling city. This high up, the noise of the city is virtually indistinguishable. All I can hear is the whooshing of the air conditioning as it filters through the heat vents, the noise soothing.

He brings his gaze back to me. His ocean-blue-eyed gaze

searches mine for a moment before he exhales. "Do you love them?"

There's something like reluctant acceptance. I wet my lips and search inside myself.

Such a simple question. Only four small words, and yet it has maybe the most complicated answer I've ever encountered.

I remember the exact time I realized I could love James though. It was within the first week of our shared time at the New York Public Library, and I had freaked out on him, accusing him of cheating on some girl by kissing me and telling him he wasn't in my summer plan. I was convinced that there was no way someone like him could be unattached—and interested in me.

"Sometimes, the best things in life are unexpected. When I'm with you, I'm with you, yeah?" He tilts my head back, so I have no choice but to meet his eyes.

A laugh bubbles up my throat, and I grasp his wrist with one hand to hold him to me. "I don't even know what that means, but I think you just went inspirational-quote on me."

James steps into me. "It means I like you too. My little punk rock princess." His lips brush mine with each word as he takes the binder from my arm and places it back on the shelf.

"Yeah?" I breathe the word into his parted lips.

He presses into me, aligning our bodies, and I can feel every hard inch of him. My emotions are so close to the surface, unlike usual, when I keep them locked up tight. His hand tightens in my hair, a stark contrast to the gentle kiss he places on the corner of my mouth. "Yeah, princess." His lips brush mine once, twice, three times before he presses them firmly to mine.

I try to deepen the kiss, but he steps back. I'm breathless; I feel strung tight and greedy. I can barely believe that the breathy noise of protest came from me. I've never felt like this before, like I'm drunk on lust.

He chuckles and pushes his hands into his pockets. He pulls out a pair of earbuds and his phone. "Patience." He tsks. "I made a playlist for you."

He puts an earbud in my left ear before putting the other one in his right ear. He scrolls on his phone for a minute before I hear the first few notes of Yeah Yeah Yeah's "Maps."

My breath hitches, our gazes lock and hold as we both listen to Karen O serenade us with her promise that they don't love you like she loves you. I lick my suddenly dry lips. This feels like a premonition and a promise. When the song ends, the next one starts, and I sink to the floor, stretching my legs out across from me. James moves to sit next to me, and we listen to this guy pour his heart out. He sings about the freckles in our eyes being mirror images, and when we kiss, they perfectly align.

By the third song, I feel warm and tingly all over. I intertwine our fingers, content to listen to this curated playlist he made for me for the rest of my life. By the fourth song, my heart feels full, and I lay my head on his shoulder. This playlist is a peek into James's soul, and I'm not passing up an opportunity to dive deeper.

THAT WAS the first moment I realized that I could love James if given the time. I think . . . I think I was given just enough time to fall in love with him. But I was sixteen. And it's drilled into us that any sort of "love" experienced at that age isn't *real love*. It's *puppy love*, they say.

But it never felt fleeting. It felt tangible and scary in that sort of free-falling way.

Of course, I had never had my heart broken until then either. No, those honors also went to James. Maybe that's why it hurt so bad. I'm sure it wouldn't have hurt as bad if I didn't care about him as much.

I bite my lip and come back to the present. "I haven't known them long." It's a copout, and we both know it.

"That's bullshit, Lainey. You can lie to a lot of people, but not to me. I know you, remember? Or at least I did."

I nod and whisper, "You're right. It was a copout. And the

truth is, I . . . I do. I'm not sure how to navigate this feeling just yet. It's so new, and I've never felt *like this* before. But what I feel for them—for you"—I look over his shoulder at the wall—"it feels a helluva lot like love. And I think I could definitely love all of you. At the same time."

Sully doesn't say anything. He just continues to run his thumb over my knuckles in long, soothing strokes.

"And that feels . . ." I blow out a breath and look at him. "Big. It feels big."

"To answer your question, yes. I do believe in soul mates." He turns my wrist over and places a soft kiss on the inside, leaving his lips against my skin for longer than usual. "Sleep now, yeah? Everything looks better in the morning."

I nod, a lock of my hair sliding against my cheek with the motion. I snuggle in closer to him, careful not to jostle him too much, and close my eyes on a deep exhale.

12

SULLY

THE SMELL of peaches and cream invades my senses, and I flex my hands in a stretch—or at least, I attempt to. I didn't account for my arm being pinned down and something to be in my hands already. Or should I say some*one.*

I've got a handful of the most perfect ass I've ever felt, and I know before I open my eyes who it belongs to. I take my time waking up, savoring the time with Lainey wrapped around me—literally. The girl sleeps like an octopus—all flailing limbs and constant tossing and turning.

In our time apart, I'd forgotten that. I think I'd forgotten a lot of things about her. Or I purposely didn't remember them. At one point, if I let myself remember even one single thing, I knew it would take me down a rabbit hole I'd never see my way out of.

No matter how much pussy I drowned myself in—and fucking hated myself for every goddamn minute of it—I never felt better. I never forgot the way she smelled or the way her nose crinkles when she's concentrating or the way just the sight of her makes my goddamn heart ache.

So, yeah, I'm letting myself enjoy this moment, because the moment I'm awake, it all goes away.

She goes back to being my ex-girlfriend who fucking left without a trace, and after the day I had yesterday, I need not to hate her for a little bit.

I memorize the way she feels in my hands and the way her body curves around mine.

"I know you're awake, asshole. You might as well stop copping a feel and get your ass out of bed. We have shit to do today." Wolf's voice comes from somewhere on the other side of the bed by the windows.

I open my eyes and lift my head up and see Wolf reclining in the chair, gaze fixed on the sprawling city below. The morning light streams in through the blinds.

"What time is it?"

"Time to get up. So kindly remove your hand from my girl before I do it for you." Wolf's voice is somewhere between a yell and a whisper. It's honestly a little amusing, not that I'd tell him that.

"Fuck off with your bullshit attitude, man. I got fucking jumped yesterday, remember?" My anger spikes a little. Not only is it uncharacteristic for him to be this grumpy, it's too early for it.

He turns to look at me, his gaze hostile one moment and softening the next. "Aye, I fucking remember. But today is a new day, and we've got a lot to do, so I need you to get up. And *don't* wake her, yeah?"

I blow out a breath, careful not to wake Lainey. "Yeah, okay. I need more pain medication first."

Wolf stands and crosses the room to stand at the foot of my bed. He studies us for a moment. "They're on your nightstand. And I'm glad you're okay, brother. It's just this shit has got me all twisted up inside." He runs a hand through his hair. "The sooner we figure it out, the sooner we can get back to normal."

I nod and begin untangling myself from Lainey. It takes me what feels like forever, but I manage to do it without her waking up and without pulling a stitch. I swing my legs over the side of the bed, biting back the groan that threatens to spill from my lips. The skin around my wound pulls with every move I make, but apparently any sort of twist is out of the question for the next week or so while I heal. I'll have to get the sling we have around here just for this sort of thing.

I swallow two more pills with a swing from the bottle of water from my nightstand and push off the bed. Standing up, I pull the collar of my shirt over to inspect my bandage. I'll have to change the dressing soon, but I'm glad that the wound isn't seeping. That's a good sign.

I wasn't lying to Alaina last night. I have been hurt worse than this before. Two years ago might've been one of the worst nights of my life. Not only did I get practically blown up, that was the same day my girl decided that I wasn't worth sticking around for. So, I had a dislocated shoulder, a broken wrist, and a fucking broken heart.

I glance at the girl in question behind me. She shifted so her face presses into my pillow, her chest rising and falling in a deep pattern. The sunlight highlights the bed, making her hair look like it's glowing. It's just the absolute perfect shade of red, and the sight of it spread out on my pillow like that goes straight to my dick.

I freeze when she sighs, but all she does is snuggle into my pillow a little more. Thankfully, she doesn't wake up. She needs the rest.

I follow the sound of my brothers talking and the smell of coffee until I'm in the kitchen. It's been a few weeks since I've been in this apartment, not since the night I walked in on my brothers and my girl getting cozy at my house. I stayed in the city a few extra days to help Matteo when his shit went south. Which reminds me, I need to call him and thank him for carrying my ass all the way to O'Malley's yesterday.

"Oh, look, brother, sleeping beauty has decided to get up after all." Wolf gestures toward me with a goofy smile on his face.

I flip him off in response, and he only laughs. I pull out a chair at the black and white table in the kitchen and sit down with a groan.

Rush slides a cup of coffee in my favorite mug in front of me. "You doing okay?"

I take a sip before I answer him, the bold coffee sending a shock of caffeine to my system. "Aye, I'll be fine. I've had worse before."

He nods before turning back to the kitchen, grabbing a platter of food, and bringing it back to the table. Wolf follows him with plates, silverware, and napkins. My brothers lay everything on the table, and I nod my thanks.

We each dish up, leaving some of everything for Lainey when she wakes up. My brow wrinkles as I take in the platter of food in the middle of the table. "Is that . . . is that all of her favorite foods?" I look between Rush and Wolf.

Wolf shrugs a shoulder. "What can I say? I'm observant. Plus, our brother's been stalking her for a year, so he—"

"I never stalked her," Rush says before he takes a sip out of his favorite mug.

Wolf rolls his eyes. "What else do you call going to O'Malley's every Friday night for a year? Don't think I forgot that you installed all those security cameras around O'Malley's. That was for her, right?"

My gaze ping-pongs between the two of them, eyes narrow.

Rush places his mug on the table with careful movements. He looks Wolf right in the eye, and says, "I'm not going to apologize, Conor. I'm not sorry, and I'd do it again."

"I'm not even that mad. I just think it's fucked up that you made some big production about going to the city every Friday night—wait a minute. *She's* the little bird you had stashed in the city?" He throws his hands in the air and stares at Rush with wide eyes.

Rush tilts his head and shrugs his shoulders in a forced nonchalance. "In a manner of speaking, yes, but it wasn't like what you're thinking."

"What about what I'm thinking?" I say over the rim of my mug.

Both of my brothers turn to look at me, but Rush is the first one to speak. "And what are you thinking, brother?"

"I'm thinking we need to have this conversation with Lainey. Especially if it involves her, yeah? She's had a lot of secrets lately."

Wolf blows out a breath. "You don't even know the half of it, brother."

I set my mug down and give them my full attention. "Then fill me in." And for the next thirty minutes, they gave me the cliff's notes version of events. Everything they could remember, the rest had to come from Lainey herself.

13

SULLY

STARING into the dredges of my coffee, I try to make sense of all the information swirling around. "So let me get this straight. Lana left Da, somehow showed up at the diner I stupidly left her without backup at, and she and Lainey both followed that motherfucker who took her from O'Malley's to some warehouse."

"More or less."

My head whips toward the doorway where Lainey stands, leaning against the wall. Still dressed in a borrowed white tee that hangs almost mid-thigh, face and eyes soft with sleep, and hair mussed. She takes my breath away.

Wolf jumps to his feet first, ushering her to the empty seat next to me. He holds out her chair like some goddamn gentleman, and I fight the urge to roll my eyes at him. "Layin' it on a little thick, yeah, brother?"

Okay, so I didn't curb my sarcasm after all.

Lainey sits down, and Wolf pushes her chair in. Rush slides the platter of food, so it's in front of her, and I find myself pouring her a cup of coffee from the carafe on the table before I even decide to do that.

"Oh, wow. This is"—she looks at each of us with a small smile—"unexpected. And really nice."

I add the sugar and cream just how she likes it and set her mug in front of her plate. She shoots me a small, private smile, reaching for it first.

"Can you, uh—maybe after you've eaten, you can fill us in a little more?" I ask and immediately want to shove the words back in my mouth. I sound like some prepubescent boy instead of the hardened criminal I am.

She slides her hand in the handle, palming the mug and sighing after her first sip. "I can tell you now. It's fine. I think . . . I think it'll be good for all of us to talk today." She looks me in the eye. "About everything."

Wolf returns to his chair and serves himself another helping of French toast. "Aye. Since everyone's up to speed on O'Malley, Rush's stalker tendencies, and—"

"Not a stalker," Rush says on a sigh at the same time Alaina giggles.

"Wait a minute." Wolf turns to look at Alaina with a raised brow. "Why didn't you tell us you knew him?"

"I told you I knew him. I just didn't give details on . . . how, exactly. And I didn't, know him, I mean. Not really. I'd only properly met him right before I met you," Alaina explains, looking at Wolf.

"Okay. That doesn't really explain why you kept it a secret. Either one of you." Wolf's tone is deceptively casual as he leans back in his chair, his eyes throwing accusations at both of them.

Alaina exchanges a knowing look with Rush, one filled with heat. She looks between the three of us. "For this to, uh, work, there has to be a delicate balance of trust and communication. While some things might stay between just two of us, we should all agree that all other lines of communication between us should remain open."

"That's assuming all of us are in this relationship." I couldn't stop the retort from leaving my lips, but it lacks any real heat and everyone knows it.

Alaina shoots me a smile like she thinks I'm being cute. I'm not. I mean, I want to have her, but I don't know if I can trust her.

How can I trust the person who's at the root of my trust issues?

Okay, so that's not entirely fair. I had abandonment issues long before Lainey stepped into my life. But that's to be expected when your mother just drops you off at some random dude's house when you're a baby.

A fucking *baby*.

Jesus Christ, what kind of fucked-up parent does that sort of thing? And then she just bails, never to be heard from again. A few years ago, Rush asked me if I wanted to know what happened to her, that he would find her for me. In the end, I decided that she'd had nineteen years to find me—I was right where she left me. So if she couldn't be bothered, then neither could I.

I made a promise to myself after that—I'd never become a parent if I couldn't guarantee that I'd be there for that kid. And that's one I intend to keep. No matter what.

Not that I'm planning on having kids any time soon. My life is much too dangerous right now. I'd never bring a kid into this chaos. We're in the middle of war, for fuck's sake.

And holy fuck. *Why the hell am I thinking about having kids and babies?*

Sweat beads on my brow and I glance around in bewilderment. I shake my head; it must be the pain meds. I'm probably just having a weird reaction like Lainey did.

Yeah, yeah, that must be it.

I look up, realizing I missed something when they're all

looking at me. I take a sip of my coffee just to give myself some-thing to do, so I don't blurt out some stupid shit again.

"Okay, so back to the diner. And my, uh, mom." She stares at the table, tracing a random pattern in the wood grain. "She told me a whole lot of things in a very short period of time."

"It's alright, baby girl, just take your time, okay? And we're here for anything you need," Wolf tells her as he reaches across the table to place his hand on hers.

She lifts her hand and places a kiss on the back of his. "Thank you."

"Why don't you just give us the facts as your mom gave them to you? That might help."

She licks her lips and nods. "Yeah, that's a good idea, Rush. Okay, so she said that my father is dead, which we already knew, but she also said that he was the heir to this company, Gallagher Industries. And she thought her wedding engagement in the paper somehow led these Gallagher Industries people to me. That's how they found me. Apparently, she'd been hiding me all these years—ever since dad left. Or was killed, I guess. Only . . ." She runs the tip of her index finger along the top of the mug, head tilted as she stares into the kitchen without really looking.

"Only what?" Rush prompts. He's leaning forward in his chair, eyes focused on her.

She turns her attention to Rush. "Only when Mom said something about Gallagher Industries to Liam at the warehouse, he said they didn't send him. But . . . but maybe I'm not remem-bering it correctly. There was a lot going on."

"Aye. What else happened at the warehouse? How did Maddie come into this?" I ask as I palm a fresh cup of coffee.

"There's something else at play here. Something I don't quite see yet." Her words are slow and measured, as if she's searching for the missing pieces as she speaks.

"What do you mean? Did Maddie say something?" Wolf tilts his head to the side.

"Hmm? Oh, no. I called her and Mary before I came out here, but neither one answered. I'll try again soon though. But, uh, something else happened. Two somethings." She takes a sip of coffee. "So apparently Mary met someone online, and they became close quickly. One thing led to another, and he started asking about Maddie. And me."

As one, all three of us stiffen in our chairs, matching scowls on our faces.

"Before you say anything, I know. But when he got aggressive, she shut it down. Not, uh, not before she shared some personal things about me." Alaina winces and looks at the table.

"Personal like what?" Wolf growls out, his hands steepled on the table in front of him.

Alaina shrugs. "I'm not sure. Likes, dislikes, and . . . my schedule. Said he'd distribute her personal photos if she didn't keep the info flowing."

I set my mug down and look at Alaina. "Listen, we might joke about Rush being your stalker—"

"Still not a *fucking stalker*," Rush chimes in with a smirk, his tone almost conversational.

I ignore him and keep going. "But that courtesy only extends to him. Who the fuck is this guy? Why don't we just go take care of it?"

"I'm not sure. Max something. And apparently, Benny already took care of it. And then he asked for payment for his *chivalry* in the form of a date. With me. According to Mary, said he'd take it one way or another."

"Benny from O'Malley's?" Rush sits back in his chair, head tilted as he looks at the wall. He looks deceptively calm, like he's holding himself so tight, one move is going to ignite him.

Lainey nods. "Yep."

Everyone is silent for a moment.

Rush clears this throat. "I don't want to tell you what to do—"

"Fuck that. I will. Our girl is not going on a date with some motherfucking prospect who's blackmailing her," Wolf yells.

"Calm down, man. I wasn't going to say she should do it. I'm just saying I'm not trying to tell her what to do." Rush stares at Wolf, furrowed brows as he leans back in his chair.

Wolf, Alaina, and I look at each other before matching smiles tip up our lips. That asshole loves to tell people what to do, but I don't need to tell anyone here that.

"Are you sure it's the same Benny?" Rush asks.

Lainey nods as she looks between the three of us. "Benny, the bouncer from O'Malley's. I'm not going to go, obviously. And I appreciate your help with that. I can try to get more information when I talk to the girls today. Which brings me to Maddie. And why she was there." She sighs. "This part is a little strange, so I'm just going to go with it. My mom was dressed like me—like in my clothes, like me—when I saw her outside the diner. She knew that someone was looking for me, so she was going to pretend to be me and get taken. Only Maddie looks a lot like me, especially from behind. So when they saw her at the diner where I should've been, they grabbed her instead."

"So who texted us that photo?" Wolf runs his hand through his hair.

"I—I don't know. Oh!" She slams her hand against the table. "We need to see my Aunt Sloane."

"All the arrangements can be made from here, baby. We don't need to leave here for a few days, at least."

Her smile dims a little. "No. I mean, yes, I know I have to contact her to talk about arrangements for . . . Mom. But that's not the only reason I need to talk to her. Mom told me that I need to tell her 'it's time.' Whatever that means. Acted like It was a matter of life or death."

"Okay. So we go see your aunt in a day or two then. You can rest, and then we'll figure it out. Hopefully, get some answers for you." I know if I suggested today, she'd jump at the chance, but honestly, I need some more downtime. And I think she does too.

"And now I want to know how you know Matteo?" she asks as she nibbles on a piece of bacon.

"He's been a sort of friend for many years." I scratch my chin, the stubble prickling against my skin. "Actually, I think you two met at Mama Rosa's one of the times we were there together. And how does he know Maddie again?"

"They had an on again off again thing in high school, until she found him hooking up with another girl right before home-coming dance." Lainey rolls her eyes and huffs.

"Speaking of high school, did you two work your shit out?" Wolf asks around a mouthful of pancakes.

I feel the muscle in my jaw tick as I stare at my brother, plot-ting all the ways I can pay him back for this shit. I glance at Alaina, bracing to see her ire, but to my surprise, she's smirking at him.

"We're working on it," she says with a casual half-shrug.

"Aye, we're doing something alright." My words are meant to be casual, but proving that this girl always keeps me on my fucking toes, she swings a glare my direction. I lean back in my chair and raise a brow. "Something to say, princess?"

"Ah, there he is. I was wondering when the moody bastard would come back." She mimes, looking at a watch on her wrist. "You lasted like an entire day. I'm impressed," she says with both brows raised and a smirk on her lips.

I cross my arms over my chest, irritation prickling along my neck.

Rush pushes his chair back and stands up from the table, stealing my attention. "I have a few calls to make."

"What about Da? Did anyone talk to him?" My words stop Rush.

He glances over his shoulder to look me in the eye. "Aye, we talked to him last night."

Insecurity prickles along the back of my neck, and I grit my teeth to stop it from spreading. I narrow my gaze on him and snap, "Without me, you mean?"

Rush's eyes flare as he turns around to regard me. Ah so he picked up on my irritation then. Good.

Rush grabs the back of the chair and leans over the table, staring at me with a smirk. "You were a little laid up, brother. And Da didn't tell us anything new."

I tip my chin up and lean back to look at him. He's my brother in every way but blood. I've killed for him—both of them —and taken hits meant for them. And I'd do it all again.

And I know they have my back—I know that in my bones. But it burns my gut a little that she wants me *and* them. And I'm doing my best to reel in the jealousy that flares up. I have half a mind to toss her over my shoulder—injury be damned—and stalk out of here.

The only thing stopping me is our conversation last night.

But what the fuck kind of twist of fate gave me back the one thing—the one *person*—who wanted me and just me. And then made her fall for two other dudes—my fucking brothers.

I wonder if I'm the only one who thinks about that.

I don't break his gaze, but I intentionally relax my muscles. I didn't realize how tense I'd gotten. "Enlighten me, then."

"Da seemed shocked about Lana's . . . involvement in the events. We didn't feed him details, but he reacted genuinely when we gave him the abridged version. So, I dunno, man." Wolf blows out a breath and runs his hand through his hair. "I don't want to think he's involved, but . . ."

"We just don't know," Rush finishes Wolf's thought. "So, we continue as if everyone is a potential enemy."

"Matteo's not." I shake my head. "There's no way he'd knife me and then take me to Jack."

"Diesel and his guys are good too. They've given us intel that we weren't privy to. It doesn't make sense for them to flip," Wolf says while drumming his fingers on the table.

"We can trust my cousins. And before you say anything, I know Mary fucked-up, but it was a one-time mistake. And I think she learned that lesson the hard way," Alaina says with a hand up, palm out.

"What about the Kings?" Rush looks between the three of us. "Which way are we falling on them?"

Alaina's the first to talk. "I trust them."

"You barely know them, princess." I raise a brow at her.

"Sometimes you just know these things," she says with a shrug of her shoulder.

"Enough to bet your life on? Because that's what we're talking about here—our lives," I counter, leaning forward and placing my arms on the table.

She looks at me, eyes solemn. "Yes. I do."

I nod and lean back, placing a hand over my bandage. The little power play I've been doing today doesn't agree with my recovering wound. "Good. I'm sure too, but I wanted to make sure you were too."

"Ass," she grumbles under her breath, loud enough for all of us to hear.

"Aye, I trust them too. So, we let them in then, yeah? Everyone else gets bare-bones information only if it's necessary. Otherwise, don't give anyone shit." Rush pushes away from the table and walks away.

Alaina and Wolf stand, push back from the table at the same time, and work together to clear the table. Meanwhile, I'm still stuck on everything she just laid out for us. It's obvious to me that she hasn't processed everything, not yet. But she will, and I have a feeling she's going to crash when she does.

But there's something missing here. And I intend to figure it out.

14

ALAINA

THE PHONE RINGS as I settle in the plush oversized armchair in the corner of Sully's room. Tucking a leg underneath me, I lean into the corner of the chair, resting my head against the back. The sun shines in through the windows, warming the room and my cheeks.

This view really is beautiful, but I think I'd miss being able to prop open a window on those perfect cool nights to let the breeze in. When you're up this high, there aren't any windows like that, just a few patio doors in the kitchen and living room.

I run the pad of my index finger along the broken cuticle of my thumbnail and curb the impulse to pick at it.

Despite the delicious breakfast Wolf made, my stomach feels hollow except for the guilt-sized boulder at the bottom.

I guess if she doesn't answer, then I get to postpone this conversation. But then I know I'll be obsessing over it until we can talk.

I'm about to end the video call request when Maddie answers. Her face is too close to the camera, and all I can see is one eye and half of her nose.

"Hey, Lainey," she says around a yawn, adjusting the phone so I can see her whole face.

"Maddie? Oh, thank god you're okay. You are okay, right? Wolf said you were, but you didn't answer when I called you earlier, and I was worried. I'm so sorry I didn't call last night. Once Sully was patched up, we came to their apartment here in the city, and I just . . . crashed. But Maddie, I'm so, so sorry for dragging you into my mess." The words come out in a rush, and my eyes well up. I don't bother wiping the tear away as it rolls down my cheek.

"Oh, Lainey, it's not your fault," Maddie says, voice thick with unshed tears.

"I think it is though. I don't understand what's going on, but I —I'm pretty sure they were trying to get me but took you by accident." I clear my throat when my voice cracks. "It was the same guy who took me on my birthday. And I just . . . You have no idea how sorry I am that you got hurt."

"I'm not mad. Maybe just a little scared though." Maddie shrugs a shoulder as she swipes a finger underneath her eyes, catching a stray tear.

I nod and grimace. "I know, and I'm sorry for that too."

"Lainey," she says on a sigh. "You're not responsible for something someone else does, and you're not responsible for my feelings. Besides, if they actually got you, I don't think we'd be talking right now. I think they would've done something horrible to you, Lainey. And I—I'm worried about you."

A small smile tips my lips up as something warm settles over me. "Always the mother hen. I'm okay. I have people watching over me."

She nods and sniffles. "And how are those Fitzgerald boys? Are they treating you good? Because if they aren't, they have to answer to me. And my new friends." She waggles her eyebrows at me, and I can't help but laugh a little.

"New friends, you say? Where are you?"

"I'm—" Her voice cuts off, and someone grabs the phone, their hand covering the camera.

"No locations, Madison. Do we need to go over this again?" His voice is firm, if not a little exasperated.

"Oh, come off it, Dante. That's my cousin we're talking about! She's the one who saved me."

"I don't care. If you can't stick to my rules, then I take your phone privileges away."

I hear her gasp, but I still don't see anything but the close-up view of someone's hand.

"Give me my phone back, or I'm calling Matteo." Her angry growl is unmistakable through the line.

My lips twist in amusement as I prop my legs up on the ottoman and wait for them to sort it out. A moment later, I hear rustling, and then my cousin's beautiful face comes back into view.

"Sorry, girl. Dante's a bossy asshole," she yells the last few words, no doubt taunting this Dante guy.

"Who's Dante?"

She huffs and rolls her eyes. "Just some asshole Matteo's friends with."

I quirk a brow. "Girl, I felt that sexual tension through the phone line however many miles away I am from you."

She doesn't answer except for a half-shrug, but the blush creeping up her neck says more than her words could.

My eyebrows shoot up. "What about Matteo?"

Maddie tips her chin up and looks down her nose at me. "Yeah, well, maybe I picked up a reverse harem novel last week after you told me all about your *situation*. And if you can do it, I thought I might try it. And what better time than when I'm cooped up in a safe house with a bunch of hot guys?"

Her confidence has always been one of my favorite things

about her. Once she sets her mind to something, she stops at nothing to achieve it. There's no doubt in my mind that she'll actually end up making her own reverse harem.

Now however long that lasts is another thing.

"It's unconventional. And . . . Sully and I, we're"—I shake my head and bite my lip—"complicated. It's not clear between us yet, but I'm hopeful."

"Damn. I'm sorry. Does that mean there haven't been any group activities yet?" At my intentionally blank look, she continues, "You know. You and at least two of them—oh my god! Has the bed seen all four of you at once yet?"

Before she can really work herself up, I hold up a hand. "No, no. There hasn't been much of that . . ."

"That sounds like a but statement," she says with an eager grin.

I chuckle. "But I wouldn't be opposed to it. We haven't exactly had a lot of time lately."

"Ah-ha! I knew it! Yes, girl. Damn the patriarchy!" She fist-bumps the air and then brings it toward the camera. I oblige her and bring my closed fist to the camera for a virtual fist bump.

"I don't think I was thinking about the patriarchy, Maddie." I roll my eyes. "But I'm not ashamed. All three of them are incredible."

"Even when Sully's being an asshole?"

"Yeah, even then." I sigh, a small smile playing along the edges of my lips.

We're both quiet for a moment, but it's a comfortable silence. I look away from the phone and stare at the morning sky.

"I'm sorry about your mom, Lainey." Maddie's voice is soft.

I look back at the phone, my sinuses tingling. "Me too. Me too."

"When you're ready, I'm here, okay?"

"Love you, cousin." My heart feels both full and empty at the same time. I'm so grateful to have her in my life—Mary too.

"Love you too."

I sniffle, feeling the tears roll down my cheeks. "It's weird, you know? I never, uh, never really spent a lot of time with her. In some ways, I didn't know her at all. And yet, I already miss her. Maybe just the idea of her, I don't know . . ."

"I can only imagine. I know Auntie Lana hasn't ever been the best mother to you, but you know my mom is always there. She's good for the kind of disapproval only a parental figure can inflict too."

A chuckle escapes my lips. "Always bringing some joy to the conversation. I don't know what I'd do with you and Mary. I pray that I'll never have to find out." My chest gets tight just at the thought.

"Well, I can speak for the both of us when I say you'll never have to find out!"

"Where is your sister, anyway? I haven't had a chance to talk to her since the diner, and I want to check-in."

"Didn't you hear? She's with some biker dudes. Apparently, Wolf vouched for them, and she didn't want to stay here with me. Said she needed 'space' whatever that means," she says with a roll of her eyes.

I jerk my head back in surprise. *Biker dudes?* "No, I . . . must've missed that somehow. I'll call her after we hang up."

"Don't bother. Her cell reception is nonexistent where she is. But I talked to her before she left, and she was okay. Told me about that creep she met online. Honestly, it's probably a good thing that none of us are in our usual routines right now." She shudders. "That Max guy sounds like a creep."

"Yeah, I'll have Wolf look into it. We have to stop by your mom soon. For arrangements and things."

That sobers both of us quickly, the smile slips from my face.

"Give her a hug for me, and call me later, okay? Don't leave me hanging, or I'll worry!"

"Always. Be safe, Maddie."

She smiles, and I end the video call. I tap the end of the phone on my bare thigh, debating on calling Mary anyway. I check the time and realize it's a little before noon.

"Screw it. I can always leave a message," I mumble to myself.

I'd rather try to get a hold of her now. I have a feeling she isn't in the best headspace, and I feel like some of that could be from me. I wince as I remember the look on Wolf's face when I told them about Benny.

Yeah, she's definitely hurting right now.

I video call Mary, holding up the phone to my face as it rings and rings. After the sixth ring, my thumb hovers on the end button when it connects.

Crunchy static comes through the line, and only frozen flashes of color are on my screen.

"Mary? Mary, can you hear me?"

"Lainey? Hey, girl, I didn't know you were here too." Mary's words are so slurred it's hard to understand what she's saying.

"Oh, shit. Are you drunk?" My jaw slackens as the picture clears up.

Mary's face is upside down, and she's taking a seriously long pull from a bottle of tequila. Her hair is wild, and she's wearing a cream peasant shirt and cutoffs.

Familiar thick bass beats fill the line, but I don't see anyone behind her. She's somewhere dark, but I can just make out the outline of a desk in the background.

I wince as she swallows and wipes the back of her mouth with her hand.

"Who's drunk?"

"Mary, turn the phone around. I can't see you."

"Whatever you say, Lainey. I always do whatever little miss perfect Queen Lainey says."

My mouth falls open at the bitterness dripping down her slurred words. My shock is quickly replaced with anger. "What the fuck, Mary?"

"Ooh, the princess is swearing. You must be mad now," she says in a singsong voice that does nothing to conceal her sarcasm.

I blow out a breath and tip my head back for a moment to gather myself. She's obviously drunk and hurting, so I'll give her a pass on this bullshit today. Guilt feels like acid inside my stomach at the situation both of my cousins are in because of me.

"I'm sorry, Mary. I'm sorry for dragging you into this mess. I still don't understand everything, but I promise that I'll do my best to keep you safe, okay?"

"Whatever, Lainey. I've got like ten hot as fuck biker dudes keeping me *safe*, so Ima have to let you go now." Mary hiccups before tipping the bottle back for another sip.

"Yeah, okay. Just . . . stay safe, okay? And call me in the morning when you're done nursing the hangover you're going to have from that," I say on a sigh.

Mary doesn't say anything else as she ends the call, and I'm left staring at my phone.

Restlessness stirs inside me, and I feel like I'm a blender, and all my insides are just swirling around. I press a hand to my stomach and focus on taking a few deep breaths.

I'm still dressed in last night's oversized shirt and rolled-up boxer briefs. Tipping my head to the side, Sully's bed taunts me with a nap.

I plug my phone in the nearby charger with a vow to check-in on Mary when I get up and crawl into bed. The last thing I remember is how soft the pillow is when my head hits it.

15

ALAINA

CONSCIOUSNESS COMES QUICKLY. One minute, I'm dreaming about beach vacations, and the next moment, I'm opening my eyes to a dark room, wondering what woke me up.

I'm overheating, and then my bladder screams its protest. Blinking a few times, I see the reason for the heat. I'm in the middle of Wolf and Sully on Sully's bed.

After some careful maneuvering and a bout of déjà vu, I wiggle out from under Wolf's bare, tattooed arm.

"Everyone knows monkeys love pineapple pizza . . ." Wolf mumbles as I slide off the bed.

I cover my mouth to stifle the laugh as I check on Sully. He doesn't look pale, and he's not sweating—all good things.

One of these days, I'm going to record all the funny things Wolf says while sleeping. They're just too good not to share.

I take care of business in the bathroom with the lights off, letting the late afternoon sun spill through the window. And then I let this magnificent shower tempt me with its built-in benches, tile walls, and three showerheads.

A quick peek inside the bedroom shows Wolf and Sully in the

same position, but no Rush. If I had to bet, I'd say he's off in *another* mini command center in this apartment somewhere. I'm not sure he knows how to let go.

Stripping out of my borrowed clothes, I take a few minutes to play with the shower settings and adjust them. I turn on all three showerheads, set it to just shy of scalding, and step inside, directly underneath the waterfall showerhead.

A shudder works its way down my body as the warm water rolls down my body, hugging my curves. I adjust one showerhead on an angle, so the water falls directly on my body, a soft sort of spray.

Tipping my head back under the spray and closing my eyes, I let the water slide down my face, over my lips, and down my neck. My shoulders loosen as the water holds me in its warm caress.

I take the time to soap my hands up with the nearby body wash container—coconut and sea salt—and run them over my body, really taking the time to massage it into my skin.

The movement is almost automatic, enough that I can let my mind wander a little bit.

I check-in with my emotions, expecting to find a well of grief with the top cracking and bulging at the seams. But instead, I mostly find the slow-moving current of rage underneath everything.

And lust. It used to be bottled up and nicely packaged, waiting until I wanted to take a sip. But I feel like Wolf and Rush and Sully have obliterated any sort of container for my lust. I feel like a goddamn walking bundle of hormones lately, and I don't know what the hell is happening.

All I know is that I want to explore it. With all three of them.

The temperature changes and I feel the beginning stirrings of lust as the water hits my body at all the right angles with the right amount of pressure.

A gasp leaves my lips at the feeling—I think I just discovered why people love these kinds of showers so much. I remember the article I read once in a women's magazine about shower-heads, and it gives me an idea. Maybe a release is exactly what I need.

Hell, at this rate, I may request a special bathroom upgrade for our dorm suite.

I detach the showerhead across from me and bring the handle close to my body, angling it so the water hits my pussy in a hot, steady stream.

"Oh fuck." The words leave my lips on a groan. Pleasure radiates throughout my body, a soft, warm sort of pleasure that has my limbs feeling light and tingly. I step back and lean against the shower wall, barely under the waterfall, and tip my head back, closing my eyes.

I feel him a second before I hear him. Tilting my face to the side, I stare at him through half-lidded eyes.

His chest rises and falls rapidly, his face the perfect look of concentration. When I flash a sultry smile at him, he takes it for the invitation it is and steps inside the spacious shower. He sits down, fully clothed in a black tee and black athletic shorts, on the bench across from me, spreading his legs and leaning his head against the tile with a thump.

I bite my lip as I aim the showerhead at a different angle, the water hitting my pussy in a new way. My eyelashes flutter closed on a moan, and fire licks up my body, heating me from the inside.

A strangled masculine groan fills the heated space, and I open my eyes. His intense gaze ensnares me, holding me captive. He leans forward, his fingers curling around the edge of the bench seat, his shoulders bunching.

He's the image of controlled desire as his gaze caresses every inch of my skin, leaving a trail of goosebumps in his wake.

"Are you just going to watch me?" I can't help but taunt him.

I know I'm playing with fire, but I'm not afraid of the heat. I'm praying I get scorched.

"I'll never stop watching you." His words sound like a promise falling from his pouty lips.

I watch in fascination as his muscles bunch and tense, his fists flexing and closing on his knees. He's holding himself back—I know he is.

What would it take to release the hold he has?

"Touch me, Sully," I all but beg him as I move the shower-head again, finding a new, pleasure-inducing angle.

He shifts forward before pushing himself against the tile wall again. "I want to, princess. You have no idea how much I want to, but I . . ."

"Pretend with me, James." I prop my foot on the bench next to me, giving him the perfect view of my pussy. And like a rubber band snaps, he springs up. I'm not sure if it was my words or my body, but I don't really care. I'm damn near giddy with antic-ipation.

With one hand behind his head, he grabs the collar of his shirt and pulls it off. I feel my jaw slacken as I take him in—all the sculpted, tattooed flesh that I'm dying to map with my fingers —and my tongue.

He turns around and presses a few buttons on the panel, and a second later, the showerhead changes its speed and pattern. It's faster and more of a pulsing rhythm. My breath hitches as plea-sure soars through my veins.

Sully stalks toward me, stopping in front of me to take the showerhead, his fingers lingering over mine on the handle. His body is angled so his wounded shoulder isn't under the spray, but our faces are inches apart.

His gaze roams my face for a moment, and I let him. I drop any barrier I might've had up and let him see *me*. I told him that we could pretend, but there's nothing make-believe about this or the way I feel about him.

He slides his hand to the back of my neck and into my hair before he seals his mouth to mine. Our tongues wage war on one another, and he taps into that passion he keeps under lock and key. I arch my back, desperate to feel his skin on mine.

He makes love to my mouth in that one kiss.

My head feels light, and my nerves are frayed, standing on the edge of a cliff and waiting to fall over.

He pulls back but keeps his lips hovering over mine as he slides his hand down to cover mine. He guides my hand to the inside of my thighs, tracing an invisible pattern that hits all my pleasure points. Lust clouds my brain, and I let my eyelashes flutter closed.

He stills our hands right next to my pussy, the tips of his fingers just above my clit. "Eyes on me, princess."

The growl in his voice snaps my eyelids open. He leans forward and presses a slow, hot kiss against my mouth, catching my bottom lip in between his teeth. He tugs softly, and it's like a straight shot to my clit.

His long, tattooed fingers tease me with light touches just outside where I need him most.

"Please," I say on a sigh, my eyes barely open as the taunting pleasure swells.

He holds my hand captive underneath his, but he doesn't torture me for long. He slides his first two fingers along my lower lips, up and down and up and down, framing my clit but never quite touching it. I lose the rhythm somewhere along the way, my hands reaching up to roll my nipples instead.

"Please what, princess?"

My chest heaves with anticipation, the flush spreading across my chest and up my neck. "Please make me come," I say against his mouth, licking the corner of his top lip.

His mouth curls into a deliciously sinful smirk before he spreads my pussy open with his fingers. He moves the pulsing showerhead directly in front of my clit, and the most intense pleasure I've ever felt takes over my body.

My back arches and a long low moan is torn from my throat. I can't keep my eyes open as I pinch my nipples and roll my hips involuntarily.

"That's it, princess. Can you imagine my cock inside you while you play with your pretty pink pussy in my shower, hmm?" Sully whispers his dirty words right into my ear, biting my earlobe softly.

"Yes," I murmur with a nod. My clit throbs in time with my heartbeat and my pussy clenches. I feel drunk on lust, and it's honestly fucking amazing. "Oh, shit. Oh, I'm going to . . ."

He angles the showerhead one more time, this time the pressure applied to my clit is almost too much, and my legs start shaking. Two seconds later, I fall off the cliff, shattering the entire way down.

My muscles clench, and my mouth falls open as the purest form of pleasure races around my veins like lightning bolts.

Sully moves the showerhead, and I open my eyes slowly, water dropping from my lashes. "That was incredible," I say on a breath.

His fingertips lightly caress me, sending little ripples of aftershocks through my body. "Aye, it was," he says against my mouth.

I slide a hand up his arm to rest on his good shoulder, holding him against me. "I'm not done pretending."

His hands tunnel into the hair at the nape of my neck. "We're just getting started, princess."

Excitement lights up inside my veins, and I push onto my tiptoes at the same moment he crushes his mouth to mine in a soul-searing kiss.

I manage to push him out of the shower and into the bathroom, never disconnecting our mouths. The tile floor is cool against my toes, and even though we're dripping water everywhere, I don't stop.

Steam billows into the air, following us into his bedroom. I guide Sully until the back of his legs hit the end of his bed.

My heart thunders inside my ears, beating a rhythm that belongs to this man. Curling my fingers into the waistband of his shorts, I slowly drag them down his hips and over his ass, breaking our kiss.

I sink to my knees, keeping my gaze on his as I slide his shorts down his legs. His eyes turn nearly black with lust, and his kiss-swollen lips part on a deep exhale.

I'm not very experienced with this—most of my previous experience was *with* him, but I'm so goddamn turned on right now, not even my insecurities can stop me. I let him see the desire radiating from my gaze—if my wet pussy wasn't enough of an indication.

I drop my gaze to his dick right in front of me and lick my lips in anticipation. "Holy shit . . ." I can feel my eyes widen at the size of him. We messed around when we were younger, but either I misremembered him, or he got bigger.

"Fuck, princess, what are you—"

I wrap my fingers around his dick, cutting off whatever he was going to say. He feels hard and soft at the same time as I stroke him, my fingertips not even close to touching.

"Goddamn." The word sounds like a groan, and I glance at him as I stroke him, twisting my hand and tightening my grip.

I lean forward and seal my lips around the head of his dick, twirling my tongue around a few times before I take him deeper.

Sully sucks in a breath, releasing it on a low groan as he slowly slides his hand into my hair. His touch is firm but undemanding as I suck his cock without a single inhibition.

I glance at him from underneath my lashes as I lick and suck and stroke his hard cock. Our heated gazes crash together and a ripple of electricity races across the room.

I know he feels it too, because in the next moment, he tightens his grip on my wet hair, twirling it around his hand. The pressure on my scalp has me gasping as I feel myself get wetter.

"Oh fuck . . ." Sully stares at me, flicking his gaze between my eyes and my lips stretched around him. His ocean-blue eyes are dark enough to look black, and I hope he can see the lust pooling in mine as I moan around his cock, flicking my tongue along the underside of his shaft.

That's as long as he lets me play though. Like a man possessed, he guides my mouth by his grip on my hair and sinks his cock into my mouth once, twice, three times before he pulls me off of him with a pop.

My eyebrows crease as I stare at him, but before I can voice my confusion, he hauls me up and crushes his mouth to mine. Our tongues tangle for dominance as he steps back against the back.

I nudge him to sit down with a hand on his chest. I place a knee on either side of him, hovering over his lap. It'd be so, so easy to just sink down on him, to claim him as mine. But doing that would shatter the illusion of pretend we're hiding behind.

Sully pulls back, his palm on my cheek and whispers, "I don't want to pretend anymore."

My heart soars, and my mouth falls open. We're definitely on the same wavelength.

He slides his palm from my cheek to the hair at the nape of my neck, his gaze bouncing around my face. His voice is low, tortured as he says, "But I don't forgive you for leaving me, Alaina. And I don't fucking forgive you for making it look so goddamn easy."

I curl my fingers around his wrist, holding him to me. "I—"

He closes the gap between our mouths, his eyes bright, and

his lips graze mine with each syllable. "Don't insult me by saying you didn't."

I strain, still hovering above him, desperate to feel him and desperate to wade into our past and finally deal with it. My heart aches at the anguish painted on his face.

"I didn't think I'd ever see you again, James. I—" I bite my lip, shaking my head in two small movements as I remember the events from that night so clearly. "I didn't leave you. I would have *never* left you."

16

ALAINA

THEN

THIS PAST SUMMER with James felt like a dream or the plot of a book or something. But definitely not real life—not my life.

And yet, here I am about to go on another date with my boyfriend. I can barely keep the giddy smile off my face.

I slip my phone out of my skirt pocket and check the time for the seventh time in as many minutes—still nothing from James. I open up the text conversation with him and read over our last messages. Maybe I misunderstood where we were meeting?

> James: Can't wait to see you tonight, princess. 8:00 at O'Malley's Pub

Maybe he's just caught in traffic. He did mention that he had something he had to do for his dad this afternoon. Traffic in the city is crazy, but it's absolutely insane on a Friday night.

Me: Hey! I'm outside O'Malley's. See you soon!

I lean against the red-colored brick and watch as a group of girls walk around me to get inside the pub. The bouncer checks their IDs and nods them inside. When the door opens, I hear the notes of The Clash's "Train in Vain" and hum along.

"You gonna stand outside all night, girlie?"

I turn my head to take in the bouncer by the door. With bright-orange hair and a matching beard, ripped jeans, and a faded Dropkick Murphys band tee, he looks every bit the bouncer to an Irish pub.

"I'm just waiting for someone."

He crosses his arms and nods his head, staring out into the NYC night. "First date, huh?"

I shrug one shoulder. "Not really, no." I shift off the wall to face him. "We've been hanging out for a while. We're meeting to check out the band tonight." My cheeks flush at my overshare and I shut my mouth with a click, hooking my thumb over my shoulder toward the pub.

"Big Clash fan, huh?" He nods toward my shirt.

"Yep. I found the London Calling album in my dad's vinyl collection years ago. It's one of my favorites."

"Your dad has good taste. I'm Jack, by the way. I own this place." He nods toward the building. "And you're going to love Jimmy and the Jazzes. They're the best Clash cover band I've seen in years. We first discovered them at our open mic night on Fridays. They were good—really good. And they brought a following with them. Eventually, we offered them a solo spotlight once a month."

There's something calming about chatting with him. The beard is a little distracting, but I think he's probably old enough to be my dad. And he doesn't give me any creepy vibes. "That's cool. Yeah, I'm excited to check them out once my boyfriend gets here. I'll have to check out the open mic night too."

My phone vibrates with an incoming text.

> James: I'm sorry. I can't

My heart thunders in my ears as I stare at my phone. Did I just get stood up? Is he . . . breaking up with me?

My face flushes and sweat breaks out along my neck that has nothing to do with the summer heat.

I knew I shouldn't have pushed him for labels. I don't even care about that kind of thing, but the girls convinced me that he would hook up with other girls if I didn't.

I bite my lip as I second-guess my conversation with him this morning. I had asked him to do the long-distance thing when he went back home to Boston, but his response was a halfhearted shrug. He was distracted by this thing he had to do for his dad, so I assumed that's why he didn't answer the way I was expecting —hoping for.

Embarrassment warms my cheeks when I remember that I told him that I had feelings for him this morning too.

> Alaina: Is this because of what I said this morning?

I watch the bouncing three dots for a moment before they stop. My heart skips for a second as disappointment so heavy fills me that I feel the telltale tingling in my nose. Shit, I'm going to cry any second now.

Stop being ridiculous, I chastise myself. I don't know that's what's going on. I just went to the worst-case scenario.

I curse my fair skin for the millionth time when I feel the

warmth on my cheeks. Taking a deep breath, I look up and blink rapidly. I will my eyes not to let go of the tears.

Maybe something happened during that errand for his dad? What if he got into another fight? Or worse? My stomach drops at the thought of James getting hurt.

> **Alaina:** Is everything okay? Are you hurt?

I bounce my heel as my nerves stretch and strain while I wait for his reply. I give him a minute to reply before I call him. It rings once before it goes to voicemail. I'm about to leave a voicemail when my phone vibrates with an incoming text message.

> **James:** Sorry, I can't talk right now.

He sent me the standard preset message. What the hell does that even mean? Oh god, he is breaking up with me.

I try to swallow past the lump in my throat.

I know I shouldn't be surprised, but I am. My mom always told me that boys will only want me for one thing—and now more than ever, I'm so glad that I never slept with him. Telling him I had feelings for him the same day he ditches me is humiliating enough.

I make up a weak excuse to the bouncer and turn on my heel as the second, third, and fourth tears slowly trail down my heated cheeks. I walk to the end of the corner and wait for the light to turn, so I can cross the street.

I can't believe that I just got stood up. Who even does that? I should've known James was too good to be true. With his perfect face and perfect laugh and perfect taste in music, he was definitely too good to be true.

I wipe underneath my eyes, trying to make sure my mascara hasn't run. I guess it's a good thing I use the stupid waterproof stuff that Madison made me buy last month. Normally, I'd be worried about someone seeing me like this, but this is New York City on a Friday night in the summer. A crying teenager is probably the most normal thing on the streets right now.

———————

BY THE TIME I make it home, I've talked myself into ten different circles with fifty different reasons why James didn't show. I decided to call him again. He already sent me to voicemail, so what's the worst that could happen?

I take my phone out of my pocket; nine-thirty and no new calls or texts. I bring up his contact and hit call. It rings once before I hear the telltale three-tone sound of a disconnected phone. My fears are confirmed with I hear the robotic woman's voice. "We're sorry. Your call cannot be completed."

I press end and call again, receiving the same three tones and automated message. I end the call and sit on the end of my bed. My legs feel weak as disbelief rolls through my body like a wave.

I look out the window as I mentally replay all of our interactions over the last few months. I thought . . . I thought James really liked me.

I fall back on my bed, one hand splayed on my heart. Is it possible to physically feel your heart breaking?

The rose-colored glasses that I've been wearing are cracking; each time we hung out, each laugh and shared playlist feels like a lie.

I thought I was falling in love with him—I thought . . . I thought he felt the same way. But now, I realize how stupid that sounds. Who falls in love with someone in a couple months?

I grab my phone and open up my group message with the girls.

> Alaina: Is that invitation to join you guys still good?

I'm not sure anyone or anything could make me feel better, but it's worth a try. This hurts way more than anyone ever told me it would. Those books got it wrong; heartbreak feels like my heart is being ripped out of my chest. And someone is pouring acid on the gaping hole.

Tears steadily roll down my cheeks, and a small sob bubbles up my chest. I feel so foolish. To think someone like him could love someone like me.

What was I thinking?

When he didn't want to introduce me to his friends in Central Park, I thought he was being sweetly possessive, like some character in a romance novel. Now though—now, I realize he didn't bother introducing us because it didn't matter—it wasn't worth it.

I wasn't worth it.

Why does everyone in my life leave me?

Ninety minutes earlier

SULLY

MY PHONE VIBRATES with a text as I step next to my brother. I slip it out of my pocket to see a message from Alaina.

> Punk Rock Princess: Hey! I'm outside O'Malley's. See you soon!

Fuuckkk. I scrub my hand over my face as regret covers me

like a heavy blanket. I should've been at the pub twenty minutes ago.

My brother, Rush, discreetly elbows me, nailing me right on my healing ribs. By the smirk tipping his lips, that asshole knew exactly where he was aiming.

While we don't look anything alike, his chestnut-brown hair and gray eyes to my dark-blonde hair and blue eyes, we're the same height and similar build.

"Pay attention, fuckers. I'm not getting shot tonight because you two idiots aren't listening." Wolf, my other brother, knocks his shoulder into mine. At six foot three with black hair and almost a full sleeve, he's the oldest of all three of us.

I cut him a warning glare. "Fuck of—"

My da interrupts me. "Something to say, boyo?"

I straighten up to my six-foot-two height and look him in the eye. "No, sir. Ready to show the Russians how we deal with thieves."

Cormac Fitzgerald, better known as the Butcher of Summer Knoll gang, and the only father figure I've ever known, chuckles. "That's the spirit, Sully. Tonight, we show them how the Brotherhood responds to threats on our territory."

When the men answer his war cry with varying cheers and yells, I pull my phone out of my pocket and type out a quick text to Alaina.

> James: I'm sorry. I can't

Before I can finish my text, my brother grabs my phone and pushes it into my chest, inadvertently sending the text. I don't have time to worry about it now. The rest of the guys are filing out of the large room we use for meetings and heading down the hallway toward our armory.

149

> Punk Rock Princess: Is this because of
> what I said this morning?

I wait behind my brothers, letting the low murmur of chatter roll off of me as I replay our conversation from this morning. I was so goddamn distracted by what I knew was going to go down tonight that she took me by surprise when she asked to stay together after summer ends. Like I'd fucking let her go anywhere. Thinking about the way her cheeks flush when she's nervous—and the other parts of her that flush—has a smile tipping up the corner of my mouth.

I regret not laying it out there for her then and letting her know that there was no way we were done in three weeks when summer break ended. But I had Rush in one ear rattling off numbers and data and other shit that he loves but no one else does.

I'm next in line for my vest and gun when my phone vibrates with a text.

> Punk Rock Princess: Is everything okay?
> Are you hurt?

Before I can text her back, my phone trills "Punk Rock Princess" by Something Corporate—her assigned ringtone. Fuck.

"Boyo! Get up here and get suited up." There's no trace of my da right now; it's the Butcher that yells at me.

I send her to voicemail and send her a quick standard message.

> Me: Sorry, I can't talk right now.

I silence my phone and tuck it in my pocket. I grab the vest and 9mm handed to me and walk over to my brothers. I need to get my head in the game. I have no intention of never seeing my beautiful juxtaposition again, she's an irresistible combination of CBGB and *Gossip Girl*—shit, she's like a punk-loving Serena Van Der Whatever. The only reason I didn't completely hate the King sisters is because they came over and watched a lot of *Gossip Girl* reruns last year, and Blake Lively is hot as fuck. Plus, Maeve always has the fucking coolest new weapons.

Unfortunately, that means I need to push her to the back of my mind and focus on what's going to go down tonight.

Hopefully, it's a quick in-and-out, and I get back to my girl. But if there's anything I learned about being in the Brotherhood, it's that you can count on shit going sideways, so you learn to expect the unexpected.

SWEAT ROLLS down the side of my face as my brothers and I carefully make our way through the overgrown weeds and around fallen trees toward the chain-linked fence encasing the abandoned industrial park in Brooklyn.

"You couldn't have pissed before we left, Rush?"

"Fuck off, Wolf. It took me like thirty seconds."

Wolf scoffs in amusement. "Thirty seconds? Bro, you were pissing for at least sixty seconds, right, Sully?"

I swat a bug away from my face and jump over a rotten log. "I don't usually keep track of Rush's dick."

Wolf throws his head back and sighs dramatically. "Whatever. The point is now we're at least a minute behind schedule, and I, for one, don't want to keep Da waiting. So, let's fucking hustle."

According to Buzz, our resident technical genius, this is where the Russians have been hanging out, and this is where we'll find our shit they stole.

The first notes of "Punk Rock Princess" pierce the air. Shit. Alaina's calling me. I could've sworn I put it on silent. It must've gotten jostled when we were crawling around like we're on the set of *Rambo*.

"What the fuck, dude?! Turn that shit off before you get us killed!" Wolf's voice is right behind me.

"Shit. Sorry." I hold the power button down to turn off my phone.

Rush stops abruptly in front of me, and I walk right into him. He grunts. "Something's not right."

I glance around. "What do you mean?"

"I mean, why is it so quiet?"

Wolf steps next to me and scoffs. "Look around you, man"—Wolf opens his arms wide—"we're sneaking around in these shitty woods at eight o'clock on a Friday."

"Exactly." Rush glares at him. "Where the fuck is all the noise? I don't hear a single goddamn cricket or branch moving."

"No shit, man. We *don't* want them to hear us." His eyes widen to emphasize his point. "What's up with you?"

Adrenaline pumps through my veins and the hair on my arm stands up. I slowly turn in a circle, trying to pinpoint the cause for my unease.

"He's right, Wolf. It's *too* quiet."

Rush tilts his head. "Do you guys hear that?"

I look to the left and then to the right. "What?"

"Shh!" Wolf steps to my right and cocks his head.

"Is that . . . buzz—"

"Ticking? It sounds like ticking." Wolf's eyebrows crease.

"Why the fuck—"

"Fuck me, that's ticking! We gotta get the fuck outta here!" Wolf interrupts me.

Before Wolf even finishes his sentence, we all turn around and run like the devil himself is on our heels. I'm not ready to meet my maker yet. There's still shit I want to do—Alaina's face comes to mind, and I can see with crystal clarity how she looks when she laughs. It's the most beautiful thing I've ever seen.

"It's a fucking trap! Get back! Get back, Da!" Rush screams into his phone as we haul ass over fallen branches, uncaring about the noise we're making.

The ticking stops.

And then everything fucking explodes.

17

ALAINA

HIS HANDS gently hold my sides, his pinkies resting on the curve of my hip and his thumbs sweeping back and forth over my ribs.

His gaze is focused on my throat as he talks. "I went back to the library for three weeks, Alaina. Three fucking weeks, I dragged my sorry ass to the steps and looked for you."

My heart stutters at his admission, and my hands tremble as they lay against his warm, tattooed skin. I can't make myself look him in the eye as I reel from the events of that night from his point of view.

"It was—it was a misunderstanding?" I whisper, flicking my gaze to his. His eyes reflect the grief I feel in my limbs as he nods. "But why didn't you just call me?"

His hands slide up and down my sides at a leisurely pace. I know it should feel a little odd that we're having this discussion while I'm sitting on his lap—and we're both naked. But, strangely, it doesn't. I feel more vulnerable, and my emotions are close to the surface, but it's the most that Sully's opened up to me since we've reconnected. So, I'm looking at it as a good thing.

"My phone was torched during the ambush, Lainey. And I didn't save shit right apparently."

"My dorm?"

He nods before I finish talking. "Aye. I went there, and one of the girls told me you were in Europe with your cousins."

I swallow the sob that threatens to escape and look at his tattoo along his ribs as I try to make sense of everything. It's a skull with a knife through the middle, surrounded by flowers. "So much lost time, James. I—I feel so foolish now."

"Too much, princess. You should've given me time to explain." His chastisement isn't harsh, but it stings nonetheless. "Though knowing what I know now—about your mom—I understand why you ran."

I dart my gaze to his. "I didn't run—"

"Princess. You literally hopped a flight hours later." He levels me with a disbelieving look.

I stroke the clover tattooed on his neck with my thumb and hold his gaze. "Alright. I can admit that. I—I don't know why I did that. I was embarrassed and . . ." I shrug. "But why didn't you have Rush look for me. I'm sure he could have found me."

"Aye. But I didn't tell him about you. You were mine—something that belonged to only me, and I didn't want to share you. Not then."

My breath hitches at his wordplay. "And now?"

He smooths his hands around my hips to rest on my ass and drags me toward him. I suck in a breath when our chests collide, my nipples pebbling. His cock, thick and hard, rests between our bodies, and lust simmers in my veins, burning out some of the grief and years-old embarrassment.

Running his hands from my ass to my shoulders, Sully whispers against my mouth, "And now you're mine." He licks the corner of my mouth and my lips part. "And you're theirs. Ain't that right, brother?"

I turn my head to the side, heart in my throat, expecting to see Rush or Wolf, but neither is anywhere behind me. I feel Sully's lips on my neck as he chuckles. I turn back to him with a mock huff and mutter, "Asshole."

One of these days, I'm going to have all three of them—at the same time. And if I have it my way, that day is coming sooner rather than later.

"Yeah, but I'm your asshole, princess. I told Wolf to get lost before I even joined you in the shower." Sully drags his lips down my body until he hovers over my nipple. "Because this moment right here, it's just for me, yeah?"

He closes his mouth over my nipple and sucks—hard. I feel the pull directly in my clit and my pussy clenches. I reach for his shoulder before I remember that he's hurt. Pulling back, I mutter, "Your shoulder though. You're hurt, Sully . . ."

"Fuck my shoulder. I've got my girl in my hands again. I'm flying high, princess. Nothing can stop me."

I don't care what he says, I'm still not convinced we should be doing this so soon. But then he tugs on my nipple, sending another shot of lust straight to my core, and I forget my own name for a moment.

I grip his good shoulder with one hand and tip my head back, letting him have better access. My damp hair tickles my back and my hips start to roll on instinct. I swivel my hips toward him, and my pussy glides along his hard cock, the tip hitting my clit every time.

He raises his head, his lips wet and shiny, and I meet him halfway for a bruising kiss. We part, foreheads touching, and chests heaving.

This is it—the moment of truth. If he's going to bail, he would do it now. I mentally prepare myself for his rejection—either polite or cruel. That tiny kernel of hope that lives inside me, etched in his name, grows with every moment that he looks at me with lust and acceptance shining in his eyes.

But I have to be sure.

"Are you mine, James?" My words are low, but I know he hears me over the air conditioning blowing into the room.

"Aye, princess. I've always been yours." He seals his declaration with a kiss that lights up my body all the way down to my toes.

He kisses all the oxygen from my lungs, but I decide that oxygen is overrated.

I can't stop my hips from rolling against him, desperately seeking friction. It's like he can read my mind, because in the next moment, he slips his hand in between us, his fingers grazing my clit with featherlight touches. It's enough to drive me mad.

"I want you to fuck me, James," I say against his lips, tugging on his bottom lip with my teeth. His hand stills as he pulls back, his gaze searching my face.

I line up our bodies together in a deliberate move, hovering above him so the tip of his cock rests against my pussy. I won't make the decision for him, but I don't want him to second-guess my intention.

I'm all-fucking-in with the Fitzgerald boys.

And I'm ready to claim them as mine.

Sully slides his hand up my stomach and between my breasts to rest at the base of my throat in a move that reminds me of Rush. I pant, my eyes half-closed as I wait for him to decide.

"Fuck, you're beautiful." I see it the moment he decides. His eyes light up, and his whole body buzzes.

In the next moment, he gently guides me down onto his hard cock, brows furrowed in concentration. I gasp at the feeling of fullness as he slides me down excruciatingly slow, my eyes fluttering closed on instinct.

His grip tightens around my hip as he stalls our movement. "Eyes on me, princess."

My eyes flash open, and my pussy clenches at the authoritative tone in his voice.

"Fuck," he says on a groan. "You like that, yeah?"

I nod several times. "More, James. I need more."

He loosens his hold on my hip but keeps his pace slow. "More what, princess?"

"You—" I groan, cutting myself off as sweat beads on my brow. He feels too fucking good.

He adjusts his hold so both hands land on my hips, and I squeeze his good shoulder with one hand, the other cupping my breast.

I open my mouth to tell him something—I don't even know what—but he thrusts up, stealing my breath and all thought.

A gasp leaves my lips, and I slam my eyes closed. I can't keep them open as overwhelming pleasure spikes along every nerve ending.

"Goddamn, you feel even better than I imagined."

I open my eyes in time to see him swipe his tongue over his lower lip in a move so sexy it should be fucking outlawed. He gives me a moment to get adjusted to the feel of him, and then I roll my hips, mimicking the movement from earlier. Only this time, it feels so . . . much . . . *more.*

He groans my name before gripping my hips again, harder this time and encouraging me to ride him faster, harder. Our mouths meet halfway as lust cascades over my body in waves. I lose the rhythm for a moment, stuttering as my pleasure spikes.

Sully takes over and starts fucking me from underneath, and I'm too busy riding that fucking wave to protest about his injury.

"You're incredible, Alaina. And fuck me if I don't still fucking love you," he says through pants and groans, his body taut.

He takes us higher and higher, and when he snakes a hand

down to pinch my clit, I free-fall over that peak. I race back down to earth, content to let these waves of desire cover me forever.

Tortured groans punctuate the air, and I fuse my lips to his, desperate to taste his passion—passion that's mine. I squeeze my muscles around his cock and grin as his breaths turn labored.

"You're going to make me come if you keep that up—" His words end on another moan as I roll my hips again and again. He tenses for a moment, and then I feel his hot cum inside me.

He rests his forehead against my chest, his hair tickling my skin and his hot breaths fanning my pebbled nipple. "Goddamn, princess. That was fucking incredible." He tips his head up, and that stupid-hot, charming grin covers his face.

There's something so disarming about his grin—probably because he so rarely uses it—but it melts my heart even further.

"That was incredible." I lick my lips, a flicker of worry creeping in on my post-orgasm bliss. "That was okay, right? You're not hurt . . . or regretting it?"

Sully places a soft kiss against my lips and slides my hair behind my ear. "It was perfect—you were perfect."

I grin and slide off of him with a small wince. "I'm going to go clean up. You stay here and rest, okay?"

The way he looks at me, with love shining in his eyes, steals my breath for a moment. I haven't seen that look in two long years. I spin on my heel and walk into the bathroom with a small smile on my face. It feels good to be his again.

It feels good to be all of theirs.

Twenty minutes and another shower later, I open the bathroom door, letting the steam pour into the bedroom again. I spy Sully's naked sleeping form on the bed, and I decide to let him rest.

I slip on a clean shirt from the top of his dresser and make my way toward the kitchen. I'm parched, and a milkshake would taste so delicious right about now. I doubt I'll find a milkshake in their kitchen, but I'd settle for any kind of ice cream.

I pause in the doorway to the kitchen when I see Rush and Wolf sitting at the table, each with a drink in front of them.

Wolf swirls his glass tumbler around, so the ice cubes clink together before he takes a healthy swallow of the amber liquid. "You're loud, baby girl."

Warmth rolls through my body, settling in my cheeks as I meet his gaze head-on. I'm not embarrassed, not really, but I'm still getting used to the idea of having all three of them. And I think they are too.

"I'm not sorry," I tell him with a halfhearted shrug.

"Nothing to be sorry for, birdie. He's just a little jealous."

I stare at Wolf, blinking a few times. "You are?"

"Hell yes, I'm fucking jealous. But not like you think, so just relax that furrowed brow, baby girl. I'm just dying to get my hands on you again. What can I say? I'm fucking greedy." He flashes a Cheshire-cat grin that's a little too feral to be considered charming.

"Well, okay then . . ." I trail off as I beeline for the freezer.

"What're you looking for?" Rush asks from behind me.

"Ice cream? I was thinking of making myself a milkshake," I tell him with my head inside their freezer. A tan, tattooed hand reaches past my face and pulls out a pint of strawberry ice cream. "My favorite," I murmur.

"I know," Rush whispers, his breath stirring the damp hair next to my ear.

A smile twists up my lips, and together, we gather everything we'll need for strawberry milkshakes. By the time I make enough for the four of us and pour them out, Sully wanders into the room.

"Ah, Sleeping Beauty is awake!" Wolf crows with a grin.

"Fuck off, Wolf." He doesn't even look his way, his gaze is

locked on me—more specifically, my bare legs underneath his shirt.

I slide a milkshake across the island, and he snags it before it hits him in the chest. With Rush and I on one side, and Wolf and Sully across from me, I let the feeling of *home* settle into my bones.

It feels amazing.

And the urge that's been riding me for a couple of days, the one that's pushing me to protect this feeling, has me opening my mouth.

"I'm ready to see my aunt, and then—then I think I'll have to deal with Gallagher Industries."

"Whatever it is, we'll deal with it together, birdie."

"Aye, as a family," Wolf vows.

"A family," Sully says with a nod.

18

ALAINA

I MOVE the side of my *Jurassic Park* shirt, adjusting the strategic rips in the sleeveless shirt made to look like dinosaur claw marks. Taking Back Sunday's "MakeDamnSure" plays through the speakers from Sully's playlist, and I smile.

Thinking about his specific song choice back at the cabin has me wondering if this song is intentional too. That man is like an onion, and all his layers are hard and thick.

That's not the only thing that's hard and thick . . .

I startle myself and a giggle slips past my lips before I can stop it. Jesus, I don't know what the hell has gotten into me. I'm on the way to see my aunt about my dead mother's last words, and I'm fantasizing about Sully's dick and giggling? What the hell is going on with me?

Well, it is an impressive dick. I roll my eyes at my inner monologue, which still sounds suspiciously like Maddie.

I sigh and stare out of the window. I'm sure I'm in some sort of denial, but I've always been able to compartmentalize. I'm a multitasker.

We stopped at a boutique a few blocks away from their apart-

165

ment so I could grab some clothes. We're going to swing by my dorm room after we visit Aunt Sloane, but for now, the artfully ripped shirt and light jean shorts will do.

My toes tap along with the beat as they sing about making sure someone can't leave, and my shoes catch my attention. Something shifts uncomfortably in my chest at the sight of the dirty shoes—is that a bloodstain? I tilt my head for a better look, and my chest eases when I see it's just dried mud.

My all-white Vans are looking a little worse for wear, but they'll be just like new after I wash them. Another reason I love my Vans? They go with just about everything.

I hadn't given much thought to my outfit when I bought it, but it just occurs to me that I'm meeting one of my mother's last living relatives—her twin sister—to discuss her funeral arrangements in a shirt designed to look like a raptor ripped it.

My mother, who was so concerned with appearances, dressing to impress, and acting however she deemed appropriate. She'd be incensed if she could see me now.

A chuckle escapes me, the idea so amusing in an ironic sort of way.

Wolf slides his hand across the space between us in the backseat. It settles against my thigh, his warm palm squeezes once. I look to him, humor dancing across my lips. His brow creases with concern.

"You okay, Alaina?" Rush asks from the driver's seat as we pull into the valet line in front of my aunt's building.

"Yeah," I sigh out the word. "It's just . . . ironic."

I meet Rush's gaze in the rearview mirror, his eyes narrowed, and I wonder if he thinks this is where I lose it. I bet they're all just waiting for me to break.

I wouldn't be surprised. I mean, that's what I'm kind of waiting for too. It's a weird notion, waiting for yourself to have an emotional breakdown. One caused by the death of your mother and the confirmed death of your father.

"Fuck. I'm an orphan." The words are pulled from my soul before I even have conscious thought to let them.

Heaviness settles on my shoulders and grief weighs me down. My eyes unexpectedly well with tears, and I chuckle, this disbelieving noise that sounds harsh to my ears.

I flick the tears off my face, and I look between these three men. Rush and Sully are twisted around to face me and Wolf has turned his whole body to face mine. Emily James sings a haunting melody in the background.

"I don't even know why I'm crying. It's just so . . . unexpected, ya know?" I blow out a breath and stare at the car's ceiling to stop the tears from sliding down my cheeks. "Orphan. I'm an orphan." The words are low in the quiet of the car. They taste foreign on my tongue.

"You make your own family, princess."

My breath hitches as I stare at my first love. His face is open —his whole demeanor has softened toward me. I think we turned a corner last night, him and I. A gift in the middle of such chaos.

Wolf squeezes my thigh once and steals my attention. His teeth dig into his bottom lip. "Mary and Maddie. Your aunt. Us."

"We're your family now, baby." Rush's voice is firm, that goddamn commanding quality I love coating every syllable.

"And you're not alone." Those four words feel like a promise from Sully's lips.

I meet each of their gazes and nod. Two tears roll down my cheeks with the movement.

A knock on the window pops the tension swelling in the car, and as one, we all turn to look at the valet standing next to Rush's door.

Rush holds up a finger to the man and looks over his shoulder at me. "Ready, baby?"

I inhale and blow out a breath as I meet his gaze. "Let's go."

Rush stares at me for a moment before turning back to the valet and opening his door.

"We're here, Red, yeah? We're right here, and if it's too much or you've had enough, you give me the signal, and we're outta there. No questions."

I unbuckle my seat belt, lean over the middle seat and press my lips against Wolf's in a quick kiss. I pull back a little, my lips brushing against his as I tell him, "I don't know what I did to deserve you guys. Thank you."

Wolf curls an arm around my lower back and sweeps me into his body. He rests his forehead against mine. "It's us who are undeserving, baby girl. But we're also selfish assholes, and I'm hoping that by the time you realize that, you'll already be so in love with us that you won't even think about leaving."

I smile, a small laugh bubbling up at his ridiculous words. I pull back, and my smile freezes when I see his expression. I expected a teasing smirk or a cocky smile, but there's neither. His plush lips are in a straight line, his eye contact unwavering.

I trace my finger over his cheekbone and down to his bottom lip. "You're serious." It's not a question but a realization.

Wolf parts his lips and scrapes his teeth over the pad of my finger before releasing it. I let my hand drop, marveling at the ease in which we touch one another. The physical act of touch is something I didn't know I was missing until Wolf came into my life. And I wouldn't trade it for anything.

The door opens behind Wolf, and I hear Rush's voice. "As a heart attack, Alaina."

"I don't like that phrase," I say, but I'm distracted by this revelation. I mean, I knew they were into me. Exchanging hushed declarations of love in the heat of the moment is one thing. But this feels like more than that. This feels like they're teasing me with the promise of forever.

"Noted," Rush says as he opens the door wider. Wolf slowly lets go of me before he turns to get out of the car. I follow behind him, squinting as the summer sun beats down on us.

I follow Wolf and Rush around the car to find Sully talking to the doorman. They shake hands and he opens the door for all of us.

"Ms. McElroy, nice to see you again."

I nod and offer him a small smile. "Thank you, Cliff. It's nice to see you too."

The air conditioning chills the lobby of my aunt's apartment building, a stark contrast to the weather outside. Goosebumps trail down my arms as I approach the desk.

"Hey, Cheryl. Is my aunt in? I guess I should've called ahead."

"No problem, Ms. McElroy. Let me just ring her and see if she's available," Cheryl says with a smile.

The thought of correcting her crosses my mind. I'm not a McElroy, not really. But I guess it doesn't really matter right now, so I let it go.

I look over my shoulder at the three men at my back while we wait. Dressed in jeans and tees, they could be mistaken for your average all-American boys.

Until you saw the tattoos snaking out from underneath their sleeves and collars. The cloud of danger that hangs around them, the matching scowls, and the aura of power that seeps from their pores.

Then your instincts kick in, and you know better. I'm not sure what that says about my instincts if they're beating down my door, telling me to run *to* them. Not away from them.

I let the smirk tip up my lips as I take them in together like this. Almost as if they can hear what I'm thinking, all three of them fold their arms across their wide chests and smirk.

"Ms. McElroy? She's ready for you," Cheryl says, stealing my attention from my three dark gods at my back.

I offer her a smile that doesn't feel as forced as it did earlier. "Thank you."

We walk to the elevator at the back of the lobby, and the doors open immediately. All four of us step on, and Rush leans over and presses the twenty-three button.

I quirk a brow. "I'm not sure that I should be surprised that you know what floor she lives on, but I am."

Rush's grin is his only response. Wolf laces his fingers with mine, and in an unexpected move, Sully slides his palm against my other hand. I look down at our hands as he slides his fingers in between mine. His grip on my hand is firm, and affection surrounds me. It feels like sunshine on a cool spring day, warming me from the inside out.

I tilt my head to look at Sully, expecting to see his eyes on me, but he's staring resolutely ahead. His gaze never strays from the closed elevator doors in front of us.

I bite my lip and look back at our joined hands. I remember the first time he held my hand.

"I made a playlist for you."

The elevator slows and dings as the door opens, bringing me out of my memory. Both of them let go of my hands as I stride out of the elevator first.

Squaring my shoulders, I walk to Aunt Sloan's apartment door. Just as I bring my hand up to knock, the door opens.

19

ALAINA

MY AUNT STANDS in front of me in leggings and a baggy sweatshirt, face makeup-free and splotchy, hair in a haphazard ponytail. Even though she was never as intense about appearances as my mother was, I don't think I've ever seen her like this before.

"Oh Alaina!" she cries before a sob breaks free. She throws her arms around me, pulling me into her apartment.

Tears spring to my eyes as I wrap my arms around her middle, squeezing her tight. In some regards, Aunt Sloane was more of a mother figure than my actual mother was.

And while my heart hurts for me, it's a different kind of hurt for her. She lost her twin sister, and I can't imagine the kind of pain she's in. I don't know what I'd do if I lost Maddie or Mary. I don't even want to entertain that depressing thought.

She pulls back and cups my face. "Oh, sweet girl. It's alright. We'll be alright." She places a kiss on my forehead and runs her hands over my shoulders and down to clasp my hands.

"I'm sorry, Aunt Sloane," I murmur, squeezing her hands back.

She pulls back, her gaze straying over my shoulder. I don't need to look to know what kind of picture the three of them make standing side by side. I can feel them at my back, their presence rolling over me like a wave—a powerful and comforting wave.

"And who do we have here?" Aunt Sloane pulls back and lets go of my hands. She sweeps her palms over her hair, smoothing any flyaways and stray locks back. Her shoulders straighten and she fiddles with the collar of her oversized sweatshirt. "Well, if I'd known you were bringing company, I'd have dressed for the occasion."

"What happened to Alejandro?" I ask with a raised brow and a smirk. I'm not surprised she's checking them out—I mean, she *has* eyes. Plus, she's known for her taste in younger men. She's mostly harmless.

Aunt Sloane stops adjusting her sweatshirt and looks at me without a lick of embarrassment? "What?" she asks with a shrug. "I'm still a woman, Lainey."

I roll my eyes. "Right, well, these are my—" I cut myself off and glance to the side. Labels are such a funny thing. A few years ago, calling someone my *boyfriend* suddenly meant something more than just a guy who was my friend. It meant there were feelings and emotional connection.

But what do you call what the four of us have?

What do you call an emotional connection that binds you to three different men equally?

Mine.

I look at Aunt Sloane, holding her gaze and say, "Mine. These guys are mine. Wolf, Rush, and Sully."

Her lips twist to the side, and she regards me with a twinkle in her eye. "Well then. Just give me a moment to freshen up, and I'll have Alejandro grab us some coffee from that cafe down the block. He's currently . . . resting . . . but I think he'll be up soon anyway. Make yourselves at home." She calls the last line over her shoulder as she walks through the sunken-in living room and down the hallway toward her bedroom.

Mary and Maddie have rooms down the same hallway too, but they rarely stay here. Most of the year is spent at school with me, and they usually travel during the summer with their mom.

As soon as she's out of sight, I feel them close in on me. Rush steps into my back, his body pressing against me from my thighs to my neck. I shiver as he snakes his hand in front of me, sliding it up my stomach and between my tits, resting against the hollow of my throat.

I grin and tip my head back before he asks me. He rewards me with a low growl against my neck, his lips vibrating against the sensitive skin behind my ear. He slides his lips up to my ear and whispers, "Yours, baby?"

I turn my head toward him, his stubble scraping against my cheek. Arching my back, I press my ass against him and feel his cock lengthen in response. "Yes, you're mine." The words come out as a hiss against his skin, and his fingers flex in response.

"You're playing with fire, baby girl." Desire coats Wolf's words.

Arousal floods my veins, and I twist to look at him. Wolf and Sully stand next to each other to my left, and the matching looks of hunger on their faces steal my breath for a moment. We're walking a fine line, the four of us. One day, something—or someone—is going to snap, and the three of them will pounce on me *together*.

I look forward to the day it happens. I shiver as I fantasize about Rush losing control, Sully letting go, and Wolf having free rein.

A cough interrupts my daydreaming, and by the time my eyes refocus on the present, I'm looking at the backs of Sully and

Wolf. I take a moment to appreciate this view, my lust still swirling around and distracting me.

"Sorry to, uh, interrupt. I'm Alejandro. Sloane's craving a cappuccino from the cafe down the street. Can I bring something back for any of you?"

I peek between the sliver of space between their large bodies, unsurprised to see the guy from Aunt Sloane's latest Instagram photos.

I step away from Rush and to the side of the boys, and after a moment, he relents with a little grumble. I flash Alejandro a smile.

"Hey, I'm Alaina. This is Sully and Wolf, and the guy in the back is Rush. Nice to meet you," I say with a little wave.

Alejandro steps forward and grasps my outstretched hand in his. "Ah, yes, the infamous niece, Alaina." He bends down as he lifts my hand toward his mouth.

Before he places his lips on my skin, Wolf steps forward and removes my hand from his with a growl. "Don't touch things that don't belong to you."

If I weren't so shocked, I'd laugh.

To his credit, Alejandro simply nods and smiles. "Apologies. When I see such a beautiful woman, sometimes I can't help myself."

Sully steps into Alejandro's space. "You better try harder, yeah?"

Alejandro backs up a step with his hands raised, palms out. "Got it. She's off-limits. Is that a no on coffee then?"

"I'll take a chai latte," I say with a smile. Wolf and Sully both whip their heads toward me, scowls overtaking their stunning features. I shrug my shoulders. "What? I could use a caffeine boost."

"We'll take three coffees. Black. And Alaina's chai latte," Rush says from behind us. I see Wolf and Sully turn to stare at their brother, no doubt shooting their disbelieving glares toward him.

Alejandro gives us a wide berth as he makes his way toward the front door. He stops to grab his keys out of a bowl that Maddie made in middle school pottery class. "I'll be back."

The front door closes with a click, and I slowly spin on my heel. "So that was . . ."

"Ah dear, did you meet Alejandro?" Aunt Sloane breezes into the room, fluttering her eyelashes with a sigh. "Isn't he dreamy?" She changed into a navy blue halter pantsuit with a low vee cut in the front and back. She looks amazing in it.

"He looks eighteen," Sully deadpans.

Aunt Sloane cuts him a look before returning to whatever fantasy is playing in front of her eyes. "He's twenty-three, and trust me, it shows in the bedroom."

"Oh, okay. That's probably more than I needed to know about the guy. Let's sit down, Aunt Sloane." I walk toward the couches in her sunken-in living room.

Her apartment is done in shades of cream—cream-colored shag rugs, toffee-and-cream-colored low-back couch, white with just the barest hint of cream paint covers the walls, and every photo is in a white frame.

I remember being younger and nervous about getting everything dirty, not that Aunt Sloane would've really cared. She'd have just gone out and bought a replacement if anything ever got ruined. But the anxiety was still there.

I sit down in the middle of the couch that faces the wall of windows. The afternoon sun shines in through partially closed blinds, warming my face.

Wolf sits next to me, Rush sits on the armchair to the left of us, and Sully stands behind the couch right behind me, arms crossed and legs spread. Aunt Sloane glances around the room, her expression unreadable, before she sits next to me.

She covers my clasped hands in hers and looks me in the eye. "Tell me what happened to my sister."

I nod and bite my lip. I glance at Rush from under my lashes, and his nod is imperceptible. I take a deep breath and prepare myself mentally to go back to that day. I'm not going to give her the whole truth—I honestly don't think she needs to hear all of it. She knows how present my mom was in my life. I give her the short version of events, surprised that I can recall them with such a level of detachment.

"I don't understand, Lainey. How did she even know these people?"

"I'm not entirely sure. I think she got mixed up with some bad people, and it all caught up with her."

Aunt Sloane sniffs. "I felt her, you know. I felt something right here"—she taps her chest right above her heart—"when she died. I felt part of my heart die that day too. She wasn't perfect, but she was my sister. And I loved her."

I nod a few times. My sinuses tingle, and I can feel the tears gathering at the back of my eyes. "I know. I loved her too."

Wolf laces his fingers through mine on one side, and I lean my head on Aunt Sloane's shoulder. We all sit in silence for a few minutes, seemingly lost in our thoughts.

I lick my lips and lift my head from her shoulder. I bring my leg up on the couch, bent so I can turn to face her. "She told me that I needed to tell you something before she died. And some of her, uh, last words were 'tell Sloane *it's time.*' Do you know what that means?"

I watch the color drain from Aunt Sloane's face, and she stares at me without really seeing me. Her mouth parts and her whole body seems to deflate. She nods, and without a word, leaves the living room.

She returns a moment later with a thick accordion file holder in her hands. She's murmuring under her breath as she sits down on the couch and hands it to me. "This is what she meant. She told me years and years ago that if something were to happen to her, I should give you this. She liked to remind me once a year. I've kept it in my safe this whole time, but I haven't ever peeked. I promise."

I run my fingertips over the worn brown leather of the file holder. It's wide and stuffed full of papers. I unwind the strap holding it closed and open the leather flap. Wolf leans in close as I pull out the top piece of paper. It's my birth certificate.

Alaina Murphy Gallagher.

Lana Murphy Gallagher, mother. Aidan Ronan Gallagher, father. I trace his signature on the bottom of the thick piece of paper. I hand it to Wolf to hold and pull out a small stack.

The next paper catches my attention. It's torn from a notebook, and it's just a list of numbers . . . almost like coordinates. It reminds me of when I had to study latitude and longitude for a school project.

"There's something . . . familiar about this," I murmur as I tap my lip with my fingertip.

"What is it, Red?"

The numbers swim before my eyes, and suddenly, it hits me. "I've seen something like this before." I look between each of them, hesitating on Rush. "When I, uh, broke into the safe in the basement at Summer Knoll. Well, I didn't break in, more like it wasn't closed all the way. Ish." I bite my lip, shoulder stiff as I wait for one of them to say something.

My gaze stays on Rush. He's the one I'm most worried about. I'm not sure what his reaction will be to that little tidbit of information. What he does next shocks me.

A genuine smile stretches across his face. "You snooped around, yeah? Good girl."

A shiver rolls over me when he says those two words in that low tenor of his, his eyes downright sparkling.

179

"What are these, Lainey?" Aunt Sloane asks, her face hovering over my shoulder.

"They're coordinates. I'm not sure what they're for, but if they're in the safe, then I know someone who might know." The three men exchange a look, and I'd be a fool not to know they're talking about their father.

"Your mom, she'd drop off a piece of paper or envelope here for me to put in this folder every once in a while. Before last week, it'd been years since she added to it." Sloan swipes underneath her eyes again, catching any stray mascara.

"She was here last week? Do you know what she gave you?" My heart pounds in anticipation.

Sloane shakes her head before I finish asking my question. "I never look or ask, but I did slip the envelope in the back."

Adrenaline floods my veins as I flip the file folder over so the back is on top. Sliding my hand in, I pull out a white envelope. My breath falters when I see her familiar handwriting on the outside of the envelope.

I swallow down the bark of nervous laughter that threatens to come out.

A letter. She wrote me a letter. I don't think she's ever written me a letter before. I don't think she's ever written me a card before. She wasn't the loving-messages-in-your-lunchbox kind of mom.

Dear Alaina,

If you're reading this, it means I'm gone. I'm not going to do that thing people do where they act like we had some amazing relationship and you're beside yourself without me. I know I wasn't a good mother to you. And I'm sorry for that.

I still remember when we found out we were pregnant. Aidan was over-joyed. He stopped strangers on the street and told them, "My wife and I are having a baby. Isn't that amazing?" He wanted you more than anything in the world.

Not a day goes by that I don't miss your father. The only thing that brings me peace is knowing that I'll see him again someday.

Life hasn't been fair to you—I haven't been fair to you. But I want you to know that I've always loved you. Always.

By now, I'm assuming you know about your real name—your father's last name. If you have no idea what I'm talking about, I've included all the papers in here. They'll explain everything.

Everything in this folder is for you. I've collected every piece of information I could over the years, but to get the full story on your father's family—your family—you need to contact the man who helped me hide you.

All I have is his address from ten years ago.
Seamus Flannery
Lismore, County Waterford,
Ireland

Give Auntie Sloan a hug for me.
—Mom

I FOLD the letter back into thirds, staring at the way the thick stationery absorbs my tears. Lifting my head, I meet Rush's gaze across from me. His posture is rigid, muscles taut, and he looks like he's seconds away from Hulking out.

A rueful smile tips up the corner of my lips at that thought. Watching Rush tear off his clothes as he kicks some ass? Sign me up.

"Words, baby." His gentle voice brings me out of the Hulk-smash fantasy of Rush ripping his clothes off.

I hold up the letter between my thumb and index finger. "Letter from Mom. She said I need to find some Seamus guy in Ireland for the whole story on being a Gallagher."

With a finger on my chin, Wolf turns my face in his direction. "Why the tears then, baby girl? Talk to us."

I lean forward, resting my forehead against his shoulder. I exhale a shaky breath and whisper, "I just don't understand why it hurts so much. She wrote she always loved me, but it didn't feel that way, not really." I lift my head and look at Wolf. The corners of his eyes are pinched like he's in pain, and his grip on my ribs is firm. "But then why am I so sad?"

"She was a shitty mom, Red, but she was still your mom. And it's okay to mourn her," Wolf murmurs.

The dam holding back my emotions breaks with his words, almost like I was waiting for permission to let go. I curl my fingers in his shirt and just let it all go.

Sobs wrack my body, and Wolf wraps his arms around me. My body expels all my pain and disappointment, attempting to purge it from my very soul.

20

SULLY

HER WORDS, so full of anguish, tug at something inside me I thought I buried years ago.

I spare a glance at Sloane when she stands from the couch, murmuring something about getting a drink.

The moment she leans her head on Wolf's chest, the saddest goddamn noise I've ever heard leaves her lips almost involuntarily. Wolf closes his arms around her and cradles her to his chest. He rubs his hand up and down her back and whispers something too low for me to hear.

I'm not sure I could hear anything anyway. My ears are ringing, and my vision is graying out on the sides. I clutch my chest where it feels like my fucking heart is about to explode.

Am I having a goddamn heart attack?

Lainey makes another noise, this one more pained than the last, and I'm moving before I even realize what I'm doing. With a hand on the back of the couch, I launch myself over it to land on the cushion behind her. I curl my arms around her middle and lean my head against the back of her neck, draping my body along the back of hers. Protecting her.

I feel my brother's eyes on me for a moment, but then his focus is back on our girl. And goddamn, she is our fucking girl, isn't she? I know what we said to each other last night, but that shit feels more like a fever dream than real life. And in all my wildest dreams, I never imagined it'd be like this.

Rush kneels next to her on the floor, shielding her body from that angle. I watch as he holds her thighs in his hands, his gaze faraway and probably calculating whatever homicide he thinks will fix this. Not that I fucking blame him.

We're a trio of shields surrounding her while she's vulnerable. I don't know how long we stay like that. Long enough that Lana's little boy toy comes back with coffee and leaves just as quick. Long enough that my legs are cramping up from this hunched-over position. Long enough for our girl to run out of tears and fall asleep like this, propped up between the three of us.

I'm almost annoyed at how good it feels to have her in my arms again. Even if it's because she's heartbroken. Which makes me a total prick.

"She's out." Wolf's voice is low.

I lift my head off of her back, sliding her hair to one shoulder to place a kiss on the nape of her neck. I'm actively tamping down the panic that's threatening to rise and overthrow me. Being with her like this—with them—letting myself care about her so quickly is fucking dangerous. It'd be all too easy to let myself get consumed by her again.

But a lot of shit has changed in two years—*I've* changed. And I have other responsibilities now—things I can't afford to lax on.

"You good, brother?" Rush asks me with a head tilt.

I nod a few times. "It's dangerous. She's dangerous—"

Wolf scoffs. "Why? Because some rich prick owns some business overseas? Please. She doesn't have anything to do with that shit. Not really."

"Nah. Not that, though I think you and I both know that if

that's who sent that red-eyed motherfucker after her, it's not just some rich prick." I eye both of them before I glance at the siren in my arms. "She's always been my goddamn siren. And you guys have no idea what I'm willing to do—how far I'm willing to go when it comes to her. I almost left the Brotherhood, you know."

Shock holds them both mobile.

Wolf recovers first. "The fuck you just say?"

I shrug a shoulder as I toy with the ends of her hair. It looks like the sunset on fire in this light. "Back in the summer I was here. I was fucking angry. Mad that I'm the one that got pinched because we had a fucking rat. Angry that I had to spend my summer away from you guys. I walked into that library with so much goddamn anger and resentment, and she took one look at me, and I was a fucking goner. That's it. She called to me like the fucking siren she is, and I haven't been able to stop hearing her call. Even all these years later."

I blow out a breath and look at my brothers. Wolf's mouth drops open in shock, but Rush doesn't look all that surprised.

"She didn't ask me to leave, not that she really knew what the Brotherhood was. But that's the fucked-up thing. I *wanted* to leave. She made me want to be a better person, to spend my teenage years going to the movies instead of securing locations for weapons deals."

"Why didn't you ever tell us?" Rush sits back on the coffee table.

I grimace. "I was going to, but . . ."

"But then that warehouse in Brooklyn blew up," Wolf fills in.

"Aye. The warehouse blew up, and I never heard from her again until I strolled into our kitchen and saw her standing next to Wolf like she belongs there."

"She fucking does belong next to me," Wolf growls the words out, his brow furrowed and gaze hard.

"You think I don't think she fucking belongs with me too?" My jaw protests at how hard I'm clenching it.

"She belongs with all of us," Rush says, his tone firm and unwavering. "This is part of our plan, both of you know that, so I don't get why you're acting like territorial dogs right now."

"And she knows that?" I glare at him.

"She thinks it was her idea. Eventually, we'll tell her the whole truth. But I don't think it's necessary right now. It doesn't change anything," Rush says with a nod.

"Doesn't it though? It changes everything. We're painting a target on her back. The Brotherhood has so many enemies, not to mention all the enemies the three of us have combined." I twirl the end of her hair through my fingers, marveling at the silky texture. "I don't want her to look over her shoulder for the rest of her life."

"Do you have anything to add, baby girl?" Rush asks, his lips twisting to the side.

Alaina tilts her head to look at my brother. "How long have you known I was awake?"

"How long have you been awake?" His eyes sparkle with amusement, but I'm still surprised.

"How much did you hear, princess?"

She adjusts her position on the couch so she can see all three of us clearly. She swipes under her eyes and runs her fingers through her hair before blowing out a breath. "I guess this is as good of time as any, right? I don't think I've made it a secret, but just so we're all on the same page. I want to be with you—all three of you. At the same time."

Her phrasing catches me off-guard, and all the blood rushes to my cock when I think about taking her in all the ways I want to. The three of us have never shared a woman like that before, but with the way their eyes light up, I'd say we're all in agreement that we're up for it.

Alaina notices the shift in the air and rolls her eyes. "I didn't mean it like that. I mean like date the three of you at the same time."

"Are you sure you didn't mean the four of us playing out those dirty little fantasies you often have?" Wolf teases.

Pink colors her cheeks and spreads down her neck. I find myself locked on the flush, desperate to know what else of hers turns pink like that. When we were together last night, I didn't have enough time to look her over properly—to explore every inch of her soft skin.

We were tangled up in our past, and we let our bodies do the talking. I'd do it again in a fucking New York minute, but this time, I wanna watch every minute of it.

She's always felt like a gift to me—something to be treasured. Only now, I want to treasure her on my knees.

She shrugs her shoulder and licks her lips. I imagine those perfectly pouty lips wrapped around my cock, and I have to fight back the groan. I don't know what the fuck is going on with me. I'm acting like a thirteen-year-old the first time he saw tits.

"I mean, would it be okay if we, you know, all played together sometimes? I like one-on-one, but I think I might like to try other stuff too . . ."

She trails off as soon as she realizes the three of us all leaned toward her as if pulled by some invisible force. And fuck me, if I was getting a semi at just the idea of her before, hearing her say she fantasizes about the four of us is enough to send all the blood to my dick.

Apparently, I'm not the only one with that problem. Wolf picks up her hand and jumps up from the couch. "This is a good plan. Let's do Red's plan now."

She laughs, the joyous sound breaking some of the tension filling the room. "I am not messing around inside my aunt's house. Besides, we still have all this stuff to look through. But— maybe someday soon, yeah?"

She tugs on Wolf's hand, and he collapses next to her on the couch. "I know you have some sort of agreement, and I don't really understand it, but if one of you wants to . . . *not* be in this foursome, then that's okay too." She licks her lips. "I know it's a little hypocritical of me to ask you three to share me even though I'm not willing to share each of you. So, I won't hold it against you if you want to bail." She looks right at me when she talks, and her gaze feels like it's staring straight into my soul.

I'm not sure if I'm ready for all that. To be with her, of course. To share her with my brothers? I'll get there eventually. But I'm not ready to bare all my fucked-up emotional shit to her, not on a day where she's up to her knees in her own emotional turmoil.

I shift my gaze to the file on the table and clear my throat. "Why don't we take this home? We can go through it a little easier."

No one calls me out on my obvious redirection, and I'm thankful. Rush replaces the few things we took out and wraps the strap around the binder, securing it.

The doorbell rings and the four of us look between each other. "Was she expecting anyone?" Rush asks, and just from the way he's gone stiff, hand hovering over the gun I know he keeps tucked in his pants.

Alaina shakes her head. "I don't—I don't know. Maybe I should go get my aunt?"

Before she can get Sloane, she appears at the mouth of the hallway. "Did I hear the doorbell? Strange. I wasn't expecting anyone."

Fuck. Okay. It could be nothing—or it could be something. And in this life, I like to err on whichever side keeps me breathing. I hand the file to Alaina and gently move her behind me as Rush grabs his gun and points it at the door, trigger finger ready.

Sloane opens the door, and I swear you could hear a pin drop.

"Da?"

21

RUSH

"GIVE me one plausible reason why you're here and not just following us," I ask my father as he stands in the doorway of Alaina's aunt's house.

My da stares at me, his face open. He raises his hands slowly, palms out. "It's just me, boyo. No one else. You can trust me."

"Answer the question." I grip my gun tighter, my knuckles white.

"Coincidence," Da answers, never breaking my stare.

"You know I don't believe in those."

"I know, son. I know. But I swear I only came to pay my respects to Lana's sister. She was my fiancée, after all. I didn't know you were here."

I stare into his eyes, so familiar to my own and try to recall my earlier conversation with him.

Did I tell him we were heading here?

I'm clenching my jaw so hard I feel the muscle spasm. I want to believe him, and therein lies the problem. I want to believe him in the same way that I want to think my father would never lie to me. But he's not infallible. He's just a man, just like the rest of us.

I make a decision then, and I hope that I don't regret it.

"We found something interesting. Looks like Lana left Alaina a list of coordinates. A list that looks remarkably similar to a list in our safe back at Summer Knoll. Know anything about that?"

Da flicks his gaze pointedly toward Alaina and her aunt with a raised brow. I get that he doesn't want to talk business in front of just anybody, but he should read the fucking room. He's the one who taught us how.

"Alaina's not a stranger. We trust her." Wolf practically growls the words, and I know he's taking it personal that Da has secrets he hasn't shared with us.

All of us have our own abandonment issues, I'm not naive enough not to realize it. It's part of why Alaina's drawn to us, whether she knows it or not. The four of us all struggle with that parental attachment. When you grow up in the kind of life we did, there's no game of catch in the backyard with your da. There are drills disguised as obstacle courses, weapons training pitched as playing ninjas, and plans concealed as treasure maps for fresh earth to bury a body. That last one is a little outdated now, ever since Sully perfected his science skills.

The dude loves efficiency.

Da shoves his hands in his front pockets and rocks back on his heels. "I was looking for Aidan. I hired a top-of-the-line private investigator who's familiar enough with the Brotherhood to know where to look without asking too many questions. The list is a collection of places he's supposedly been before—either on a job or traveling with his family."

"Then how did Lana get one?" Sully asks, his tone guarded.

"Dunno, boyo. I suspect she hired her own investigator. Did her list say anything else?"

I shake my head. "We'll let you know if we find anything worthwhile to you."

He understands my dismissal right away. A muscle in his cheek twitches and I idly wonder if that's what I look like when I'm curbing my anger. What an interesting thing to pass down a generation.

There's a charge in the air, compressing the space between us as neither one of us speaks. What is there to even say?

He knows better than anyone how easy it is to breed distrust in this life, and right now, there's enough to fucking choke on.

I look him over and notice how fucking tired he looks. Dark circles shadow under his eyes, and his beard is a little rougher than I'm used to seeing. Almost involuntarily, something inside me softens a little.

Fuck.

At the end of the day, he's still my fucking da. Doesn't that deserve the benefit of the doubt?

I open my mouth to, I don't fucking know, throw an olive branch, but Alaina beats me to it.

"It's fine. We were just leaving anyway," Alaina says as she steps around Sully.

I don't like her being out in the open like that. It makes me feel fucking twitchy. I relax my hold on the gun just a little bit. Not enough to stow it, but enough to not be a single second away from firing.

It's like he senses my small yield. Da steps inside the apartment, but he doesn't stray past the entryway. Sloane stands off to the side toward the kitchen, and Alaina beelines for her.

Wrapping her arms around her aunt, she murmurs something too low for me to hear.

"It's all in the file, Lainey, but your mom didn't want a traditional funeral. She just wants her ashes to be spread at sea, where she always found peace."

195

Alaina nods and hugs her aunt again.

I keep her in my peripheral vision, but I don't take my eyes off my da. He turns to face me, his broad shoulders stretching the fabric of his gray shirt. We've been about the same size for a few years, but I've got an inch on him now.

Looking at him, it's like a glimpse into the future. Except for maybe that beard. I don't know why the fuck he keeps that thing. I can't imagine having something that long and scruffy attached to my face all the time—a few days' worth is long enough for me.

I feel my brothers on either side of me before either one of them says anything.

"You ready to tell us what the fuck is really going on?" Wolf challenges him.

Da glances between the three of us before his gaze rests on Alaina talking quietly to her aunt. He exhales, his shoulders falling with the movement. He focuses back on us, meeting each of our eyes before settling on me. "Meet me at home tonight."

"Now's better," Sully says.

"Alright. Your apartment, then," Da says as he folds his arms across his chest.

I'm already shaking my head before he even looks at me. "No. That's not an option either. Somewhere neutral."

"O'Malley's at nine tonight," Wolf suggests. I glance at the clock hanging in the foyer. That gives us almost five hours to get back to the apartment, grab food, and go through the file from Lana. I can make that work. I nod my agreement at Wolf.

"Aye. I'll see you boys tonight. Jack'll make sure we have some privacy. We're going to need it for this conversation."

I stare at him then, apprehension and a tiny kernel of hope mingling inside my gut. "Don't make me regret this, Da."

A wide, satisfied smile blooms on his face, and he tips his chin up at me. "You'll do just fine, boyo, just fine."

My chest puffs up a little involuntarily—a leftover side effect of forever searching for my father's approval.

Alaina steps next to me, close enough that her arm brushes against mine. She glances between the four of us, her eyes guarded. "Everything okay?"

I toss my arm around her shoulders, bringing her closer to my body. It's more of Wolf's style, but I felt compelled to. And I'm not in the business of denying myself anything when it comes to her.

"We're good, birdie. Let's go home," I say into her hair before placing a kiss against her head. I don't miss the shiver that skates down her spine at the word *home*.

I guide her toward the door, Wolf and Sully behind us when Da steps into our path.

"I'm sorry for your loss, Alaina," he says. His voice is low, and his eyes actually look a little glassy. Fuck me, did he actually have feelings for Lana? I thought it was more or less a sham?

Alaina clears her throat before she says, "Thank you. I'm sorry for your loss, as well."

Da nods his head, but he doesn't say anything else before he steps to the side.

The four of us are quiet as we leave Sloane's apartment and head to the car in the parking garage.

22

ALAINA

Chapter Twenty-Two—Alaina

Cobi's "Don't Cry For Me" plays when Rush starts the car up again. I stare at the buildings as we drive back to the apartment. I close my eyes against the late afternoon sun shining in my window and lean my head against the headrest. The warmth feels nice against my flushed face. Comforting. Rejuvenating.

I guess I was wrong. I guess I fell apart fairly quickly, all things considered. I take a moment to look inside myself, search for a way to put my feelings into words.

Rolling my head to the left, I open my eyes to see Wolf staring right at me. "I'm not sure I've ever felt so much and so little at the same time."

He scans my face, his big body taking up most of the space in the backseat. He's propped in the corner, an elbow propped up on the windowsill, leaning half his big body against the door. "What are you feeling?"

I close my eyes and open them again. "Grief for losing someone. Grief for the loss of possibility. Joy at having all of you in my life. Guilt for feeling joy during such a sad time."

Wolf nods and the sounds of "I Should Live in Salt" by Ásgeir fill the car. I cut my gaze to Sully. Once upon a time, we shared a love of music, and I distinctly remember telling him how much I loved The National. He doesn't turn around or meet my gaze in the mirror, but I know he did it.

I lean forward to flutter my fingertips along his shoulder in gratitude. "Thank you." He nods but doesn't offer anything else.

Leaning back into the seat, I notice the look Wolf's giving me. Curiosity and something a lot like wonder.

"You don't need to feel guilty for feeling two different emotions at the same time, even if they're on the opposite spectrum of emotions. Whatever you're going through is unique to you, and you don't have to apologize for it. But most of all, you're not alone, baby girl."

I reach over and slide my hand over his as a tear slides down my cheek. "Thank you. Thank all of you. I . . . I don't know what I would've done if I didn't have you guys."

"You wouldn't be here." Sully's words are low but not unkind. "If you never met us—if Lana never agreed to marry Da—then you wouldn't be here."

His words sting. Even if they aren't delivered to be blows, they land just the same. I flinch without thinking.

"What the fuck, man?" Wolf growls the words. Rush just shakes his head and sighs.

"What? It's true," Sully says as he crosses his arms.

I clear my throat, wading through all my initial hurt. My emotions are raw and on the surface right now. "He's right. I wouldn't be here—with you all—if Mom didn't meet Cormac."

"That's not entirely true . . ." Rush hedges as he shifts in his seat, adjusting his grip on the steering wheel.

Sully glares at him. "Explain."

"Ah, is this where you tell us all about how you had a plan for Red all along?" Wolf laughs under his breath.

My gaze ping-pongs between them, curious to see how this is going to play out.

Rush shifts in his seat again. It's such an uncharacteristically nervous gesture that it catches me off-guard. I tilt my head, even more intrigued to see how this will unfold.

Rush clears his throat as he turns a corner and pulls into the underground parking garage to their building. The air is already charged with tension and then "Rebellion (Lies)" by Arcade Fire starts. The irony of the name of the song isn't lost on anyone.

"The playlist ended and it automatically played this song, so don't side-eye me, man. Although . . . it is kind of timely." Sully smirks.

Rush pulls into the same spot he was in earlier, the open one between Wolf's car and a charcoal gray SUV.

He shuts off the engine and tips his head against the head-rest. "She's funny and smart and kind and absolutely fucking perfect, and I won't apologize for wanting her the moment I laid eyes on her."

Warmth unfurls inside me, flushing my cheeks at his words. A kernel of confusion worms itself inside the bubble of affection.

He got all that from watching me sing on Friday nights?

Wolf must be on the same wavelength because his next words echo my thoughts. "And how did you come to know all of that about Red, hmm?"

"You already know I went to O'Malley's on Fridays."

"Aye. And I also know that you two didn't interact much until recently. So, explain it to me, brother."

Rush meets my gaze in the rearview mirror. His stare bold. "I watched her."

"How?" Sully asks.

"Because I had cameras installed." His gaze doesn't flinch away from mine.

"I fucking knew it. No wonder you're always glued to your computer," Wolf says with a humorless chuckle.

"Where?" Sully demands.

"O'Malley's. And a few surrounding streets." Rush is unapologetic about his little foray into surveillance.

Surprise and something darker floods my veins. I think I should be alarmed that he was essentially spying on me. Maybe I'm just on emotional overload because those are not the thoughts swirling around. Looking back on the last year, there were so many times I felt like there were eyes on me, but I always chalked it up to living in New York City. But now . . . now I wonder if it was Rush's eyes on me the whole time.

A shiver of awareness works its way through me. Would it be such a bad thing to have Rush looking out for me? It certainly doesn't feel like it now—and I didn't know him then, not really, but I have a feeling I wouldn't have minded then either.

"Okay. Okay. So, what does that have to do with our current situation?" Wolf asks, bringing my thoughts back to the present.

Rush shifts his gaze to his brother. "I was going to bring her in. For us."

Wolf's lips twist to the side as he taps his leg twice before he looks at Rush. "See, that's the thing, brother. I can't figure out why you didn't bring her up to us earlier if that's what you were thinking. No, I don't think you had any intention of bringing her in for our agreement. Not right away, at least."

Rush twists around in his seat, his calm facade cracking. "Do you want to do this in the car? Because I'd rather not get blood on the seats. I just got it detailed."

It's like the gauntlet was thrown down with those words. Wolf flings open his car door and stalks out of the car, rounding the trunk to stand in the driving lane. Sully's not too far behind him, and Rush watches both of them with his neutral expression. He turns to meet my gaze; his face softens and I can read his expression again. "Don't step in, okay? Just stay in the car."

I only stare and nod, confusion taking center stage.

I watch in fascination as Rush blanks his face again and prowls out of the car to meet the boys in the driving lane. I twist around to keep them all in my line of sight, but I can't quite hear what they're saying. I have a pretty good hunch it's about me, at least indirectly.

I make a quick decision and get out of the car. On quiet feet, I walk to the back of the car and lean against the trunk. Wolf's in Rush's face while Sully stands to the side of them, his arms crossed over his chest.

It happens in slow-motion. One minute, they're talking, and the next, Wolf's fist is flying toward Rush's nose. Their flesh meets with a sickening crack, and I don't realize I'm moving until I feel a strong arm band around my stomach.

"C'mon, princess. You know stepping in would be bad. Let them work it out, yeah?"

"Jesus Christ, Sully! Don't just stand there, stop them!" I try to pry his fingers from around me, but his grip is too firm.

"You should've fucking told us, Dec! All that bullshit about being a family, and here you are making plans to play house with Red without us?" Wolf's breaths are choppy and his chest rises and falls in fast, heavy breaths.

"Aye. I should've told you both earlier. I'm sorry. But I won't apologize for going to O'Malley's to see her every week. Or for wanting her."

"Fuck, man, I'm not mad about that—not really. I'm—my feelings are fucking hurt, okay? You lied to us after you were adamant about no secrets." Wolf rakes his hair off his face, leaving his hands in his hair, biceps bulging.

"I'm sorry, Con."

I watch in fascination as both men stare at one another, and with each exhale, their chests deflate and so do their tempers.

"But how the fuck was I supposed to know fate would bring her to us like this?" Rush rakes his hands through his hair.

I'm calm enough now, and I tap Sully's hands three times. He loosens his hold, and when I don't immediately try to run toward them, he steps back so he's standing next to me.

"I don't know, man. Maybe from all the other shit that you somehow just always know." Wolf throws up his hands and turns to face the side.

The aggression in the air has faded. No sooner than the thought crosses my mind when Sully steps right up to Rush, cocks his fist back, and lets it fly.

A gasp leaves my mouth before I can stop it, and I shove both of my palms across my open mouth.

"Sully, what the fuck?!" My words are high-pitched and echo around the cement walls.

Rush moves his jaw back and forth, trying to work out any injury. He cuts his gaze to me. "It's fine, baby. They were owed those, but we all know that I'll only allow one free shot."

And then they do something that surprises me even more. The three of them move toward one another, and then they hug. Like straight-up hug each other without any preamble. And when they pull back, smiles spread across their faces.

"What the hell is going on?" My words are whispered as my brow furrows. "I don't understand."

"You wanna see me toss some more punches, baby girl?" Wolf digs his teeth into his bottom lip as he tips his head back in that stupid move hot guys do.

"What? No." I shift on my feet, my cheeks flushing a little.

Rush tosses an arm around me, the other hand pinching the bridge of his nose as blood trickles out of one nostril. "It's fine—

we're fine. Sometimes we just need to throw a punch before we can move on."

I glance at him from under my lashes and hesitantly nod. I don't understand though. If I'm enraged enough to start swinging, then I'm not sure I'd be hugging the person I just punched a few minutes later.

Maybe it's a sibling thing, or maybe it's a lifestyle thing. Or maybe it's unique to them, but I think it might take a little getting used to.

I let Rush guide me into the elevators, the other two following behind us. With my arm wrapped around Rush's middle, I let my head rest against him as we both lean against the far wall.

"Did you really put cameras all over the city? To look for me?" My words are muffled against his shirt, and my eyes are halfway closed. I feel totally drained from the events of the last few days.

Rush adjusts his hold on me, tucking me under his arm more. He places a kiss on the top of my head, murmuring against my hair. "And if I did?"

"I know I should be weirded out by that, and maybe I will be tomorrow, but for now—for now, I think I'm okay with it."

Exhaustion threatens to take me under its spell, but I hold onto consciousness with both hands. At least until I can collapse on a nearby soft surface.

23

ALAINA

THE NEXT COUPLE hours pass by in a blur. After some grumbling, Sully finally agrees to rest. I think the reasoning that finally got through to him was the idea that if things go sideways tonight—or any time really—he might be a liability.

I still don't fully understand all the moving pieces, but they've explained a few different things.

Like in addition to Rush's skills with computers, he's also their unofficial general. He keeps tabs on the moving pieces when it comes to the Brotherhood, scoping out possible problems—and enemies. And he owns an online security company. Given everything I recently learned, I'm not all that surprised.

And Wolf is an assassin for the Brotherhood. A fact that he wasn't too keen on sharing, but I'm not stupid. I knew the Brotherhood—and them by extension—would be into some sort of crime. I mean, they all casually carry guns. He also works at the Brotherhood-owned mechanic garage.

And Sully is the muscle in more ways than one. Apparently, he runs the underground fighting ring they have—and he's said he's been known to jump in the ring a few times. I don't love the idea of him willingly putting himself in harm's way, but he assured me he's rarely even there anymore. Some other guy mostly runs it now.

They also explained what went down that fateful day at the warehouse. Six different places were met with violence around the same time Sully was stabbed. All of the places belonged to people they know—but they're not all Brotherhood members—like Matteo. I'm still unsure how that connection started.

And thankfully, only a few of the places hit belonged to the people who were present in our little basement meeting weeks ago—meaning the violence wasn't done in retaliation.

God, has it only been a couple of weeks since then?

Time feels weird here, with them. Or maybe it's just this specific time in my life. It feels almost fluid—one minute, I'm sipping a latte and binge-watching *The Vampire Diaries* with Mary and Maddie, and the next, I'm dodging a crumbling building that blew up.

We're sprawled out around the coffee table in the living room of their apartment, trying to go through Mom's file folder. It's a hodgepodge of information—family tree lines from Mom's side of the family, medical records, random pieces of paper torn out of a notebook with notes that don't make a lot of sense.

Papers cover every available surface—some are laid out on the couch while others are in a pile in the corner of the rug. It looks like a hoarder's dream in here. All four of us are spread out on the floor, each reading something and attempting to make sense of it, trying to place meaning on it other than the obvious keepsakes.

A lot of it is personal stuff—some love letters from my dad to my mom, photographs of my grandparents with their arms around me at a picnic table somewhere, a couple baby photos of me, and then my parents' wedding photo. There isn't a single photo of my dad and me together—not in here at least.

It's depressing the hell out of me, but Rush said he might be able to do some digging and find something. I'm not hopeful, but I appreciate the gesture all the same.

I'm sorting through a small stack of papers when I find it. Our first real clue. Bank statements—lots and lots of bank statements. I thumb through the packet of paper stapled together in the corner, the numbers and lines blurring together in front of my eyes. I blink them rapidly, but they still show me the same absurd numbers.

"Oh my god . . ."

Rush lifts his head from behind his laptop. He started bringing it in here to work, and even though he didn't say it, I'm pretty sure it's because he wants to keep an eye on me. "What is it, birdie?"

Shifting through the papers, my jaw drops and I look at him. "These are all in my name. They're . . ." I pause and swallow. "They're account statements. From several different banks."

Rush stands, but Wolf reaches over first and grabs them. He whistles under his breath as he flips through the pages. "Damn. There's gotta be a hundred million in this one, at least."

I sputter and choke on absolutely nothing. I literally choke on air, the thought of that much money is astounding. "I'm sorry, did you just say one hundred *million*? As in dollars?"

"Aye," Wolf says without taking his eyes off the handful of papers. "Looks like some are offshore, one in the Swiss Bank, one at some bank in Ireland, and two here."

"I . . . I don't know what to say. Where did this come from? I didn't think we had that kind of money." My mouth sort of hangs open at the idea.

"Baby girl, you go to one of the most elite boarding schools. How did you think your ma paid for it?" Wolf raises a brow.

My mouth snaps shut with an audible click. "I hadn't really ever thought about it."

Wolf makes a noncommittal noise as he flips through the stapled stack of papers.

"Wait. Could it be like an inheritance from my mother's parents? They passed away a while ago."

"Most were opened before you were born and transferred to your name nineteen years ago. The paperwork for it is right here. One looks like it's just yours though. The one in Ireland." Wolf's voice is low as he scans the information.

"Damn. I—I don't know what to say to that." I sigh.

"Nothing to say, *princess*," Sully says with a cheeky grin.

I flash him a grin and toss a balled-up piece of paper at him. It goes wide and lands a few feet away from him.

He arches a brow, smirking at me and flashing that dimple I love. "We need to work on your aim, princess."

"You going to give me another self-defense lesson?" I tease with a smile playing around the corners of my lips.

Sully's eyes darken to a dark blue as he looks at me. "Aye. I'll be giving you a self-defense lesson tonight."

"We've got to meet Da at O'Malley's, so your lesson will have to wait until tomorrow, man," Wolf murmurs without looking at either of us.

"I don't think they're talking about exercise, Wolf." Rush's tone is droll, and I let the smile break free with a giggle.

Wolf lifts his head, his brows furrowed. "What?" He looks between Sully and me, and a sly smile crosses his face as he waggles his brows. "Ahh. A *self-defense lesson*."

Now it's Sully's turn to toss the crumpled-up piece of paper at Wolf. "Green isn't a good color on you, Wolf."

He watches it hit him square in the chest and fall to the floor before he moves his gaze to me. Lust shines from his espresso-colored eyes, darkening them. My smile slips as a shiver of arousal zips up my spine at the unspoken promises in his gaze.

Rush slaps a stack of paper against Wolf's chest, breaking the spell. "Read through these."

I blink a few times and return to the folder in front of me.

"Later, baby girl."

I glance at Wolf from underneath my lashes, nodding at his words that sound a lot like a promise.

Silence descends on us as we continue to wade through the information from Aunt Sloane's safe.

Not all the papers on the floor are from my mom's file folder either. Some are different things Rush has found online that we thought might help connect the dots. Like printed out aerial maps of a few different addresses we found. And one particularly interesting article from an Irish newspaper detailing a conspiracy theory about Gallagher Industries.

I scan the article again, my mind stuck on the timeline of events. It reads like the plot of an action movie, but there's a ring of truth to it. I pick up the piece of paper and read it again.

"So, my dad was the oldest and the heir to Gallagher Industries—which by the way, I still don't really understand what they do—and he bailed, so his younger brother, Brady, took his place. The author of this article notes that this was the first time any first-born Gallagher has ever stepped down, publicly at least. And that upset the balance of the board. *Whatever that means.* But then he goes on to detail that four additional men attempted to step up and claim they were Gallagher heirs too, but"—I scan the rest of the paragraph—"those claims were either disproved or discredited."

I glance up and notice three pairs of eyes are locked on me.

"Gallagher Industries is listed as a technology company, and after a little strategic digging, I found that they also develop weapons. They're a privately-owned company that's been around for at least a hundred years, and they have several military contracts. I don't know the specific contracts yet, but I could probably find out with a little more time," Rush offers.

I nod, flicking my gaze back down to the stack of paper in front of me. "Okay. So, this journalist goes on to write two more articles about Gallagher Industries. This one explains the events that happened eight years after Brady took over."

"What's it say?" Wolf asks.

"Ten years after Dad stepped down, which would put it right about the time he met Mom, Brady stepped in. Four years later, Oscar Gallagher—their dad and my grandfather—died." A small thread of grief winds its way around my heart. I never had a chance to know my father's parents.

"Then two years later, Dad, uh, went missing and Brady died." I look at the stack of paper fanned out next to me, sliding a few around until I spot the one I'm looking for. Plucking it from the floor, I reread the dates. "The time between when Dad left for his job and the time Brady died is two weeks. They called it a mugging, but this journalist thinks it's part of a bigger conspiracy—that either members of the board staged a coup or that an outsider wanted a position on the board and found a loophole."

"What sort of loophole?" Sully asks.

"The loophole that says if no Gallagher sits on the board and there are no heirs, an extended family member is appointed."

"But there is a Gallagher heir—you." Wolf's gaze is intense as he stares at me.

I nod, the motion slow. "Something that my mom went through great lengths to conceal for eight years."

Rush stands up. "What's the journalist's name?"

I scan the article for the byline. "Christopher Lein."

He walks to the edge of the rug to a pile of paper ripped from a notebook. "Your mom wrote that name down on here."

"And I just looked him up online. It looks like he died . . ."

Sully trails off and looks from his phone to us. "Eight years ago. Mugging in Lismore."

"Lismore, County Waterford? As in the same small town Seamus Flannery lived?" Rush asks. "There's only like fifteen hundred people that live there."

I sit back against the couch with a thud. "So, the guy who publicly pointed a finger at the company that deals in weapons and technology for various government agencies died around the same time my father and Brady died? In the same small town as the guy who apparently helped my mom hide me?" My mouth parts as my mind races. I blow out a long breath. "I'm not sure if I've watched the *Bourne* movies too many times, but this feels like an actual conspiracy or one hell of a coincidence."

"Nah, I don't believe in coincidences like this, Red."

My heart starts to pound. I know what I'm about to suggest sounds a little crazy, but part of me also thinks that it's the next logical step. I stand up and face them. "Okay. Let's do it, then. Let's go to Ireland and get to the bottom of this."

No one speaks for a moment, and then Rush nods and says, "Aye. I'll call in a few favors to get the trip off the books. It's best if we leave the country undetected."

I tap my lip with my index finger, nervousness jumping around inside my veins. "When can we leave? I'm eager to figure all this out."

Rush is already typing on his phone. "Tomorrow. Tonight we have to meet Da." He eyes Sully with a frown. "But I'm not too sure you shouldn't stay here and rest. And before you get mad, someone should stay with our little bird."

I bristle and glare at Rush. "First of all, I'm perfectly capable of taking care of myself. And maybe I wanted to tag along."

"Do you?" Rush arches a brow.

I huff and shift my weight. "Well, not really, no. But it's the point. And I—"

The doorbell rings, interrupting me. All three of them whip out guns from places I didn't even realize had guns—under the coffee table, the side table, and next to the couch. Sully moves to stand in front of me, and Wolf and Rush turn toward the door.

I clear my throat as the doorbell rings again. "Oh, I forgot to tell you. I invited the King sisters over."

24

WOLF

I RELEASE the breath I was holding and relax my grip on the gun I nabbed from underneath the side table. Red moves around us to look at the screen next to the door that shows the feed from the hallway. Even from here, I can see the faces four of the King sisters are pulling—tongues sticking out and other weird shit. All except Maeve. She's all-business, staring right at the camera hidden in the corner of the doorway with a serious expression.

Red opens the door, and a wave of noise greets us. I always forget how fucking quiet it is with the entire apartment sound-proofed. It was a precaution Rush insisted on when we bought this place years ago, since we frequently discuss Brotherhood business here.

All five Kings stride inside like they own the place, none of them flinching at our aggressive formation or the guns in our hands. I'm not sure if it's a testament to their upbringing or their familiarity with us—probably both.

"Damn, Fitzgeralds, pretty fancy place you got here," Roisin says with a whistle.

Rush tenses before he glances at Red. "A word, birdie?"

She follows my brother into the hallway and into his bedroom, closing the door behind them. Sully and I share a look, but neither one of us follows them.

"I don't suppose anyone bothered to tell her Rush doesn't like people in his place?" Maeve asks as she walks into the living room.

"Nah. It wasn't really a priority today," Sully answers her.

"I heard you guys had a busy few days." Fiona settles into the armchair with a sigh.

I pivot to give her my attention. Something about the way she said that doesn't sound right. "Where'd you hear that?"

Fiona leans her head back, tilting it to look at me over the arm of the chair with a smirk. "A little birdie told me."

Sully sighs. "Please tell me you didn't go snooping again. One of these days, you're going to get caught, Fiona, and then what?"

"You act like I didn't learn to shoot a gun for my sixth birthday. Besides, I have allies—and my sisters."

The youngest King sister steps next to me with her arms crossed and her gaze trained on the paper littering the floor. "What's all this?"

"Get that gleam outta your eye, kid. This is above your pay grade." My tone is firm, but I swear it's like talking to a fucking brick wall. Roisin King never met a challenge she could step back from. I swear that kid goes *looking* for trouble.

"*Kid?* Pfft. You're like four years older than me, Wolf. Besides, I bet I could teach *you* some things."

"You better not be hitting on him, Ro! He's a taken man now, aren't you, Wolf?" Ava yells from the kitchen.

I turn around to look at her. When the hell did she go in there? She's rummaging around in the fridge, probably looking for something sugary as usual.

"I swear to god, you guys are like fucking gremlins—"

"Imagine what happens after midnight, Sully!" Ro flashes a maniacal grin at my brother and he narrows his eyes in response.

"So, what's goin' on that your girl called us?" Maeve asks as she picks up a piece of paper at random.

I tip my head back and look between all of them. Sully's imperceptible nod encourages me to give them some insight—but not all. No need to give away all of our secrets, even if I trust them.

"Red's ma died, and someone's stalking Red—"

"*Still?* You guys didn't take care of it?" Ava asks, her shoulders tensing and her eyes narrowing.

Her accusation hits the mark, and I grit my teeth against the shame that threatens to bubble up inside my chest. "Aye. Still. We're working on it, which is why I suspect she called you."

"More lessons from the infamous Kings?" Kiera asks with a grin. "I've got a new crossbow I've been dying to try out."

"Ki, I've been telling you for a week now, a crossbow is just not that plausible for everyday weaponry," Maeve says with a roll of her eyes.

Kiera cuts her sister a look. "I know that. But it's fun to play with. And I think Red could use some fun in her life. Don't you think so, Wolf?"

I let the irritation of *my* nickname for Alaina out of someone else's mouth roll off my back. It's not as bad as if some random dude called her that, I suppose. Then I might have to introduce him to my favorite gun.

"Oh, for fuck's sake. Wipe that murderous look off your face, brother."

I snap my gaze to Sully, who's leaning against the wall facing the hallway. I purposely let my shoulders drop a little and paste a smile on my face.

Rush and Red walk out of the hallway, both looking a little

flushed. "Did I hear something about murder?" Red asks as she adjusts her shirt.

Jealousy courses through me, stinging my limbs. Not the kind of violent jealousy, more like a low simmer. Honestly, I'm mostly cursing myself that I didn't think to sneak her away for ten minutes earlier.

I'd bet my fucking left arm they were messing around in his room. "Lucky bastard," I murmur. I'm already envisioning all the ways I can get her alone tomorrow. A smile twists my lips when I remember the jet has a king-sized bed in the back.

"You guys don't mind if I stay here, right? You'll fill me in on your conversation?" Red asks, looking between Sully and me.

"Nah, we're good, Red. You stay here, and I'll fill you in when we get back."

She crosses the room to stand in front of me. Pushing up onto her tiptoes, she brushes her lips across mine. By the time I try to deepen the kiss, she's already easing back.

"Thank you. Be safe, okay?"

"Always am, baby girl." I swipe my tongue across my lips, savoring the taste of her. I'm fucking salivating for more of her.

Soon, I promise myself.

She moves toward Sully, and he reaches out and curls his hand around her shoulder, bringing her in for a kiss. It's just as brief before she leans back. "Take it easy, okay? We need you well enough for our trip."

Sully, that moody fucking bastard smiles, and it's this blinding white thing that takes me by surprise. It's been a hot second since I've seen that smile.

"Damn, girl. Did you break him with your magic va—"

A chorus of "Roisin" interrupts her before she finishes her sentence.

Roisin throws her arms up in the air. "What? It's a valid question. I didn't even *know* Sully had a dimple, and one very modest peck, and he's all smiles? It's weird, okay?"

Sully scowls at everyone but Red as he folds his arms across his chest. "I'm not that bad."

Roisin points at him from across the room. "See! That's what I'm used to."

"Alright. As fun as this is, we gotta leave if we want to make it on time to our meeting," Rush says before he slides his hand down the back of her hair and places a kiss on the top of her head. "We'll be back soon, birdie."

"Alright. Be careful, all of you." She watches us as we leave the apartment. I glance over my shoulder as the door shuts and our gazes connect. She hasn't moved from her spot in the living room as she holds my gaze until the door closes with a click.

"Get your heads in the game, brothers. We need to be sharp for this meeting."

O'MALLEY'S IS UNCHARACTERISTICALLY quiet for this time of night. Patrick, one of the prospects, was monitoring the door when we got here. He told us that Jack wasn't in tonight, but he set up a few things to make sure we had the privacy we needed. I guess part of that means the decreased clientele tonight.

Da sits in a corner booth mostly concealed in the shadows. His mouth stays in a flat line as he eyes the three of us striding toward his table. I scan his posture, looking for clues to his mood.

Like usual, he has whatever emotion he's feeling locked down pretty tight. His parenting style is usually warm, all things considered. But his leadership style is arctic—his low tolerance for bullshit is widely-known.

His trigger finger isn't as itchy as Cillian Kelly's, but there's a reason Da's friends with the head of the original Brotherhood, and it's not for just camaraderie. That motherfucker is crazy as hell and just as likely to shoot you as to hug you.

Fuck.

We're going to have to set a meet with him or his nephew, Quinn, when we reach Ireland. There's no way we can land in his country without paying our respects to him. That alone would sign our death warrants.

My gut clenches at the idea of Red in the same room as either of them. Though we might have an easier time with Quinn. I make a mental note to bring it up with Rush and Sully when we're done here.

There's a pause, heavy and stiff, when we reach the booth. Da's gaze flicks between the three of us before he nods and tips his head toward the bench seat across from him. He leans back and signals the bartender for another drink, looking every bit the image of authority.

Rush slides in first, sitting across from Da. Sully takes the seat next to him, leaving me in to sit at the end. With a hand on the back of the chair from the empty table next to us, I pull it over, leaving it far enough away so I have plenty of room to spread out at the end.

The air around us is thick with tension as Patrick, one of our prospects, brings us four lowball glasses of whiskey. "Thanks, man. You helping out tonight or something?"

"Yeah. Jack asked me to fill in for him for a little bit tonight. I'm shit at making drinks, so I just run them out while Carter pours 'em."

I nod and take a sip of the whiskey, relishing the burn as it slides down my throat. "Who's at the door then?"

Patrick shrugs, the movement stiff. His gaze keeps darting to Da and back to me. "Jordan's there tonight. Benny's supposed to be here sometime too, but he hasn't been around the last few days, so I dunno."

I nod, making sure to school my face into something that doesn't show the rage bubbling right now. I haven't forgotten that asshole's attempting to blackmail a date outta my girl through her cousin. "You let me know if he shows, yeah?"

"Sure thing, boss." Patrick nods, three quick motions, his gaze darting around and unable to stay on one of us.

I take another sip as I watch him spin on his heel and head toward the bar.

"I'm not too sure about that guy. He's like a frightened rabbit," Sully says with a scowl.

"Aye. Maybe he'll pull out of it though," I muse, swirling my ice cubes around in the glass.

"Enough chitchat. We have questions." Rush stares at Da, unblinking.

He raises a brow and takes his time sipping his drink. I watch the muscle in Rush's jaw clench at the obvious power play here.

It's silent as the four of us stare at one another, but it doesn't last long. Da's the first one to break the silence. "Where's Alaina?"

"She's safe. What do you know about her? And don't bother bullshiting us," Rush says.

Da sighs and leans back against the booth. He looks around us, as if to make sure we're alone. "I know what it looks like—"

"You mean you know that it looks like you're doing some backroom bullshit deals that may or may not be connected to the recent run on our people and our livelihood and those of our allies?" Sully's voice is low as he stares at Da.

He spears Sully with a glare. "You know I wouldn't do that."

Sully nods, the movement slow and reluctant. "Aye, but I didn't think you'd pick up some random woman, move her in, and propose to her after a few weeks either. So, I'm inclined to think that anything's possible."

Da clenches his jaw so tight, a vein pops out in his forehead.

"I already explained what happened with Lana. And I already explained that I was looking for Aidan, for a time. I had no way of knowing your history with the girl—or that you'd develop this kind of relationship with her."

I find myself nodding before I even realize it. I stop the motion immediately and look at him. "Then why all the cloak and dagger bullshit? What aren't you telling us? And why the fuck were you called into a surprise family meeting?"

Da tosses back a healthy swallow of whiskey and pins me with a look. "I was protecting you. Despite what you all think, you're still my boys. You'll always be my boys. And I didn't fill you in on our family reunion because the less people that know, the better."

"Know what?" Rush asks.

"That Cillian's stepping down early. He's not well, and his prognosis is less than a year."

"Fuck," my brothers and I say at the same time.

Da nods a few times. "I see you're understanding the implication now. The Brotherhood is progressive in a lot of ways, but this is not one of them. We've been doing things the same way for too long. And Quinn isn't quite ready—he hasn't been in the junior council for long enough and he doesn't have the connections yet. It seems that our enemies might already know about Cillian."

"Another fucking *rat*?" Sully seethes.

"Probably. But the damage is done. Someone knows, and we all know secrets between two men only stay safe if one of them is dead."

I lean forward, bracing my forearms on the table. "So, they're swooping in during the chaos."

"And if they're smart, they'll do it strategically so the Brotherhood's own members start to question whether or not Quinn is capable of leading them," Rush adds. "It's what I'd do."

I nod my agreement. "So, what now? How do we get in front of this?"

Da runs his hand down his beard. "We have some things in place. Cillian's planning one of his famous *tea parties*. The rest should work itself out."

"And you couldn't just fucking tell us that? Jesus Christ, Da. We thought you were fucking double-dipping or some shit." I run my hand through my hair, the motion more agitated than smooth.

His gaze hardens as he pins me with a look. I'm not looking at my da anymore—it's the Butcher. "I'm the motherfucking president of the East Coast Brotherhood. I'd sooner die than betray my family. And don't you ever forget you're my fucking family, boyo. All of you are." He looks at Sully and Rush, pausing on each of them for a moment.

Rush clears his throat. "Okay. We'll await updates then, yeah?" The Butcher nods his agreement. "And one other thing: We're leaving for Ireland tomorrow."

"We've got business to sort out with Lainey's extended family," Sully offers with his chin tipped up.

Da looks into the bar, his brows creased in concentration. "I'm not going to tell you not to go. Just be safe. And for fuck's sake, check-in with Quinn when you arrive. We'll wait to hold a small service for Lana until you're back then."

"Aye, it's already set up."

Da tosses back the rest of his drink and sets it down on the table with a clink. "Are we good then?"

The three of us look at each other and then look at him, and as one, we nod. Damn, we couldn't have timed that better if we tried.

He taps the table twice. "Good. I'll see you when you're back stateside."

25

ALAINA

"OH MY GOD, THIS IS INCREDIBLE." My eyes widen as I take in the grandeur of the private jet we just boarded.

An older woman in a black skirt and matching jacket greets us as she walks down the aisle toward us. "Welcome aboard, Fitzgeralds. I should've known you'd be early." She winks at them before turning her attention to me and extending her hand. "And you must be Birdie. I'm Alice. I have to say, I just love your name. It's so unique."

I grasp her hand and politely shake it as I raise a brow at Rush. He shrugs a shoulder and stows our bags inside a compartment next to the first row of seats.

"Thank you. It's so nice to meet you, Alice."

She lets go of my hand and says, "Now you let me know if you need anything. Usually these boys are pretty self-sufficient, but I've been informed of the longer trip today, so I'll be preparing a meal in our dinette kitchen onboard. If you'll excuse me, I've got some things to help the pilot with before we take off."

Alice walks past me and heads down the aisle toward the

cockpit. Wolf laces his fingers with mine and gently tugs me further into the plane.

It's all done in grays, whites, and dark charcoals. It looks more like the lobby of a ritzy hotel than the inside of a private jet. Though I suppose I don't have any experience with a private plane before now, so maybe this is how they all come?

"Who's plane are we on?"

Wolf squeezes my hand once. "Rush called in a favor from a friend. Not only is he keeping you off the books, but we're adding a couple extra small stops, and on paper, changing passengers. So it'll look like we went to Atlanta and seven businessmen boarded it to London. Where a married couple fly to Ireland."

My jaw falls a little. "You guys arranged all that in a day?"

"You'd be surprised what we can do in a day, princess," Sully says as he takes a seat on one of the plush white leather single seats along the sides. There are two single seats on each side, facing one another and a set of four facing seats behind them. Little tables are between the seats with white linen tablecloths and a small vase with fresh flowers.

I'm content to let Wolf lead, so I can take everything in. Even the lightly designed gray-and-white runner rug is plush beneath my sneakers.

We pass a wall in the middle of the jet with what looks like a fifty-inch TV mounted on it. Beyond that are the bathrooms and a bedroom.

Wolf pushes open the door, but he doesn't step inside. "You can lay down here if you need to. It's pretty comfortable and quiet. And they change the bedding after each flight, so you don't have to worry about anything gross."

"Good to know. I'm okay now, but last night was long, and I have a feeling I'm going to crash soon."

"Mm-hmm. And how was your time with the Kings? Did they teach you any new moves? You know I'm always available to be your guinea pig, Red." Wolf smirks at me, and I resist the urge to kiss it off his face.

"They taught me a few things. And gave me a few things too." I pat the side pocket of my slightly flared black skirt where the knife Ava gave me sits. It hits me mid-thigh, and I thought it'd be comfortable to travel in, but I did bring leggings too.

Wolf's eyes lower, and he deliberately gives me a once-over, his gaze lingering on my hand over my pocket. "And what did they give you, baby girl, hmm?"

I roll my eyes. "Get your mind out of the gutter, Wolf. Ava gave me this." I pull out the three-inch, slimline, lightweight blade and wiggle it.

"Damn, Red, that's not pulling me outta the gutter."

I chuckle and playfully nudge him with my shoulder as I pocket the blade. "I thought it might come in handy. You know, since we're confronting my long-lost family who may or may not be sending psychos after me."

He throws an arm over my shoulder and places a kiss on the top of my head. "Smart, Red. But you won't need it. You have us. Let's settle in. We'll be taking off soon."

I sink into the seat next to Wolf in one of the four seats grouped together. It feels more like a luxury armchair than a seat on a plane. I sigh, tip my head back against the headrest, and close my eyes.

A few moments later, I feel someone's gaze on me and crack an eye open. Sully stands right in front of me with his arm outstretched. He uncurls his fingers, revealing a set of white earbuds in his palm.

Déjà vu hits me like a tornado, and my heart skips a beat.

"I made you a playlist."

Those five little words send my heart spiraling to a different time. A time when two kids fell for each other in between the stacks of the library during one summer.

Holding his gaze, I take the earbuds from his hand and put them in my ears. I spare a moment to worry that I won't be able to hear anything over the pounding of my heart, but then I hear the first few notes of The Clash's "Hateful."

I feel the smile tip up the corner of my lips as a buried memory resurfaces.

I quietly sing along to my playlist as I walk further down the dimly lit aisle. "Anything I want, he gives it but not——"

"I didn't take you for a Clash fan, princess."

I whirl around with a shriek and see the guy from earlier standing in front of me with a smirk on his too-handsome face.

"Shh!" Faster than I can imagine, he takes a step toward me and gently presses his hand to my mouth. "Jesus. If you don't stop screaming, they're going to think I'm murdering you or some shit."

My heartbeat races and my mouth falls open in surprise. But his warm hand is still on my face, and it smells strangely good, like saltwater taffy.

He raises a brow. "Did you just sniff my hand?" I will myself not to flush, and I curse my fair skin again.

Do you know how hard it is to hide your embarrassment or arousal—not that I've had a lot of practice with that—when you're a redhead?

At my flat stare, he removes his hand, but he doesn't step away. "You good?" I nod.

"You scared me." I press a hand to my chest. "Who does something like that?" I glare at him accusingly.

"I called out to you like five times. I figured you were playing hard to get or whatever it is chicks do." He shrugs and puts his hands in the pockets of his faded jeans.

I take out my earbuds and hold them up. "I don't even—I wasn't. I didn't hear you." I'm flustered, and I can only imagine how red my face and chest are getting. I can feel my ears getting hot.

I look at Sully, and judging by the grin on his face, he's remembering the same thing I am.

He nods once as the song changes and "Punk Rock Princess" plays, propelling me into another memory.

James turns to look at me, and his shoulders relax. "That's me. What about you, princess? What's your story?"

I lean against the shelf and give him my undivided attention. "I'm just a regular girl." I shrug a shoulder.

James matches my position and leans against the shelf across from me. His gaze slowly roams over my face before making a leisurely sweep down my body. I swear I feel tingles every place his gaze touches. "A pretty princess who loves The Clash?" He scoffs. "Somehow, I doubt you're just a girl."

"It's Alaina." I keep my gaze on him, despite my pounding heart.

He smirks. "I know. See you around, punk rock princess." James pushes off the shelf and walks toward the aisle. As he turns the corner, he looks over his shoulder and gives me the cockiest smirk filled with promises I've only experienced in books.

It takes me several minutes before I can peel myself off the shelf. I don't know what just happened, but I have a feeling that everything is about to change. I glance at my phone and realize the time. Shoot. The program ended ten minutes ago.

My heart beats so hard it feels like it's trying to escape my chest. I have a hunch that he made me a playlist of all the songs we used to listen to together.

My theory is proven correct when I hear The Smiths followed by the Yeah Yeah Yeahs and more. I close my eyes and let my mind wander as the sweet songs roll over me like a soothing wave.

A few minutes later, Rush joins us and sits next to Sully, across from Wolf, and pulls out his laptop. Alice comes by with drinks for everyone—whiskey for them and champagne for me.

I see their mouths moving, but the music in my ears drowns them out, so I let my eyes drift closed again and just listen.

SOMEONE SHAKES MY SHOULDER, startling me from sleep. My eyes are quick to pop open, and for a second, I forget where I am.

"You fell asleep, Red. Why don't you go lay down on the bed in the back?"

I blink a few times, and tilt my head to the side to stretch out my neck. "How long have I been out?"

The music is no longer playing in my ears, so I pop out the earbuds and place them on the table.

"Not long. Twenty minutes or so," Sully answers, his gaze intense.

His eyes are the color of the middle of the ocean, the richest blue that seems almost unnatural, and my heart swells inside my chest. Just like two years ago, Sully invited me to look inside his soul through a playlist. And this playlist had almost every song we ever shared with one another the summer we met.

This wasn't just a glimpse inside his head, it was a remembrance of who we were then—and who we could be now, together. My fingers tingle, and my heart pounds at the gesture.

A smile spreads across my face, wide and joyous.

It's a modern-day love letter.

That tattoo-covered, scowl-loving, broody alphahole made me a playlist of love songs and handed it over like he was giving me the newspaper. I beam at him, laughing to myself.

He spots my amusement and that ever-present scowl returns. Shifting in his seat, he folds his arms over his chest, his biceps bulging. "What?"

I twist my lips to the side to quell the laughter, but I can feel the sparkle in my eye. Without a word, I unbuckle my seat belt, shift the table to the side, and launch myself at him. He has just enough time to uncross his arms and catch me.

I crash my mouth to his with a leg on either side of him. My skirt flares around my legs as I hover over his lap and pour all my emotions into this kiss. He holds me against his chest with his hands on my ribs.

I pull back before I get carried away. "Thank you," I whisper against his lips.

"Thank you, Lainey. For not giving up on me." His voice is rough and low—a moment just between us.

"Never, I swear it." My vow is met with another soul-searing kiss.

The plane dips, and the glasses on the table rattle as we experience turbulence. "Just a small bit of turbulence here, folks. Should be out of it in two minutes or so, but until then, please make sure you're in your seat with your seat belt fastened," the captain says over the speakers.

I move off of Sully and settle back in my seat, fastening my seat belt as the glasses rattle again and my stomach pitches. I don't usually get motion sickness, and I don't want to start now.

"I take it you liked it then? The songs I chose?" Sully asks, stealing my attention from the turbulence.

"Yeah, it was alright," I tease with a feigned shrug.

Sully arches a brow and tips his chin up. "Alright, she says. I'll show you *alright*, princess."

I don't miss the innuendo in his statement, and judging by the way Wolf and Rush are both staring between the two of us, they didn't either.

"Bro, are you . . . teasing Red?" Wolf's mouth parts in disbelief.

Rush hides his grin behind his hand as he watches everything unfold.

The tips of Sully's ears get pink and he huffs. "No."

Wolf chuckles and nods a few times. "It's a good look on you, man. Fuckin' weird to see you teasing and making playlists, but I'm glad to see you've worked your shit out with our girl."

Sully eyes me, his gaze smoldering as he says, "Aye, we worked it out, but we might need to work out some more."

My mind immediately goes back to the huge shower in their apartment—and the bedroom—and the bedroom again. Warmth rolls over me, and I shift in my seat.

"Alright, folks, looks like we're out of it. You're free to move about the cabin," the captain says.

I unbuckle my seat belt and stand up to stretch. I feel all three pairs of eyes on me, but I do my best to ignore it. For now. "Where's the bathroom again?"

Wolf stands before the others even open their mouths. "I'll show you, Red. Follow me."

26

ALAINA

I DRY my hands on the soft hand towel in the bathroom while staring at my reflection in the mirror. This is easily the biggest airplane bathroom I've ever seen. It has a full shower in the corner and a double vanity, all done in the same black-charcoal-white theme. It's probably as big as my bathroom in my dorm suite. I could spread my arms out as wide as I can, and I still would have five feet of space on either side of me.

I eye the bench along the wall as a sliver of lust slides around in my veins. A smirk curves the corner of my lips up at the idea of joining the mile high club in this bathroom. I've never done anything like that before, but with this much space—and this much privacy—I can't deny the thrill of it.

You should totally take advantage of the opportunity to mess around, my inner voice that sounds a lot like Maddie encourages.

I smooth out the wrinkles in my skirt and fluff my hair up a little. I blow out a breath and square my shoulders. I open the accordion door to the bathroom, and Wolf is leaning against the wall facing me—exactly where I left him. He looks up from his phone in his hand, and before he can say anything, I reach out

237

and grab a handful of his black tee and pull him into the bathroom with me.

I know he could take control if he wanted to, but he lets me be in charge, at least for a moment. I slam the bathroom door closed and flick the occupied lock, my fingers still curled around his shirt.

"You ever join the mile high club, Conor?"

That cocky little smirk that I hate to love crawls across his handsome face as he stares at me. He sinks his teeth into his full bottom lip, letting it slide out slowly as he looks at me from head to toe through half-lidded eyes.

Goddamn.

My desire was at a low simmer, but with that one look, he keys it up.

"Oh, baby girl, I thought you'd never ask."

I push onto my tiptoes, and he slams his mouth to mine as he hooks his warm palms underneath my thighs, lifting me up. I wrap my legs around his waist, feeling his thick cock harden as he absolutely devours me.

Our tongues fight for dominance as we chase our lust together. With an arm curled around his neck, I wiggle my body closer to him, desperate to feel him against me.

He groans into my mouth, this desperate, heady sound that sets my blood boiling. He spins us around until my ass hits the countertop. I don't unlock my legs from around his waist as his hands tunnel underneath my shirt and settle on my bra.

His fingertips dance along the lace trim on the cups of my bra. I pull away from his mouth and he immediately moves it to my neck. I bunch up his shirt and get a good look at his mouthwatering abs and chest—and that goddamn *vee*.

He pulls away from my neck when I tug on his shirt, understanding what I'm asking without words. Reaching behind his head, he grabs his shirt by the collar and pulls it over his head in that move that has women everywhere short-circuiting.

He flashes me that charming smile of his. "You alright, baby girl? You got a little something here," he says as he drags his finger along my bottom lip.

I swipe my tongue out between my parted lips, tasting the oranges he ate on his fingertips. His eyes darken and his chest expands. All those delicious muscles and tattoos are right in front of my face, but his gaze holds me hostage.

Hunger.

Raw hunger shines from his eyes, and I can tell by the way his body tenses that he's holding himself back.

I pull my shirt over my head and drop it to the ground. He holds out for three whole seconds before his gaze flies to my tits. I'm suddenly glad I wore my favorite lacy black bra today.

Wolf's tattooed fingers cover the swell of my breasts before he flips the cups down and toys with my nipples. I arch my back as pleasure shoots straight down to my clit.

He leans forward and wraps his lips around my nipple. My breaths come in short bursts as he pinches the other nipple with just enough of a bite that arousal floods me. I feel myself growing wetter by the second.

Lust makes my head feel foggy as I reach for the waistband of his pants with one hand, desperate to feel him. I make quick work of unbuttoning his jeans and shoving them down his hips. His hard cock springs free between us, and I wrap my hand around it, marveling at the size. He groans against my breast, his other hand flexing against my nipple.

He's big enough that my fingers don't touch, and I have a second of panic interrupt my lusty haze.

He skims his mouth in between my breasts and up my neck as he murmurs, "Don't worry, Red. It'll fit."

239

I feel my cheeks flush as I remember the first time I held him in my hands, I had the same sentiment. "You're just . . . so *big*."

He chuckles against my ear, the laugh dripping with sexual intentions. "Keep up the dirty talk, baby girl. I like it." He punctuates his words with a nip against my neck that has me groaning.

I pump my hand up and down his shaft a few times before I swirl the pre-cum around the tip.

He lets me play for another few moments before he takes a step back. A noise of protest leaves my lips as my fingers slide off his cock.

"Patience, Red," Wolf says as he takes my hand in his and puts it flat on the counter next to my hip. "Keep 'em here, yeah?"

I nod and he trails his fingers along my inner thighs. The feather-light touch has me practically panting in anticipation, my heart thundering in my ears.

He inches up my skirt at an agonizingly slow speed, exposing more skin to the cool air-conditioned air. "You are so beautiful, Red. So fucking beautiful, and so fucking mine." His words end on a growl as my skirt sits around my waist, his fingers tracing the lace trim along my inner thigh.

I tense my muscles to keep from moving. I want to reach out and touch him so bad, I can practically taste it. Lust sits heavy on my tongue like triple chocolate cake, and I'm two minutes away from begging him to put me out of my misery.

His fingers caress me with long, light strokes through my underwear, teasing me by stopping right before he reaches the spot that's aching for him.

I rock my hips against his hand, impatience and lust turning my rhythm choppy.

"Stop teasing me, Conor."

"You have no idea how badly I want to be inside you, Red. But first . . ." He curls his fingers around the flimsy side of my panties, and with a hard yank, rips them off of me. With his hands splayed on my hips, he pulls me to the edge of the counter and kneels on the floor.

My breath catches at the sight of him—head bent, hair tousled, and those dark, expressive eyes zeroed in on me beneath hooded lids.

He looks every bit the dark god I always imagine him as. And he's on his knees for *me*, begging to pay fealty and worship me.

That's the last coherent thought I have before he leans forward and swipes his tongue through my slit. Once, twice, three times. The desire to touch him becomes too much, and I thread my fingers through his dark hair, holding him against my core. He moans against my pussy, his tongue relentless in his teasing licks.

My hips buck against his face, and my eyes slide closed as I whisper, "More, please." I barely recognize the breathy voice coming from my lips.

"You want more, baby girl?" he says against my clit, his lips grazing but never quite touching it.

My eyes pop open, and I stare at him through the fog of arousal. The look on his face matches exactly how I feel inside—desperate hunger.

"I want it all, Conor."

His eyes flash before darkening to nearly black. He flashes one of his panty-dropping smirks at me, holding my gaze as he licks my pussy in a long, long wet flick of his tongue before he wraps his lips around my clit and sucks. *Hard.*

My eyes slam shut and my breath hitches as I run toward my orgasm. In the next moment, he slides two fingers inside me, curving them toward me to hit that perfect spot that sends me flying high.

I'm on the edge of coming when he does the unthinkable and pulls back. "What?! No, don't stop," I practically beg him as he gets to his feet. My hands skim over his sculpted muscles.

"Damnit, Wolf. I was so close." I don't even care that I sound like I'm pouting because I am. I feel robbed, my orgasm hovers just outside my reach, taunting me with its euphoria.

He grabs my chin and turns my face toward his. "The next time you come, it's going to be on my cock."

If I wasn't already dripping wet, my panties would be soaked from that sentence alone.

He picks me up, and I instinctively wrap my legs around his waist. It takes me a moment to realize that we're out of the bathroom and heading to the bedroom at the back of the plane. I don't even have enough time to be embarrassed that Wolf's half-dressed and I'm in a bra before we're inside the bedroom.

WOLF

I DON'T GIVE her a chance to get spooked as I march her pert ass down the hallway and into the bedroom. There was no way I was going to slide into my girl's tight pussy for the first time in a fucking airplane bathroom. Regardless of how nice it is.

But this bed back here is the perfect place.

She surprised the hell outta me when she opened the bathroom door and asked if I've ever joined the mile high club. I wasn't about to pass up the opportunity to help my girl cross something off her bucket list.

Her arousal slicks against my abs, and I have to concentrate on putting one foot in front of the other and not pinning her against the nearest wall and sliding into that perfect pussy.

I kick the door shut with my foot and set her down on the bed. Before she can say anything, I cover her body with my own, careful to keep some weight off of her, and steal her mouth. The fact that she's tasting herself on my tongue makes me impossibly harder. I can't stop my hips from grinding into her as our tongues tangle.

Fuck. If I don't slow it down, I'm going to come before the show even gets started.

I break the kiss and trail my lips down her perfect fucking skin until I reach her nipples.

"Conor." She sighs my name when I use my teeth and tug her already hard nipples.

I can't stop staring at her tits and envisioning my cock between them. If my goal was to slow down to make it last for her, I'm doing a fucking shitty job of it. Reaching a hand between our bodies, I rub my fingers against her pussy, making little circles around her clit. Her desire coats my fingers instantly, and she moans my name. I gently tug on her other nipple with my teeth at the same moment I slide two fingers inside her and press down on her clit with my thumb.

Her back comes off the bed in an arch so sudden, I have to adjust my hold on her. My name comes out in a strangled moan, and deep satisfaction courses through my veins.

Fuck anything else, this is the best goddamn high of my life.

"Enough teasing, fuck me, Conor. Now."

A condom lands on the bed next to us and my head whips to the side. I was so wrapped up in her that I didn't even look to see if anyone else was in this room.

Rush sits in the armchair in the corner facing us. A lowball glass with an inch of whiskey dangles from his fingers as he stares at us—Red—with barely concealed lust.

"Why'd you stop—oh. *Oh*," Red says from underneath me. I didn't realize that I stopped moving.

My brows lower as I stare at my brother. I'm usually pretty good at analyzing people, but he's keeping most of his shit locked up tight, like usual. Worry churns in my gut, replacing some of the desire. It's one thing to talk about sharing a girl in hypotheticals, but it's another thing entirely to see it in front of your eyes.

When Sully kicked me outta his room, it was bad enough assuming he did it so he could mess around. And then I heard her moans, and then my jealousy flared. But fuck, she sounded like she was in ecstasy, and fuck me if I'm not selfish enough that I wanna make her see fucking stars too.

Even though this whole fucking thing was Rush's grand master plan, I'm unsure how he's going to react to watching me with Red. I glance at the woman in question, and her gaze is locked on Rush's. Her chest heaves, and she rolls her hips, encouraging me to continue my exploration of her. So, with a wary glance at my brother, I do.

27

ALAINA

IT ONLY TAKES a moment to get over my initial surprise at finding Rush in the corner of the bedroom. I shouldn't be shocked, not really. Watching is Rush's thing, it's where he feels comfortable.

I have a hunch that he's waiting for my cue—for me to say it's okay for him to join in. I've made my feelings for the three of them clear, but I never asked if they're okay sharing me . . . like this.

There's only one way to find out.

I circle my hips a little, getting Wolf's attention back on me. He takes the hint and glances at his brother before he slips his fingers back inside me, dragging them in and out slow enough that I feel like I'm losing my mind a little.

My breath leaves my lips in little pants, and when he dips his head, and his tongue laves against my clit, my lashes flutter closed and I moan his name.

I make myself open my eyes and stare right at Rush, daring him to come closer. Still, he stays in the armchair, his grip on the glass tight enough that I see the whites of his knuckles.

So, I up the ante again and slide one hand to cover my breast, plucking and tugging on my hard nipple. The other hand goes to Wolf's head, tangling in his hair and keeping him against my core.

I stare at Rush as I ask, "Are you going to stay over there all night?"

He licks his lips, his gaze straying to my hand on my breast. "Are you sure?"

"I'm sure. Come here."

Rush is by my side in an instant, his glass forgotten on the floor. He hesitates by the side of the bed. "Wolf?"

Wolf lifts his head, his lips shiny with my arousal, and says, "I won't deny our girl. Will you?"

"No. I won't deny her anything. Not in this life or any other." Rush stares at me with a burning intensity that I feel in my soul. "Do you trust me, baby?" I nod before he even finishes talking. He runs his fingers down the side of my face, stopping on my bottom lip. "Good girl. Fuck our girl, Wolf."

I flash Rush a grin that borders on giddy. His commanding tone sets my blood on fire. And with a nod of encouragement from me, Wolf slides his fingers from my soaking core before sticking them in his mouth.

"Fucking delicious," he says with a carnal smile. He tears open the condom with his teeth and rolls it down his erect cock.

He lines us up, and as he seals his lips to mine, he pushes inside of me. My breath stalls in my lungs as the feeling of fullness invades my senses.

I roll my hips, loving the way he feels inside of me. "Conor." His name leaves my lips on a moan as I start that delicious climb toward my orgasm again.

I inch my hand toward Rush, holding his gaze as I unbutton and unzip his pants. He doesn't stop me, just watches me with stormy-gray eyes. My heart races, and I don't know if it's from the feeling of Wolf sliding in and out with an excruciating slowness or if it's from the fact that Rush isn't wearing anything underneath his jeans.

Curling my fingers as much as I can around his impressive length, I slide my hand up and down and delight in the velvety smoothness of him.

"Harder, baby," Rush commands.

I squeeze my fingers tighter around him and adjust my speed to match Wolf's. My heart slams against my ribs when I feel the telltale signs of my impending orgasm.

Wolf drags his palm down my body, leaving a trail of fire in its wake. "You feel like fucking heaven, baby girl. I can feel you clenching around my cock."

His words feel like a match to my already-lit fire, and I can't stop myself from clenching around him again. His speed picks up, but he still maintains those smooth strokes. "Oh, god, that feels good. Don't stop," I beg him.

Wolf clucks his tongue. "Our girl likes the dirty talk."

"Mm," Rush responds with a twist of his lips.

Wolf stretches his body across mine and whispers against my lips, "Come for me, baby girl." His tattooed fingers encircle my clit softly before he changes it up and pinches.

I distantly hear Rush's hiss as I squeeze my fist tight around him, but I'm too busy floating on a cloud of absolute bliss to pay attention. My vision blacks out for a moment and stars dance across my vision.

"Goddamn," Wolf grunts a second before he comes, holding his hips flush against mine, our chests heaving in tandem.

After a few moments, he pulls out and collapses next to me on the bed, throwing an arm over his eyes.

I just had one of the best orgasms of my life, but I'm not done yet. Not today. With lust coursing through my veins giving me courage, I push onto my knees with my hand still wrapped around Rush's hard cock.

I curl my hand around his neck and he fuses his mouth to mine, carrying me over to the armchair he was sitting in earlier. He sits down without breaking our kiss and I straddle him. I feel his dick hard against me and rock my hips without a second thought.

He tilts my head to deepen our kiss, and my lust burns brighter, hotter. Quickly, I start that climb toward my orgasm again.

I break our kiss to reach between us and roll a condom down his length. I position him at my core, desperate to feel him inside of me. Rush tightens his grip on my hips, stopping me from sinking down.

"Eyes on me, baby."

He bunches my skirt in one fist and holds it to the side. Cool air washes over me, leaving goosebumps on my heated skin. His other hand smooths a path up my body until it's resting against the hollow of my neck. I arch my back into his hold, my pleasure mounting at being in this position.

"Go slow, yeah?"

I nod my head twice before slowly lowering myself onto his cock. My breath hitches and my heart stutters. He feels easily as big as the other guys, and it doesn't seem statistically possible for all of them to be so large, but I'm thanking my lucky stars for my good fortune.

I pause when he's fully seated inside me, giving myself a moment to adjust. When I start to roll my hips, Rush pulls me in for a bruising kiss. "You're everything, Alaina."

I blink a few times at his intensity. He lets me control the pace for another moment before he takes over and starts fucking me from underneath. I put my hands on his shoulders and enjoy the ride.

Pleasure infuses my limbs, making me feel boneless and heavy at the same time. My lips part in amazement. "I—I think I'm going to come again."

His pouty lips curved into a carnal grin. "I want to feel you soak my cock, birdie."

I whimper at his words—something about his tone and his words sending me spiraling higher and higher.

The fabric of my skirt flutters around my hips and his palm goes back to my hip before smoothing down the curve of my ass. He encourages me to ride him faster and harder, and I meet his request with every dip and roll of my hips. His big palm covers my cheek, his fingertips grazing the one place I've never explored.

A shiver zips down my spine at the possibility. And when he dips his fingertip to lightly graze me there, I see stars. My breath completely leaves me, and I can't move as pleasure too overwhelming electrifies my body.

Rush groans against my mouth as he finds his own pleasure, his hands flexing on my skin for a moment.

I rest my forehead against his and try to collect myself. I feel like I left pieces of myself in this room today—or more likely, my inhibitions. I'd do it again in a heartbeat.

Something has awakened inside me since I met them, and for the first time in ten years, I feel like I'm right where I belong.

I arch my back and tip my head back to meet the ocean-blue gaze of my missing piece. Sully leans against the closed bedroom door with his hands shoved down his pants. I watch the slow up and down movement of his arm, and somehow, a fresh wave of arousal slithers over me.

His gaze narrows as he leisurely pumps his cock beneath the fabric of his pants. He's the picture of desire with his bedroom eyes and tousled hair.

I rake my teeth over my bottom lip as I look my fill of my boyfriend.

Rush groans beneath me. "Fuck, baby. You keep clenching around me like that, and I'm never going to leave."

I chuckle and place a kiss on his lips before I rise off of him with a moan. "Patience, Dec."

My skirt flutters around my thighs as I cross the room to Sully, swaying my hips with each step. I stop in front of him and hold his gaze as I slowly unzip my skirt, letting it fall to the floor in a puddle of fabric at my feet. Then I reach behind my back, and with a flick of my wrist, I unhook my bra and slide it down my arms before it joins my skirt on the floor.

His gaze flares, and his jaw clenches as he takes me in. It's not the first time he's seen me like this, but it's the first time he's had an audience.

This isn't the place for any insecurities, so even though he's quiet in his perusal, I don't let it affect me. I let the high of my previous orgasms embolden me and erase the space between us. I trail my fingertips down his chest until I reach his waistband and tug. His gasp is ambrosia to my ears.

I slide his pants over his hips and gently bat his hand away, revealing his hard cock. I hold his gaze as I wrap my hand around him and sink to the ground. A low groan spills from his perfect lips, and I flash him a sultry smile before I take him in my mouth.

"Goddamn, princess."

I run my tongue up and down his length before teasing his head. My hand covers everything my mouth can't reach, and I relish in the feel of him against my tongue.

Sully moans my name and tangles his fingers in my hair, holding it in a tight grip to keep me against his cock. I moan at his unspoken request, and a curse falls from his lips.

He guides me off his cock with gentle pressure, and I can't

help the noise of protest. He thumbs my bottom lip as he stares at me with lust darkening his gaze. "I love your mouth, princess. But I wanna feel that tight pussy squeezing my cock."

My lips part on an exhale, and he slides his thumb inside my mouth. I flick my tongue against it, tasting his skin. Before I get carried away, he says, "Get on your knees on the bed."

I make quick work of crossing the room to the bed, a trio of chuckles fill the air. I guess they could feel my eagerness too. I smirk at Wolf as he reclines on the bed, leaning against the headboard. And as much as I'm eager to turn my fantasies into reality, I don't think I'm ready to take all three of them at once. Not today, at least.

My hands and knees sink into the plush comforter, putting my pussy on display. Just as I'm about to turn around, Sully slides his big palms over my cheeks and around my hips. He smooths his hands up and down my back, resting them on my hips. I wiggle my ass and scoot down on the bed until I feel him flush against me.

"You know I don't like to be teased, James." My voice is raspy with desire.

He curves his body over mine, trailing open-mouthed kisses down my back and slipping his fingers inside of me. "Fuck me, Lainey. You're fucking soaked."

I groan his name, rocking my hips against his hands as he finger-fucks me into oblivion. I've never come so many times so quickly in my life, but as pleasure infuses my limbs and my chest heaves, I'm rapidly approaching my next orgasm.

"I can feel you clenching around my fingers. You're close, aren't you, princess?" Sully's whispered words against my back send shivers down my spine. He removes his hands and lips from my body, and just when I open my mouth to protest, I hear the familiar sound of a condom wrapper opening. And in the next second, I feel his hard cock at my entrance. "Hold on, Lainey."

I sink to my forearms and curl my fingers into the comforter, bracing myself as Sully slides inside of me. If I wasn't already so wet, he'd probably have to take his time. But my arousal drips down my inner thighs, and Sully thrusts all the way inside of me. This position is different, and he feels bigger—deeper.

"It's too much. This angle. Too good." My words are choppy and my breath comes out in pants as Sully starts that delicious rhythm that has me tingling all over.

It starts in my toes—this feeling of pins and needles—and it crawls up my legs and over my hips. When he reaches around my hip and tweaks my clit, the feeling races up my spine and sets off an explosion behind my eyes that steals my breath. I swear I black out for a moment as pleasure so intense takes over my body.

My name on Sully's lips draws me back to earth in time to feel him lose himself inside of me. He grunts, holding his hips flush against my ass as I feel my walls flutter around his still-hard cock.

I hold on for another second before my arms and legs give out and I fall onto the bed in a puddle of post-orgasmic bliss. Sully pulls out of me with a groan and lands on the bed next to me.

With contentment and three explosive orgasms riding me hard, I feel my eyes flutter closed. "I just need to rest my eyes for a moment."

"Rest now, baby. We'll take care of you," Sully murmurs as he rolls over to pull a blanket over us.

With his assurances, I let myself relax and trust that they'll look after me.

28

ALAINA

AFTER OUR EVENTFUL FLIGHT, I crashed hard for several hours. I woke up as we landed for one of our layovers. I was nervous that it would be awkward between the four of us—or worse, hurt feelings and resentment—but to my delight, there wasn't anything like that. If anything, Wolf and Rush were down-right giddy.

Pairing that with Sully's general mood improvement, and our in-flight dinner on our second layover was honestly weird. Good but weird. I could definitely get used to this—having three boyfriends who take care of *all my needs*. Maddie's gonna die when I fill her in. Honestly, she's probably living out her own reverse harem fantasies by now. Once we're home, and the danger dissipates, I'm going to spend an entire weekend with her and Mary, just catching up.

We landed thirty minutes ago, and Rush insisted on driving to Seamus Flannery's house first thing. I'm jet-lagged as hell with all the seemingly random layovers, but Rush always has a plan, and I trust him.

Apparently, we already have someplace to be tonight, and

maintaining the element of surprise is paramount when you have no idea who's after you.

I'm dozing in the backseat, admiring the rolling green hills on our drive. The sky is overcast, but it doesn't dampen my appreciation for this beautiful country. I know I have some second or third cousins and other distant relatives somewhere in this country, but I haven't seen them since I was really little—young enough that I wouldn't even remember them if I didn't see the photos.

After another hour, Rush turns down a gravel driveway located between two huge leafy bushes. I sit up straighter and smooth out the wrinkles in my shirt. Suddenly, I feel nervous. Maybe I should've packed nicer clothes in my carry-on.

After I woke up in the bedroom on the plane, I changed into a plain white v-neck and a dark-purple skirt, this one flared around my thighs.

Rush cuts the engine, the silence interrupting my thoughts before they spiral too much. "Everyone ready? We go in, get our answers, and get out. This isn't a social visit. We have no way of knowing how he'll react or who he's loyal to. A lot can change in ten years."

I nod along with Rush and expel the deep breath I didn't realize I was holding. I inhale and square my shoulders. "I'm ready."

As if they were waiting for my approval, all three of my men open their doors at the same time. I follow suit a second later and stand next to Sully. "Here goes nothing."

I let Sully lead me to the bright red door of the country house. Green ivy crawls along the front, concealing most of the brick underneath. I blow out a breath and ring the doorbell, immediately stepping back two steps. Sully and Wolf flank me on either side, and Rush stands behind me.

A tall man with salt-and-pepper hair answers the door in a black sweatshirt and black gym shorts. "Can I help you?"

"You Seamus Flannery?" Wolf asks.

The man in question folds his arms across his chest, the action taking up more space in his doorway. "Who's asking?"

There's a moment of hesitation, and I send a quick prayer that I'm making the right decision. "Alaina Gallagher."

All the color drains from his face and he drops his arms. "Aidan's girl?"

I nod, my body tensing as my fight or flight instinct kicks in.

"Well, I'll be damned. Please come in, come in."

We follow Seamus inside his home and into the first room off the entryway. It's decorated with a midcentury modern twist on a cottage—all cherry-colored woods and off-white trim. A large red and tan rug covers the floor, and two pastel blue couches face one other with a glass oval coffee table between them.

"We have some questions for you, Seamus," I tell him as I look around. "You are Seamus, right?"

"Of course, yes, I'm sorry. You can never be too careful, right? I'm Seamus Flannery, and your dad was a dear friend of mine. We were actually second cousins by marriage. Oh, look at me, diving right in before I even offered you refreshments. Please, sit down, and I'll be right back." He gestures to the couches as he spins around and jogs to the kitchen.

I take a seat in the middle of the couch with Sully and Wolf on either side of me and Rush behind us.

Seamus returns a moment later with a tray of assorted cookies and a bottle of whiskey and five glasses. "I'm sorry. I'm all out of tea."

I wave his apology off. "It's fine. We're fine. Thank you, though."

Seamus pours himself a generous portion and throws half of

it back before he even sits down. He sinks into the couch across from me, holding my gaze. "What do you want to know?"

We'd agreed that I would do most of the talking at first, and one of them would only step in if necessary. But now that we're here and talking to him, I'm at a loss for words. I don't even know where to begin.

"What do you know about Gallagher Industries?" Rush asks, saving me from floundering for another minute.

Seamus tosses back the rest of his glass before leaning forward and refilling it. "That's a hard one."

"Specifically, your involvement in Lana Gallagher's plot to hide Alaina from the rest of the Gallaghers." Wolf goes right to the point, his body language deceptively casual. Since we already know the gist of it, this is a question designed to make sure he is who he says he is.

Seamus looks at me. "Your ma came to me years after Aidan stepped down from Gallagher Industries and begged me to scrub you from anything traceable. The only exceptions were a few banks—one I helped your da set up for you when you were born, by the way." A proud smile spreads across his face. "And even though those accounts are in your name, I have it buried enough that it's not easily tracked."

"So, you helped her. Then what?" I ask, turning all the information over in my mind.

"Then nothing. Then I never heard from her or your da again."

I clear my throat. "He died. My dad, I mean. I just officially found out recently, but he died ten years ago."

"Hell, I'm sorry, kid. I assumed as much when your ma came to me all those years ago, but I kept hoping he'd turn up one day, ya know?"

I nod and look over his shoulder at the framed artwork on his wall.

"Does the name Christopher Lein mean anything to you?" I ask, staring at the black and white photo of a circus tent.

Seamus blows out a breath. "This path you're walking down, it'll only lead to more bad. Sometimes things should remain in your past."

I focus on him and narrow my eyes. "The bad is coming to me whether or not I walk this path. I can't properly arm myself if I don't have the right information. And I think you might have what I'm looking for."

A muscle in his jaw tenses and I feel rather than see all three of my guys tense in response. I know that they're all a hair's breadth away from pulling out their guns.

"So are you going to help me?"

"Aye, kid, I'll help you. But first, I need another drink. You sure you don't want one?" he asks as he pours himself another drink.

"We're good, thank you."

"Alright, I'll tell you everything I know. For Aidan." He holds his glass in the air as a toast before he takes a healthy sip.

———

As LUCK WOULD HAVE IT, Seamus knew a lot. A whole lot. The silence is loud as we all process the information he just dumped on us.

"So . . . the most likely scenario is one of my extended family members is trying to kidnap me? Because he or she assumed control of the board at Gallagher Industries? Right? That's what we're all thinking?" I squint as I try to work all the logistics and loopholes out in my mind. Where's the dry erase board when you need one?

"Aye. That's what I'm thinking. Do you know who the

261

extended Gallaghers are, Seamus?" Rush asks with his hands braced on the back of the couch behind me.

"No, I'm afraid I don't. They remain elusive around these parts."

I sit up straight as something occurs to me. "What about a guy named Liam? Six-two, dark hair, and favors wearing red contacts. Does that ring any bells? He was last seen in New York City not too long ago."

Seamus scrunches his face for a moment. "I do seem to recall a kid who wore red contacts a lot, joined some sort of gang and terrorized folks for fun. Mason was his name, Liam Mason. Red eyes are hard to forget, ya know?"

"Liam Mason, age twenty-five, lives on Melbourne Ave in Dublin," Sully says with his head bent over his phone. He wiggles it in my direction. "I searched for him online."

I smirk at him and push off the couch, Wolf and Sully standing too. "Thank you, Seamus, for your help today and all those years ago. I'm grateful."

He rises off his couch, a little less steady on his feet. "It was my pleasure. Best of luck to you, kid."

We're almost out the door when Rush turns around and says, "One more thing. How did you scrub her so securely? Even my custom programs which find everyone didn't find her original files."

Seamus flashes Rush a toothy grin. "Not everyone, I guess, eh? A magician never reveals his secrets." He ends his sentence on a laugh, and I take that as our cue to get out of here.

I watch the cottage house get smaller as we drive down the gravel driveway toward the street. My mind spins with what to do next.

29

WOLF

RUSH PARKS the car down the street from Liam Mason's flat. It took us three hours to get here, plus an additional thirty minutes when we stopped for food.

The evening stars have just come out, and we've been parked in the same spot for the last twenty minutes. Arcade Fire plays quietly from the speakers and Red hums along.

The flat in question is dark, but that doesn't mean anything. So we wait until we're sure that someone's home—preferably him.

"From everything I can find, he lives alone in a flat, doesn't have a steady job on record, and is well-known as muscle for hire," Rush murmurs. The glow from his laptop lights up his face as he types some shit in that looks like legit gibberish from here.

"So what does that mean?" Red asks.

"We wait until he comes home," I say, settling in my seat.

I let my mind wander as I scan the street, looking for the red-eyed punk. This street isn't busy, making it much easier to keep an eye on people coming and going.

Ten minutes later, a small, two-door, piece of shit car barrels down the narrow street and parks in front of his flat with a screech of tires. A guy unfolds himself from the driver's seat, slams the door, and stalks toward the front door. I sit up straight and watch his movements like a hawk. "Head's up."

"It's hard to tell from here, but that looks like it could be him," Alaina murmurs next to me.

He pulls a key from his pocket and shoves it in the lock in the front door. It swings open and the guy in question walks inside without a backward glance.

"That's gotta be him, unless it's an unregistered roommate." My gut tells me this is our guy, but I'm kind of surprised that he didn't even look around when he walked inside. Anyone could've been in there—fuck, *we* could've been inside.

"For a criminal, the guy sure doesn't have any self-preservation," Sully muses.

I grin at my brother. "I was just thinking the same thing. So" —I rub my hands together—"how are we gonna do this with Red here?"

All three of us look at our girl. We're no strangers to extracting information from anyone, but we're usually doing it at the carriage house on Summer Knoll, and we've never had a non-member of the Brotherhood witness these . . . conversations before.

"What do you mean? What do you usually do?" Red blinks those big whiskey-brown eyes of hers at me, and I fight the urge to take her mouth. There's just something about that girl that brings out my inner caveman.

That, and I can't get the image of her spread out underneath me out of my mind. In fact, it's been sitting center stage in all my thoughts since it happened.

I shake my head to refocus. "Sometimes a conversation is all we need. And other times, we have to get a little creative." I pin her with a look. She's been around enough lately to read between the lines.

"Like what—beat him up or something?" She tilts her head to the side and her brow wrinkles in this adorable way.

And I'm just going to gloss over the fact that I just thought something was adorable while talking about the possibility of torture.

"Or something," Rush says with a smirk.

Red nods a few times. "Alright. Let's go then."

She opens her car door and has a foot on the ground before any of us register what she's doing. The three of us scramble to stow our shit, turn the car off, and get out of the car while she's halfway across the street. I leave my brothers behind us as I jog to catch up to her.

"Whoa, Red. We can't just march up to his door. He'll recognize you, remember? We want the upper hand here."

Her steps slow and she looks over at me. It's enough for Sully and Rush to catch up to us. "You're right."

"I don't see any security cameras, so Sully and I'll just go to the door. You guys stay to the side and out of sight, yeah?" Rush says as he heads toward the front door of the dark-brown flat.

I grab Red's hand and lead her to the overgrown bushes along the side of the house, far enough away that he won't see us, but close enough that we'll be able to step in when the time's right.

Rush knocks on the door and the same guy opens it with a beer in his hand.

Red leans forward, her hand clutching my forearm. "That's him."

Rage surges in my veins, so swift and deadly that it steals my focus for a moment. I'd checked that anger and fear from when Red was taken from us and from when she was coerced into that walking death trap called a warehouse. I shoved it down deep and let it simmer until I could do something about it.

The time has come.

Rush wraps his hand around Liam's throat and pushes him into the house, quickly followed by Sully. I tug on Red's hand and jog up the two steps to the porch and walk into the house. Red shuts the door behind us, and I take a moment to peer out of the window to make sure no one saw that little exchange before locking the door.

Once I'm satisfied that we're in the clear, I follow the sounds of my brothers' voices.

"Stay by me, yeah?"

"Alright. But I wanna look him in the eye right before you mete out his punishment. I know that's what you're going to do, Wolf. You don't have to sugarcoat things with me, you know."

I fight the smile tipping up the corner of my mouth. "Sure thing, baby girl."

We find them in the small kitchen with Liam sitting in a metal chair in the middle of the yellow linoleum floor. His lip is already split and bleeding.

"This is him? This the guy that you saw?" Sully asks Red with a fistful of Liam's hair, holding his face up.

Red eyes spit rage and retribution at us, but I'm having none of that shit. This is our retribution for what this motherfucker did.

Red nods, her mouth a harsh slash against her beautiful face. "That's him. You killed my mother." Her voice is even, calm even, so what she does next shocks me more than it should.

She steps forward, winds her hand up high and plunges a knife into Liam's thigh. His scream is loud in the quietness of the kitchen, with only Red's heavy breathing.

She brings her hand up again, but I grab her trembling wrist and gently guide it down to her side. "We need answers, baby. If he passes out from blood loss, we may never get them."

It's true, we do need our answers, but a bigger part of me wants to see her fucking destroy this asshole who dared to lay his hands on her—indirectly or not. Blood rushes to my cock, my body's way of letting me know that I wouldn't mind seeing her slam that knife into his leg for other reasons too.

She nods and licks her lips, her hair sliding forward over her shoulder. "Okay. Who do you work for?"

Liam groans and spits a wad of bloody saliva on the floor. "Are you fucking kidding me? I'm not going to say shit to you."

"Okay." Red shrugs and jerks her hand from my grasp, winds it back, and punches him in the face.

"Damn, baby girl." I adjust my hardening cock in my pants and shrug when she looks at me with a raised brow. "Don't stop on my account. I'm just over here enjoying the show."

She flashes me a mischievous smile while she shakes out her hand. Her knuckles are red, but they don't look too bad. Sully must've been teaching her something for her right hook to land so well.

"Fuck you. I don't even get why he wants you anyway." Liam sneers.

"Who wants me?" Red takes a step closer, and I tense. If Liam breaks free of his bindings, she's within his reach now. It makes me fucking jittery.

Liam snaps his mouth shut with a clink, and Rush's patience snaps. He pulls out his gun and points it at Liam's head. "Who fucking hired you, Liam Mason of Debra and Harold Mason, born May twenty-second in St. Mary's hospital?"

The color drains from his face, and finally, the first real traces of fear enter his eyes.

"Good. We have your attention now. I'll ask you one more

time. Who hired you?" Sully asks as Rush pushes the barrel of the gun against his forehead.

"Fine! Fine. I'll tell you. He didn't even pay me enough to deal with this bullshit." He sighs and looks up. "He paid me a hundred k to pick up Alaina McElroy slash Gallagher. He handed me an unlimited pass for his personal jet, a list of possible places she'd be, a recent photo. But when everything went down at the warehouse, I hopped on the jet and came home. I told him I needed more money since she was such a fucking handful."

"And Lana McElroy?" Rush presses.

"The hot ma? She made me when I was following Alaina and her cousins one day. That bitch had a set of balls walkin' right up to me like that. Said she could get her daughter to cooperate and go with me willingly if I split the money with her. Said to arrive at the Blue Lotus Diner at one, and Alaina would be there alone."

Red gasps and Liam sneers at her. "That's right. Your ma gave you up, sweet cheeks. How does that feel?"

Red steps forward, fists clenched and anger rolling off her in waves. "I could kill you, you know. Right now, I could put a bullet in your gut just like you did to my mom, and there's nothing you can do about it. How does that *feel*, mm?"

Fuck me. I don't know what it says about my psyche or whatever, but when Red talks all murderous like that, I wanna bend that tight ass over the nearest surface and fucking worship her and her dark thoughts.

"Ah, but you won't. You need me. Ain't that right?" Liam taunts.

"Until it's no longer necessary—until *you're* no longer necessary." The ice in Red's voice sends a chill skating down my spine, and I'm not even on the receiving end of that threat.

The tendons in Liam's neck strain and he clenches his jaw. I don't like the way he's staring at Red with murder in his eyes, so I step forward and partially block her view. "Tell us what happened after you took the wrong girl."

Liam's nostrils flare as he stares at me. "I did everything right. I went to the right diner at the right time. A redheaded girl was sitting in the booth alone, and she looked like Alaina, so we grabbed her."

"We?"

"The boss paid a few of his local guys to help. They bailed once we realized the mistake. So, I had to go back to the diner, and that's when I saw you—and your mom."

Red nods, and all the pieces are starting to come together. The only question now is: Who's pulling the strings?

"So, ready to tell us who hired you, or are you ready to die for that secret?" Rush asks, placing his finger over the trigger.

"Aeron. Aeron Briggsby hired me," Liam grits out between clenched teeth.

30

ALAINA

WOLF LACES his fingers through mine as we follow Rush and Sully to the red door of Three Dogs. "Stay close to one of us at all times," he murmurs.

"I know, Wolf. Trust me." I look at him out of the corner of my eye as we approach the man outside the door.

"It's everyone else I don't trust." Wolf punctuates his statement with a squeeze of my hand.

I lean into him and tip my head against his shoulder for a moment as we stop behind Rush.

"We're here for Quinn Kelly."

The guy at the door is as tall as he is wide. With a shaved head and biceps bigger than my head, he looks like he bench presses school buses for fun. He brings his wrist up to his mouth and says something too low for me to hear. After a moment, he nods at us and opens the door.

"Mr. Kelly is expecting you. He'll find you when he's ready."

I murmur my thanks as I pass him, and I don't miss the way his eyes linger on all the exposed skin. From the low-pitched growls reverberating around me, I don't think I'm the only one who caught that.

Wolf turns around and snaps, "Keep your eyes to yourself before I tear them out of your fucking skull."

The man just smirks with a raised brow and shrugs his big shoulders, looking away.

I pat Wolf's chest with my free hand. "I'm fine, see?"

"I knew this was a mistake," Rush snaps.

We walk into the pub, though it feels more like a club than a pub. "We agreed that it was best for everyone to stay together, remember? Relax, Rush, it's not like I haven't been checked out before." I roll my eyes with a smile on my face.

"Aye, but surrounded by your men?" Rush raises his brow at me for a moment before he looks over my shoulder, no doubt aiming that glare at the bouncer. A shiver rolls down my spine at the mention of being surrounded by *my* men.

"Some people are into getting their ass kicked," I say with a shrug. "But I'm not going to let it ruin my night, and you shouldn't either."

Rush reaches out and palms my waist, pulling me toward him and untangling my hand with Wolf's in the process. "I didn't account for the sheer number of assholes that will be getting intimately acquainted with my fists tonight. You look like a goddamn wet dream, baby."

"They can look—"

"Oh, princess, they're already looking," Sully cuts me off with a growl.

Sliding my hands up Rush's hard chest, I lean back and tilt my head with a raised brow. Looking from Sully to Rush, I let the smirk crawl across my face.

The feeling of having these three men salivating over me is intoxicating. I feel powerful with their hungry gazes eating up every inch of me. I feel bold and maybe a little bit reckless.

"Well, they can look, but they can't touch. Right, boys?" I can't help the taunt; I'm leaning into this feeling of power.

Rush runs his lips from my collar bones up the front of my neck. I let my head fall back and close my eyes at the sensation. His stubble just barely scrapes my skin, and I can't help but think of the way his stubble will feel against my inner thighs.

His lips follow the curve around my jaw, placing open-mouthed kisses until he pauses underneath my ear. "No one touches what's ours." His possessiveness is woven into each word, and I don't bother suppressing the shiver of arousal.

Sandalwood fills my nose as Wolf steps in behind me. His warm palms encircle my waist, his fingers splayed to touch more skin. He runs his nose down my neck on the opposite side of Rush. "And when we get back, I wanna see you in this. Just this." His fingers toy with the material at my waist.

I chose a black mesh long-sleeve top with a black bra underneath. It's not a push-up bra by any means, but honestly, it makes my tits look great. It's tucked into a pale-pink short skirt that hugs my curves. I was a little nervous when I threw this outfit into my suitcase, but I wasn't sure what to expect over here, so I packed a little of everything. And some things that push my comfort levels —like tonight's outfit.

The moment I walked out of the bathroom back at our rental place is one that I'll remember long past tonight. All three of them were waiting by the door, and as one, they turned to watch me walk toward them at the first click of my heels on the hardwood floor.

The matching looks of hunger boosted my self-confidence like nothing I've ever experienced before. I look at them now, and the hunger in all of their gazes stirs the flames of desire inside me. I'm already counting down the time until I can get my hands on all three of them after we leave here.

Someone bumps into Rush, and even though he barely

budges, it's enough to shatter the spell we've woven around us. Rush lifts his face from my neck to growl at someone over his shoulder, never taking his hands off of me.

I lift my lashes, slow to come out of the lusty spell they cast over me. Rush is backlit from the lights inside the club, and from this angle, he looks every bit the dark king I imagine him as. He's a wolf among sheep, and he's one nudge away from snapping and teaching everyone a lesson.

I war with myself. I want to see him deliver a warning, and some small part of me actually salivates at the idea of him commanding the room like that. But the practical side of me knows meeting Quinn is important. We can't get intercepted before we resolve all the stuff with the Gallaghers. And from what Wolf said, the Brotherhood's presence over here is stronger than anything back home. It'd be disrespectful to come to their town and not check-in.

So here we are. At some club on the outskirts of Dublin.

I curl my fingers around the soft cotton material of Rush's shirt and tug to get his attention. He whips his head back to face me, the snarl still in place. "Eyes on the prize, Dec."

He loses some of his anger and his face softens with a sigh. Leaning in, he places a small kiss against my lips. "You're right, baby."

I try to deepen the kiss, but he pulls away before I can. Pink lip gloss shines from his pouty lips, and I don't know how the hell it's possible, but he looks even hotter.

"Alright, let's get this done, yeah? Sooner we're done, sooner we can get Lainey back home." The intent behind Sully's words is clear. I eye the distance between us.

Rush takes a step away from me and runs his hand through his hair. I watch in fascination as an emotionless mask comes over his face. He shoots me a knowing smirk, and I roll my eyes at him.

I think I might love playful Rush just as much as I love commanding Rush.

Wolf squeezes my waist before he steps back too. "He's right. Let's get this over with, yeah?"

All of us nod, and then we turn and make our way to the bar on the side of the club. The music gets louder the closer we get to the dance floor, and I noticed that there are stairs that lead up to another level. I can't see anything beyond the two bouncers in black polo shirts. They're standing in front of the staircase with matching scowls. A quick glance only affords me a glimpse of people in the balcony areas, but it's darkened, so I can't really tell who's up there.

Not that I expect to know anyone here. But there's a small part of me that expects Liam to jump out from behind every corner, no matter where I'm at. The only time I ever feel safe from him is when I'm surrounded by my men.

I do feel better equipped since the King sisters have scooped me under their wing. But I don't think I'll stop looking over my shoulder until Liam's taken care of.

Permanently.

And whoever the hell his boss is.

Once we hit the bar, I turn around and face the crowd. Sully's next to me, Wolf scans for threats, and Rush orders our drinks.

"Stick to the plan, yeah, princess?"

I flick my gaze to the man next to me. In his old band tee and jeans that hug his ass, he looks like every bit the boy I fell in love with years ago. Only now, he's not a boy anymore. I'm not sure if he ever was a boy, but he's been aged by more than just years since we parted.

"You and me are down here until Rush and Wolf get done—I know."

He looks at me for a moment, his gaze bouncing around my face. "Good."

"I took the liberty of ordering you a fancy, fruity drink with lots of vodka. I think you'll love it." Wolf passes me a red and orange drink and a whiskey for Sully before he turns around to grab his drink off the bar top. Whiskey for all three of them—I'm not even a little bit surprised.

I hum in delight as I take a sip of my drink. Citrus bursts on my tongue, and I decide on the spot that it's my new favorite drink. I mouth *thank you* to Wolf, who's had his eyes on me the entire time.

After another mouthful, I turn around and survey the space. It's crowded for a Wednesday night. Especially since this isn't located in the heart of the city—in fact, it's so off the beaten path, I thought we had the wrong address for a while.

A big, burly dude comes out of nowhere to stand in front of us. I take a deep breath and press my palm to my chest to calm my racing heart.

No one says a word as this random guy thoroughly looks between the four of us. After a moment, he returns his gaze to Rush and nods, tilting his head to the side, motioning for Rush to follow.

Rush glances at me, and with that single look, I know he's telling me to behave.

It's kind of amazing that I can pick up on whatever he's trying to convey with just a look. It's like I'm finally learning the secret language. I watch as Rush and Wolf follow the guy over to the VIP staircase. The bouncers don't stop them as they follow the guy up to the balcony area.

After another moment without movement, I turn back to people-watching. I'm not even sure what we're watching for, but I'm looking nonetheless.

People are seated at the handful of booths on the back wall. They're underneath the balcony area, so they're somewhat shadowed. There are more bar tables at seemingly random places around the space, and each one has someone posted up there, sipping a drink and chatting.

The lights dim even further, and red, blue, and white strobe-like lights start a pattern over the dance floor. When the song changes, the music gets louder and a dozen people rush the floor, dancing the whole way there.

There's a DJ spinning records on the small stage in front of the dance floor. He's wearing a hot pink beanie with black head-phones covering his ears and a light pink track jacket over a white tee. He's grooving to the song that's playing, and I get an idea.

I put a hand on Sully's shoulder and lean in close to his ear. "I have an idea."

Sully turns his head, bringing his drink to his lips as he people-watches. "Your last idea was risky."

"It was hardly risky. You guys invited the King sisters into the fold a long time ago—I thought you trust them. Besides, I like them. And we need help."

Sully slides his arm closest to me around my waist and leans closer, putting his mouth right against the delicate skin on the shell of my ear. "I don't trust anyone, not when it comes to you."

His words are delivered with a promise, and I press closer to him, my chest flushed with his. I used to think that I never needed anyone to protect me, and now I realize that was my own way of coping with the fact that I never felt protected by the two people who are supposed to do that.

"Ready?" I start, toying with his hair at the nape of his neck.

He wore it pulled back into a small knot at the back of his head. I never thought I'd be into this look, but maybe my tastes in men are changing. More likely, it's him. I think anything they do would get me hot.

"Hmm?" His voice vibrates against my skin.

"Time for my idea. C'mon, loverboy." I sip the rest of my drink through the straw and place it on the bar behind me. Sully swallows the last of his whiskey, and his Adam's apple bobs with the movement. I swear to god, my panties get wet just watching him.

I shake my head a little.

Get it together, Lainey.

He reaches over my shoulder and sets his glass on the bar behind me, and his sea salt scent invades my senses. I can't stop myself from touching him. I slide both hands over his chest and across his shoulders to meet behind his neck. He looks impossibly big from this angle, and it's working for me.

It's really fucking working.

It's like I'm having my very own sexual awakening. But like times three. I don't know how else to explain it. It's like my hormones threw a party, got a taste of them, and now they're fucking ravenous.

My breath hitches, and I fight my imagination trying to over-throw me and play out my fantasy.

Sully follows behind me as we cut through the people dancing on the dance floor and reach the DJ's table. The guy holds up one finger as he bobs his head to the music, headphones on and hand spinning. Huge stacked speakers frame the table he's spin-ning at, but otherwise, he's kind of tucked away over here.

A moment later, he slides his headphones off to rest on his neck and yells, "What's up?"

I lean over the side of the table and ask for my request. I watch as he scans Sully from head to toe, no doubt cataloging every six-foot-two inch of him, from his full-sleeve tattoos to his general intensity. He flicks his gaze toward the darkened balcony area and his eyes harden before they quickly clear.

"Yeah, sure thing. Next, okay?"

"Perfect. Thank you." I turn around and look at Sully, a mischievous smile curving up my lips. I can't wait to see how this plays out.

31

ALAINA

SULLY LEANS in with a hand on my waist. "What's that look for?"

I turn my face into his neck. "There's no look," I say on a laugh. Before he can question me further or call me on my shit, the song changes. The deep bass of a familiar song pipes through the massive speakers just behind us, and I can't contain the smile spreading across my face. I lace my fingers with Sully's and walk to the middle of the dance floor.

Sully spins me around to face him. "This your doing?" He tips his head toward the DJ.

I nod and bite my lip. "Good idea?"

His bright blue eyes stare intently in mine. My heart pounds as I wait for his reaction. It's a calculated move, a small one, but an intentional one all the same. I requested a song that we listened to at the cabin.

We had a breakthrough, Sully and I, but it'll take a while for that trust to grow to what it used to be—what it *will be* one day. Right now, he needs a nudge—or ten—and if I get some benefit out of it, so be it. When he doesn't immediately pull away, I slide my palms up his arms, along his shoulders, and into his hair at the nape of his neck. I'm close enough to touch him, but not nearly as close as I want to be.

Looking into his eyes, I don't know if it'll ever be close enough for me. Sully's like a tidal wave. Just his very presence is enough to overwhelm me, and on most occasions I try to temper that force, he leaves me upside down and underwater.

But he didn't always.

He wasn't always so volatile, and once upon a time, he welcomed my attempts to tame him.

I see him wrestle with indecision, jaw taut and eyes almost narrowed. "What are you up to, princess?"

My fingertips dance along the back of his neck, and I push on to my tiptoes to whisper against his lips, "Dance with me, James."

He palms my waist, his hands branding his signature on my body in more ways than one. In one swift movement, he pulls me toward him and slides a hand to the back of my neck. Using his grip, he pulls me into him, his mouth meeting mine in a soul-shattering kiss.

My nipples tighten and something low in my stomach clenches. This—this is why I push him. He's got so much passion bottled up and buried that when he lets himself go, it's an explosion. And I'm going to reap the rewards with a fucking smile on my face.

I don't know who breaks the kiss first, but I don't open my eyes right away. I tip my head to the side, our foreheads pressed together. Determined to make this last, I turn myself over to the moment. The song changes and I let the sounds of Hey Violet infuse my limbs. Surrounded by Sully, I start to sway and swivel my hips.

I'm not at all surprised when Sully tightens his grip on my waist, keeping my head right where he wants it with his hold on the back of my neck. He brushes his lips across mine with each sway of my hips.

One song bleeds into two, and two into three, and then I lose track of how long we're on the dance floor. Sully's hands roam my body as we dance out more unsaid and unresolved feelings toward one another.

I've danced at clubs before, not often, but enough to know that this is anything but *just* a dance.

There's nothing friendly about the way our bodies are communicating. It's demanding and intoxicating. And I don't ever want to stop.

Sully and I might as well be in our own little world. Nothing else exists right now but this bubble we've created on the dance floor. Lust swirls around us, entwining us together, almost as if it was a tangible thing.

Sweat dampens the hair on my neck as the temperature in the club rises. Energy swirls around the club, and it feels like there are more bodies around us, but I can't bring myself to tear my gaze away from Sully.

He looks like a goddamn fantasy. All those bold tattoos stand out in sharp contrast against his stark-white tee. His muscles flex as he keeps his hips in line with mine.

We've started a slow grind, him and I. A sensual dance that would only be better if we didn't have so many layers between us. The beat drops, and I roll my hips. Without missing a beat, he slips his knee in between my legs, his hands drifting down to hold onto my hips. He drops his gaze to watch the way our bodies move against one another as The Glass Animals's song fills the charged air. With every roll of my hips, I feel his cock, hard and thick, rub against me, and my arousal spikes. Flashbacks of our night together dance in my vision, spiking my lust higher. I don't think my thong will survive the entire night if we keep this up.

I'm five seconds from begging him to take me to one of those darkened booths when I feel them. Wolf steps in behind me, molding his body perfectly to mine. He swivels his hips in time with me, and I tip my head back on his shoulder to look at him. Leaving my right hand gripping Sully's shoulder, I reach back with my left and bring Wolf's hand to my hip.

"You're the most captivating woman on the dance floor tonight. I couldn't keep my eyes off of you." His voice is low, drenched in lust.

I lift my chin, searching for his mouth, when I feel long fingers gently wrap around my neck from the left. Without looking, I know it's Rush. I roll my head to face him, leaving it resting on Wolf's shoulder, never stopping my slow grind in the middle of the dance floor. He's wedged along the side of me, as close as possible, considering I'm sandwiched between his brothers.

Rush steps impossibly closer to me, bringing his mouth to mine. I part my lips, hungry for his mouth on mine. Anticipation claws at me, my desire nearly overwhelming.

He pushes into us and groans into my mouth, "Mine." His tongue tangles with mine, and I feel my nails dig into Sully's shoulder and Wolf's wrist. I moan into the kiss, losing some of the rhythm I had. I didn't need to worry, though, Sully and Wolf keep the slow grind dance going. I'm rewarded with feeling Wolf at my back. His cock is hard and thick, and rubs against my ass in the most tantalizing way.

I can't stop myself from fantasizing that the four of us are back in our rented room instead of a packed club. I've had a taste of all of them, and instead of satiating my hunger, it left me salivating for more.

Rush fucks my mouth with his, and I'm *this* close to coming from all the stimulation, but then Rush rips his mouth away from mine. His chest heaves and the protest is on the tip of my tongue when Wolf tips my head back and claims my mouth as his.

"Mine." The word is groaned into my mouth, this tortuous

sound that turns me into a puddle. My neck strains as I try to claim more of his mouth. He's uncharacteristically restrained in this kiss, and I've had enough.

I break the kiss for a split second to spin around, and then throw my arms around his neck and reconnect our mouths. He moans into my mouth, and I hitch a leg up along his side. Strong, warm hands slide underneath my thighs from behind as one of my dark kings steps in close behind me. The smell of sweet citrus invades my senses.

Rush.

My quiet one. The one who always has my back—who's had my back long before I ever realized I needed someone to watch it. I often wonder what would've happened had I gotten the courage to confront him a year ago—or even just a couple of months earlier.

What would my life have looked like then?

Would I still be here, now? Would I be with all of them? Had Wolf not picked me up from the train station, and had my mother not gotten engaged—the thought of my mother stops my train of thought and threatens to kill my libido, so I squash it down. Way down. To someplace only a therapist can access many years from now.

The three of us move as one, and I tip my head back to look for my missing piece. Concern overshadows my lust for a moment when I don't find him right next to me. The lights flare and dim with the beat of the music, so half of his face is in shadows. I hold his gaze, my brow furrowing as Wolf kisses a path down my neck.

Sully takes a step forward, his face coming into the light. He gives me a slow, purposeful once-over, and goosebumps race across my skin. The intense desire on his face only fans my flames. He bites his lip, his eyes low and hooded as they take the three of us in. He gives me another slow perusal as he thumbs his lip in that stupid hot way guys do.

His gaze fucking smolders when it connects with mine. My lips twist as the realization becomes crystal clear.

Sully has voyeuristic tendencies.

And I like it—no, I fucking *love* it.

He's next to us, not quite touching, but close enough that I can reach out and touch him. So, I do.

They say a look is worth a thousand words, right? Well right now, Sully's looking at me like he wants to consume me.

And I plan on letting him.

In two steps, he eliminates the space between us as he smoothly steals my attention from his brothers. He slides his palms on either side of my face and growls out, "Mine." It sounds ripped from his very soul, and my body goes pliable in response.

He seals his declaration with a kiss that feels like it shakes the floor beneath my feet, and my body goes liquid.

It's not until the screams start that I pull away from Sully, slowly blinking to clear the lust from my eyes. Silently, I preen, pleased to see I'm not the only one affected.

Another scream sounds, reverberating off the walls. I scan the area, but all I can see is chaos. The people from the tables are running around, but the people on the dance floor are slower to move. Fear slithers inside my veins as I look for our escape route. A big warehouse-style place like this is sure to have more than the one standard emergency exit.

Sully curls his fingers around mine. "Time to go, princess."

"Aye, let's move out. I saw another exit behind the bar," Rush says before he strides in that direction. The rest of us follow behind him, Sully's grip never waivers. We weave around a few people, but otherwise make it outside unscathed.

None of us talk as we hurry toward the place we parked the

car. Wolf didn't want to park the car in the lot with everyone else, and now I'm a little suspicious.

"Did you know what was going down tonight?"

Sully squeezes my hand. "Crazy shit always happens around Quinn." He looks at me with a smirk. "That, and we like to give ourselves another exit. You know how Rush likes his backup plans."

My lips curve into a wry smile. "Of course."

"That, and we got an address on Aeron Briggsby. We're going to pay him a little visit tonight," Rush adds, spinning around to face us and walk backward down the block.

"Where'd that intel come from so quick?" Sully asks as his head in a continuous swivel around us.

"We bartered our allegiance to Quinn for the information— which he had ready to go, by the way. I may or may not have put some deliberate feelers out."

"That's a risky move, brother."

"Aye, but I had some insurance lined up if we needed it." Rush smirks as he scratches his stubble.

The car comes into view, and after Wolf checks it out, we all pile in and head for our next destination.

32

WOLF

RUSH and I walk along the sidewalk closest to the homes, staying out of the pool of light from street lamps.

"You think it's safe to leave her there?" I ask my brother.

"Sully's got her. And we really do need a lookout. We have no idea what we'll find here—or who. We might need them if we run into trouble. If this guy has a personal jet at his disposal, I'm expecting a lot of manpower."

I nod and step over a puddle. The air smells like rain, enough that I search the sky for an impending storm. But it's late as hell, so I can't see too much. "What does your gut say?"

Rush glances to the right and then left, his guard is always on. I mean, so is mine, but his is next level. I think it's because he spends so much of his time plotting and planning and maintaining his position—which is usually two steps ahead. He's always glued to his *command center*, as Red calls it, looking for deceit and watching every*one* and every*thing*.

"My gut says this Acron person is the only lead we have, so I'm hoping it leads to something. And if it *is* him, then we just have to figure out his connection to Gallagher Industries, how he found out about Alaina, and if he's working alone."

"Right. So, we're on a wing and prayer? Just another day in the life, eh, brother?" I roll my eyes.

A dog barks in a nearby yard, and I cut my gaze toward the sound. I'm only satisfied when I realize the dog isn't barking at us. We do not need any witnesses for our b and e tonight. We have connections—and they're fucking good ones—but I don't want to have to depend on them. Quinn's fucking crazy, and I don't want to owe that psycho a debt.

"What if we want to get married?" The question slips out before I realize it, and I feel my shoulders tighten on instinct.

Rush slows for a second before he recovers. Out of my peripheral, I see him stare at me, but I keep my gaze on our surroundings. I don't know where the fuck that thought even came from, but now that it's out there, I don't want to take it back.

"I think that's a conversation we all need to have together."

"Aye. Together."

"731. Here," Rush murmurs, slowing his stride and walking down the paved driveway.

We keep to the shadows as we move toward the backyard of the small colonial-style house. A single lamp is on inside, but it's otherwise dark, quiet. It's a little shabby, but not neglected. More like whoever lives here just doesn't keep up with it like it needs. That's the problem with these old houses—they need a lot of upkeep.

Overgrown green bushes line the driveway, spilling into the concrete and concealing our movement from prying eyes.

We move toward the detached single-car garage in the backyard on silent feet. I slide my gun out of the shoulder holster and hold it at the ready should we run into the kind of trouble we can't talk our way out of.

"I'll keep watch. You look inside there," I tell my brother with a head tilt to the side.

Rush jogs across the grass, the wet blades absorbing any noise he might've made. He peers inside through a dirty window. "Nothing. Looks like some old computer equipment, but not much else."

I nod my head toward the house, holding my gun chest-high and breathing in slow, easy breaths. Everything fades to the background as I focus on what we're about to do.

There's only one window in the back, and it's on the second floor. Rush unholsters his own gun as we get into position. This isn't the first time we've been in a similar situation, but we usually have Sully with us to watch our six. But if this sick fuck is home, we can't have Red here. I won't risk it.

I won't risk her.

Rush and I lock eyes, and like we've practiced a thousand times, we open the door. The door creaks with disuse, and we step into the dark house.

We pause to listen for any movement. If there's anyone home, there's no way they didn't hear that noise. After a few moments of silence, we start the process of securing the house, room by room.

When we're sure someone isn't hiding with a shotgun and a shaky trigger finger on the first floor, we head for the second floor.

Walking down the narrow hallway toward the staircase to the second-floor loft, I see something that stops me in my tracks. A gallery of black and white photos line the wall, all eight-by-tens in frame. "Rush, get a look at this."

He stands next to me, gun at his side and brow furrowed. "Is that Coney Island? And this looks like New York."

"Aye. And doesn't this look like the fucking New York Public Library?" I ask, pointing to the photo next to it.

"Mm-hmm."

I move a few feet down and look at the next photos. "And this looks like an outdoor music festival."

We follow the photos to the end of the hall, most of which are familiar. None of them were in color, and none of them had any faces.

The second floor is more of a loft area, with just one big room and a small bathroom off to the side. But there could've been a goddamn mariachi band in the corner, and I still wouldn't be able to tear my eyes off the shitshow in front of me. "What the fuck."

Shock holds me immobile for a minute as I take in the enormity of what I'm looking at. Rush doesn't have the same hesitation. He strides right for the far wall that looks like it's from the set of some detective show. He holsters his gun and whips out his phone, photographing everything he can.

The action is enough to pull me out of my shock, and I do the same thing. There's so much shit here, I have no idea if we'll be able to get it all on camera.

A map takes up a good amount of space with different places circled in red and photos and cut-out newspaper articles about Gallagher Industries stapled against it. Sticky notes with barely legible words and red string connecting a few things.

I move to the opposite wall. It looks like some fucked up obsession wall. And Red is the star. They're almost all paparazzi-style photos except for a few that look like they're printed from her Instagram account. At the café, on the street, with her cousins, at fucking O'Malley's. In front of her dorm room window in her fucking underwear.

"Who the fuck is this guy? I'm gonna fucking rip his eyes out just for this." The words come out in a growl, and I feel the beast inside me flexing against the chains I've kept him in. I can't unleash him. Not until we find a worthy opponent. Liam Mason

294

was barely a blip, and despite my need to extract my rage on him, I couldn't deny Alaina the opportunity to get her own vengeance.

There's one photo in the middle of all of them that stands out. Mostly because it's been circled with red marker enough that it's nearly worn through the paper. It's a wide shot, so it shows more than just Red like the others. But the other thing, the thing that fucking freaks me out more than I'd like to admit is that it's from inside O'Malley's. I'd recognize that bar and stage anywhere—and I'd recognize my brother too.

"Fuck. Get over here. Now," I bark the words at my brother, and he's next to me in a flash.

"What is it?"

"When was this?" I ask, pointing to the circled photo.

His eyes narrow and his jaw clenches the moment he sees what I saw. "That was shortly after I started going to O'Malley's every week. A month tops."

I nod and look at the ground, my mind spinning in too many directions. There's only one thing to do though. "Fuck it. Let's take it all."

I stare at Rush, expecting him to tell me we can't make such a bold move until we know who the fuck this Aeron Briggsby piece of shit is.

His jaw flexes. "Call Sully. Tell him change of plans and to come get us. We're going to need to find something to carry all this shit in. Don't leave a single piece behind, yeah?"

I send a quick text and start searching for a box or a laundry basket to get all this. I've seen enough crime dramas to know that whoever this fucking guy is, he's lethal to Red. My gut churns with anxiety and fear coats my skin. I think we made a mistake in bringing Red to his doorstep.

He could be anywhere.

33

ALAINA

I ROLL down my window as Sully shuts off the engine. The warm breeze filters through the car, ruffling the hair that's fallen out of the loose braid I pulled it into earlier. I was sweating pretty good by the time we left the pub, and it felt nice to pull my heavy hair off my neck.

"Do You Realize?" by The Flaming Lips plays softly through the speakers, and crickets sing in the distance. The moon is low in the sky, its bright light giving everything a pale glow.

We're parked a mile down the road from a stranger's house, waiting for my other two . . . boyfriends—men—I'm still getting used to the idea of having all three of them as my own. Boyfriend seems like something *less* than what this is, but there's still a certain thrill to it.

I lean against the car door, shifting so I face Sully. I look at his profile. Dark-blond scruff covers his angular jaw, his longer hair curls over his ears, and his nose has a bump in it from an obvious break. His dark, sooty lashes frame his ocean-blue eyes, and even now, he still takes my breath away sometimes.

They all do.

"So how does it feel to be my boyfriend again?" My lips twist to the side with my tease.

I'm not sure if he's going to lash out at me like a scared puppy or not. We've grown close the last few days, but his default setting is to run from feelings. And knowing his past, I don't even blame him. Nothing but time will help that.

It's okay. I'm onto him now, and his little barbs don't hold as much weight as they used to. Or maybe I've changed. Grown. That's all we can ask for in life, isn't it? To grow, to become better versions of ourselves. Change is never easy, but it's necessary. I imagine the rest of my life if I didn't change—didn't start the journey to figuring out who the hell I am. It's bleak and lackluster and sad.

Sully's need to push people away rides him hard, and sometimes he can't help himself. It's alright, I can be patient. I've waited years to get him back, now that I have him, I can wait a little longer until he's ready to talk without snapping anytime someone gets too close to his emotions.

He looks at me from underneath his lashes, his lips twisting to the side. "I'm not your boyfriend."

For the briefest moment, I'm shocked. Then I get over my own shit and do what I do best: push him. I unbuckle my seat belt and place a hand on the middle console.

Sully raises a brow. "What are you doing, Alaina?"

I move my hand from the console to his shoulder and climb into his lap. His hands automatically move to my waist as I hover above him. Sliding my arms up his arms, over his shoulders and around his neck, I lean in and sink down. The skirt of my dress rides up my hips and exposes us to any prying eyes. Not that there's anyone around who can see anything. "What does it feel like I'm doing?"

Sully slides his warm palms along my ribs, stopping when his thumbs reach the curve of my breasts. He tips his head back and holds my gaze, his eyes lighting with interest. "We're on lookout, princess."

I move from side to side on his lap, the movements small. "I know. But you said you weren't my boyfriend, and I think"—I pause and roll my hips over him, my teeth digging into my bottom lip when I feel the hard ridges of his cock—"we need to remedy that misunderstanding."

Sully uses his grip around my ribs to press me into his lap, stilling my movement. His cock hits me at all the right angles, and I swear he did that on purpose. I thread my fingers in the hair at the nape of his neck, tugging slightly. He groans, closing his eyes for a second. When they open again, they sear me to the spot. A shiver tiptoes down my back with the intensity in his gaze.

He moves one hand to the back of my neck and brings my face closer to his. "Nothing to remedy, princess. I'm not your boyfriend." He leans in, so his lips graze mine with each syllable. "I'm your motherfucking man." He crushes his mouth to mine, our lips sliding against one another, fighting for dominance.

Victory sings in my veins.

He tilts my head, deepening our kiss. My skin feels hot and tight, and I'm itching to remove some layers between us. They got me all worked up on that dance floor, and like a match to a flame, I'm burning within moments.

I crave the feeling of his skin on mine. Of the way his muscles flex and bulge when he gets me right where he wants me —where I want to be.

I groan into his mouth, rolling my hips against his. His answering moan heightens my desire, and I tear my mouth away from his, intent on removing his shirt at the very least.

I slide my hand underneath his tee, the soft fabric a juxtaposition with his hard muscles. I legitimately never thought eight-packs were real until I met the Fitzgerald brothers.

Before I can slide his shirt up any further, he breaks the kiss and traps my hand with his. Leaning his forehead against mine, his kiss-swollen lips brush mine with each word. "We can't, princess. We gotta stay focused." He places a soft kiss against my lips, and I return it eagerly. "But once we're back at the room? You're all mine."

A shiver of awareness trickles down my spine. "Promise?" I ask with a raised brow.

"Aye." He fuses his lips to mine once more, tongue dancing with mine in a dance only the two of us know. It's amazing how similar all the Fitzgerald boys are in some ways, and in others, they couldn't be more different.

Their personalities shine through each kiss. Wolf's kisses always have a playful side—even when he's making me see stars. Rush always has control in his kisses, which allows me to lose my control. I know he'll always be there. And Sully kisses me with all the unrestrained passion he's harboring inside that delicious, tattooed body of his.

His phone rings, interrupting us, which is probably a good thing. I shift back over into my seat, adjusting my skirt and leaning my head against the window, letting the light rain mist over my overheated face.

Somewhere between parking and now, the clouds moved in, mostly covering the moon, and rain began to fall.

Sully answers the phone and puts it on speakerphone. "What did you find?"

"Fuck. What didn't we find. There's so much shit here. So much shit about Red. It's a lot. I sent you a few photos of what we found. Come get us in twenty minutes, and make sure you don't have a fucking tail. We're taking all of it with us, and we can't carry it all to you," Wolf says.

I lean over the console and look at Sully's phone. He has his text thread up, and six photos fill the screen. He zooms in on each one and ice fills my veins. "Fuck me. Who the fuck is this guy?"

"I don't fucking know, brother. But I'm sure there's something in all of this that will help."

"Aye. We'll see you soon." Sully ends the call and turns the car on. "Buckle up, princess. Time to go."

I click my seat belt in place and roll up my window as Sully pulls away from the curb. The rain starts to come down harder, but visibility is still okay. If it gets much worse, I'm afraid we'll have to pull over until we can see.

Five minutes later, headlights from the vehicle behind us shine into our car. Sully curses under his breath and flicks his turn signal on. "We're detouring, Lainey. I don't know if this is a tail, and we just saw it now, or if it's a coincidence."

I peek in the side mirror, but all I can make out is some large black SUVs. They make the same turn, and my heart starts to pound. "James . . ."

"I know. It's fine. This isn't my first time, princess. Just hold on, yeah? I'm going to lose them up here."

We're approaching a town square shopping area with several side roads branching off, and Sully turns the wheel at the last minute, racing down the streets. A quick left turn later, and we're on another road. I'm completely lost after so many twists and turns, but one thing is for sure—we didn't lose our tail.

"Motherfucker," Sully growls under his breath when the rain starts to pour even harder, reducing our visibility. A last-minute right turn has us skidding along the pavement, the screech of the tires loud in the car.

Sully swings the wheel to the side to avoid oncoming traffic, and the car hydroplanes. The black SUVs behind us keep pace, their bumpers dangerously close to ours.

I twist around to look out of the rear window, my mouth falling open. "They're boxing us in!"

Sully flicks his gaze to the rearview mirror. "I know. The

streets get narrow up here. We should be able to lose them then. Hang on."

I face forward just in time for Sully to take the car onto the curb connected to the sidewalk. I'm thankful that it's nearing ten o'clock at night, and this little block of shops is closed for the day. I can't imagine what would happen if it was the middle of the day. Sully would never risk innocent people like that, and we'd be caught for sure.

The car rumbles and groans as two of our wheels protest being higher than the others. I plant my feet on the floor and hold onto the handle above the window to brace myself.

"Watch out for the—" The front bumper clips the patio table and chair from a closed cafe. "Table."

Sully grips the wheel, his knuckles white. "Sorry, princess. Call Wolf again, yeah? We should've heard from them by now."

I slip my phone out of my skirt pocket and dial Wolf's number on speakerphone. Ringing fills the air, and a second before his voicemail clicks over, he answers.

"'Lo?"

Relief tingles in my fingers. "Wolf. Where are you? Are you guys okay?"

"We're fine, Red. Ran into a hiccup, so it took a little longer than expected."

"What hiccup? What happened?"

"Nothing we can't handle, baby girl. We'll debrief you when we see you. Where are you?" Wolf asks.

"Well . . . the thing is, we had to leave." I wince.

"What do you mean you had to leave? You're the fucking lookout, Sully!" Wolf yells.

"Aye, we are. And then two blacked-out SUVs came creeping up on us, and I made an executive decision to get us—get Alaina—the fuck outta there," Sully rationalizes.

"Where are you now? We'll meet you," Rush says. It takes me

a moment to realize that Wolf must've put the call on speak-erphone.

"I don't fucking know. We passed the town square five minutes ago. All these backroads are winding, and I can't quite shake them yet."

I hear Wolf curse before Rush says, "Keep your tracking app on. We'll hotwire a car and come to you."

Two more black SUVs pull in on either side of us at the same time. The narrow road feels even smaller now.

"Goddamnit," Sully curses, turning the wheel to avoid hitting one of them. At this speed, surrounded by vehicles, a small hit is enough to total us.

"What's going on?" Rush demands, his tone hard.

"Two more, on either side of us. Four total. We're fucked if I can't get rid of 'em." Sully's jaw clenches as he grips the steering wheel tight.

"Hold on, brother. We'll be there soon. And take care of our girl," Rush orders.

"And don't be a fucking hero, Red," Wolf warns.

I roll my eyes. "It was one time. I walked into a building one time—"

"A building that was crumbling and on fire," Wolf growls out.

I scoff. "I'd do the same for any of you, so—"

"As touching as this trip down memory lane is, I need to concentrate. Get here soon."

"Be safe," Rush says before he disconnects the call. I make sure my location settings are on and shared with him before I slip my phone into the pocket of my skirt.

Sully presses down on the accelerator, and the force of the speed has my back hitting the seat with a thud.

"Hold on, princess," Sully warns, yanking the wheel to the right hard and turning into a narrow alleyway. The side mirrors scrape along the brick walls on either side, sending sparks flying.

We fly out of the alleyway, the car airborne for a few seconds before we land on the road with a crash. The car fishtails as Sully overcorrects the movement.

I twist in my seat to look out the rear window. "I think we lost them."

"I think so—oh fuck," Sully curses, and he slams on the brakes to avoid hitting the parked cars to the right.

Three SUVs come out of nowhere. And the way these ones are driving make the previous ones look like child's play. I have no idea if they're new SUVs or the same drivers, but either way, they're playing for keeps. They're not messing around anymore.

I hear the accelerator ramp up right before I feel the tap—they bumped us from behind! Sully tightens his hold on the steering wheel, his gaze on a swivel all around him.

The other SUV swerves to drive alongside us, and my heart pounds double-time at the road ahead.

It's a bridge.

The bridge isn't wide enough for both cars to drive down it like this—it's only a little bigger than a single-lane. Sully doesn't slow down, and neither does the SUV—we're playing a dangerous game of chicken here.

Sweat beads on my brow as I grab the handle. "James . . ." There's a warning in my voice, and it doesn't go unnoticed by him.

"I know, Lainey," he says through clenched teeth. He pushes the accelerator a little more, and I feel like we're flying. We're going so fast that by the time I see it—it's too late.

A fourth SUV comes from the cross street and plows right into the back end of our car, sending us in a dangerous spiral. We turn and turn and turn, the motion sending my body slamming into the door with every rotation. My head cracks against the window, and stars dance in my vision.

After what feels like an eternity, we finally stop, and I grab my forehead with a groan. My heart leaps out of my chest when I realize we've stopped halfway down the bridge.

"Lainey! Lainey, you okay?" Sully's panicked voice sounds muffled, and it takes me longer than it should to focus on him.

"I'm okay," I say with a groan. "Are you hurt?" I scan him, looking for visible injuries. Through the driver's side window, I spot a black SUV racing down the bridge, heading straight for us.

Sully spots them at the same time and yells, "Alaina!"

That's all the warning we get before the SUV clips our rear bumper. The car groans, and something scrapes against the road, the sound shrill. It's not until we start to tip forward that terror unlike anything I've ever experienced races up my spine.

The deep blue river beckons me into its icy depths. It taunts me with its promise of a watery grave.

I push myself back into my seat, my hands flying to my window and the middle console and my feet pushing against the floor in a futile bid to stop our movement.

But gravity isn't on our side. And we're trapped in a two-ton machine that wasn't made to float.

"Oh fuck. Fuck. Fuck. Fuck." It's all I can say as my chest heaves and my vision starts getting dark around the edges.

"Stay with me, Lainey. You fucking stay with me!" Sully yells. I cut my gaze to his and latch onto the commanding tone of his voice, begging my body to obey.

The SUV hits our bumper again, this time harder than the last. It's enough to tip us over the edge.

And then we're free-falling.

34

ALAINA

THE SCREAM GETS LODGED in my throat as the car careens off the bridge. The seat belt locks into place as my body fights gravity. My eyes feel like they're going to bug out of my face they're so wide. Breath gets trapped in my lungs as something beyond fear takes over all my senses.

"Brace, Lainey. Brace!" Sully roars, moving his hands to the steering wheel in the ten-and-two position.

I look at Sully instead of the impending river. His gaze is already on mine, and for a moment, it feels like time stands still. Nothing exists outside of him and me and this moment.

Then we hit the water.

I don't think I'll ever forget the sound of metal hitting water. It sounds like an ominous thunderclap.

Streaks of my dark-red hair fill my peripheral vision as my body flies forward with the impact. The seat belt cuts across my chest, knocking the wind out of me. And it feels like my brain slams against my forehead.

It takes me precious seconds to recover enough to talk. Panic threatens to overtake me, rising up my throat as we sink further into the lake.

"James?" I unclick my belt as I look over at him. My heart stops when I see his head hanging forward, the driver's side airbag expelled. Blood smears across the powdery surface, and I can't stop the tidal wave of panic. A sob breaks free as I reach over and clasp his face. "Come back to me, James."

He groans low in his throat, and it's the sweetest noise I've ever heard. "Lainey?" He cracks an eyelid, his gaze focusing on me.

"Oh, thank god. We have to get out of here. We don't have much time." I unlatch his seat belt just as a foreboding gurgle reverberates around the cab of the car. "Hurry, James."

"Oh, fuck. Okay. Okay. We can do this. Open the back window, princess." His voice is clearer than it was a second ago, and I imagine all the adrenaline flooding his veins is helping him focus.

I climb over the middle console into the backseat. Because the car tipped over the edge like it did, it's sinking at an angle that's almost perpendicular to the water, and I'm almost kneeling on the back of the passenger seat. The water hasn't reached the rear windows yet, and I send up a prayer of thanks to whoever is listening.

I push the button to lower the window, and my breath freezes in my lungs when it doesn't move for a second. I release and push the button again. Still nothing.

"James!" My voice is shrill, echoing around the car. "They won't open. The windows won't open!"

I look over my shoulder to see Sully pushing the limp air bag material away from him, fanning the powder away from his face. "Fuck. Hang on, I think I saw . . ." He fiddles with something on the arm of the driver's side door.

I try not to let my growing panic take over as I see the water rising out of the corner of my eye. Ten more seconds, and we won't be able to open it at all.

Nine.

Eight.

Seven.

"Try it now."

I slam my finger down on the button, and a sob of relief escapes me as the window rolls down. I eye the slow roll of the window and the rising water, mentally urging the window to go faster. Sweat breaks out along the back of my neck, and my hands tremble. The window is almost down when it stops.

"What? No." I release the button and push it again. "No. No. No." I push the button over and over again. Panic wraps its icy fingers around my throat, choking my air from my lungs.

"Hey, hey, hey. It's alright, princess," James says next to my ear. He's crouched on top of the middle console. "There's plenty of room to get out. I want you to go through the window and swim to the edge of the lake, yeah?"

My lower lip trembles as the car groans under the pressure from the water. "You'll be right behind me, right?"

"I'll always be with you. I love you, Lainey." Sully cups my face in his hands and presses his lips against mine in a quick, hard kiss. "Now go. And don't stop swimming until you're at the shore, yeah?"

Water pours through the open window, splashing against the upholstery and filling the car up faster than I thought possible. Each drop that hits my bare legs feels like a tiny cold needle.

"I love you too. Right behind me." I stare at him for a moment longer, my heart beating hard enough I'm afraid I'm actually having a heart attack. He nudges me forward, and I wiggle out of the open window, half underwater. It takes a little maneuvering, but I'm able to kick myself free of the window, splashing like crazy as I tread water.

I do as Sully says and swim toward the bank right away. I make it two terrible strokes before I look behind me. Fear chokes me when I don't see his familiar blond head.

Something's wrong. He should be out by now. The top of the car is still visible, but the entire window is submerged.

I don't hesitate. I channel my inner mermaid and swim back to the sinking deathtrap. I take a deep breath and dive underwater. My eyes sting as I search the murky water for my boyfriend. He's hanging out of the window, stuck on something. He's yanking on his jeans and pushing on the sides of the window, trying to wiggle his way out.

I swim closer and pull on his shoulder, but it's not easy to get any traction when you're underwater. Terror seizes me as my lungs strain, but I fight the urge to inhale.

I swim closer to the window and see that he's stuck on the gun wedged inside the back of his pants. With quick fingers, I push him inside the car a little, wedge my hand inside, and take out his gun.

Sully pushes against the car one more time, his muscles flexing and straining with the exertion. And like a rocket, he shoots out of the car. He grabs my hand and pulls me through the water and toward the surface.

I break through the surface a second before Sully does, and immediately, I wrap my arms around him.

"Oh my god. Oh, my fucking god." My words are choppy and coming out in broken sobs.

Sully wraps an arm around me and starts swimming the both of us toward the shoreline. "It's alright, princess. We're alright. Just hold on, yeah?"

"I can swim," I say as I try to untangle my hands from around him.

"Your doggy paddle won't get you very far. Just hang on, I've got you."

I don't argue with him, and five minutes later, he's pushing my butt onto the shoreline. It's a rocky little patch, and the drop off to get to the water is steeper than a usual beach. I've never been happier to see land.

I land on my knees, and Sully collapses to his back beside me. Shivers wrack my body as I sink my fingers into the earth, feeling the rocks dig into my skin.

I've never been more grateful to be here than I am right now. The cool night air breezes across me, sending goosebumps in its wake. It's not particularly cold here this time of year, not compared to New York. But I'm wearing ten pounds of lake water in a mesh shirt and tight skirt.

I wring out the sides of my skirt as much as I can and watch Sully's chest rise and fall in a deep rhythm. Walking on my knees until I'm leaning over him, I ask, "Are you okay?"

His eyes pop open, and something about the way the color shifted to an endless blue has me tongue-tied.

He curls upward to wrap a hand around the back of my neck and guides my mouth to his. Our tongues tangle in a kiss filled with so much passion—the kind you experience after you nearly die. One that's rooted in a zest for life and love.

I give him my weight as I lean into the kiss with everything inside me. I pour all my fear and hope and love into this kiss. It feels like a defining moment, this one. The kind that people write songs about.

I'm not sure if it's because I really thought we were going to die, but an overwhelming sense of gratitude washes over me, and tears slide down my face.

Sully pushes my face back an inch and searches my gaze. "What's wrong, Lainey?"

"Nothing. Everything. I think my adrenaline is crashing." I swallow the sob that threatens to break free as tears roll down my cheeks and fall onto Sully's chest.

"Shh, shh. It's alright, princess. We're alright." He pushes some of my wet hair off my face, leaving his hand on my cheek. I lean my head into his hand, grateful that he's still here. "We're not safe here, though. We have to move, yeah?"

I nod and press my lips to his once more before I crawl backward off of him and offer him a hand to stand up.

A slow clap starts from somewhere close by, and both of our heads turn toward the noise. My head protests the quick movement as stars dance behind my eyes and nausea bubbles up my throat.

The clapping gets louder as it picks up speed. I search the area around us, but the moon has gone behind some clouds as the rain lightens to a drizzle.

Out of nowhere, four men in black hoodies step onto the pebble beach, two on either side of us.

"James, look out!" I yell, but I'm not quick enough. One of the guys grabs him with an elbow around the neck and slams a cloth over his nose and mouth. He struggles and lands a few punches, but he's no match against whatever chemicals they used.

"Good. You're alive. Take them to my warehouse."

It's the last thing I hear before one of the guys behind me places a similar cloth over my nose and face. I don't have a fighting chance, and I'm out in seconds.

35

SULLY

I OPEN my eyes with a groan. It feels like I just went ten rounds in the ring.

"James? Can you hear me? Are you okay?" Lainey's panicked voice instantly spikes my own anxiety.

I crack an eyelid open, immediately closing it against the harsh light aimed at us. I wet my lips and open my eyes again. It's a little easier to see this time. "Lainey? You good?" A gash by her hairline is bleeding pretty steadily, and I notice a few more cuts and scrapes along her body, but she seems mostly okay. We're both secured to metal chairs in the middle of a warehouse, I guess.

"I'll be fine. I—I don't know where we are though. Some kind of warehouse, I think."

"It's alright. We'll figure it out together, yeah?"

She looks at me with her big whiskey eyes, and I know that she believes me wholeheartedly. And because of that, I make a promise to the fucking universe that I'll deliver on it. No matter what.

Another slow clap starts, and I squint my eyes against the

spotlight to view the shadowed frame of a man walking toward us.

He steps closer to us, on the other side of the light, and suddenly, I can see his face.

His very fucking familiar face.

I laugh. I can't help it. "You've got to be fucking kidding me. What the fuck are you doing here?"

"I believe you were at my house tonight, Sully."

"This weaselly little punk is the mastermind behind all this? You're Aeron Briggsby?" My eyes widen as some of the pieces fall into place.

Benny pulls his gun out and points it at Alaina's head. My heart leaps into my throat at the gesture, but pride oozes into my veins at the brave face my girl has. She tips her head back and looks Benny right in his manic gaze with a small smile.

"What the fuck are you smiling for, bitch?" He brings the gun down against the side of her head, and her head snaps to the right with a deafening crack.

Rage boils in my gut, and I feel like I'm coming unhinged. My muscles grow tight, and I flex against the zip ties holding my hands to the back of the metal chair I'm sitting in.

Apparently, he considered me more of a threat than my girl, because her hands are tied with some sort of skinny rope to her chair.

Ultimately, that will be his downfall. He's underestimated our girl, and she fucking loves a good challenge. Even now, as she slowly brings her head back to face him with blood trickling down her forehead, her fingers are busy twisting and turning the rope. I have no idea if she knows what she's doing or if she's just hoping she gets lucky.

But if there's one fucking thing in this life I believe in, it's her. She's the most amazing thing I've ever met.

And I need to buy her enough time to work herself out of those knots.

"You know, I'm not even that surprised that you're obsessed with my girl. I mean, I get it, man. She's a fucking ten in a world of fives. But there are other ways to get a girl's attention than kidnapping." I force my tone to stay conversational, so he keeps his eyes—and his fucking hands—off her while she works.

It works, and Benny swings his crazy-eyed gaze toward me. He scratches his cheek with the end of the gun as he walks two steps, so he's in front of me, head tilting to the side. "You think I'm obsessed with her?"

I hold his gaze. "Aye. I think anyone who takes as many photos as you did with a telephoto lens has an obsession."

Benny laughs, the sound crazy and manic. "I'm not *obsessed* with her." He sneers at me, throwing his arm—the one with the gun—in Lainey's direction. "You can't be obsessed with something that already belongs to you."

I see Lainey stiffen out of the corner of my eye, but I keep my gaze on the asshole with the gun. "I don't follow."

Benny sighs, then makes a big production about pulling over another metal chair. He drags it across the concrete floor, the noise cutting through the stale air with a screech. He situates the chair and sits down with a huff.

"Alaina Gallagher. The lost princess of Gallagher Industries." He sneers at me. "She was promised to me—"

"By who?" I interrupt him, risking his ire. He's not walking out of here alive, and I'm not above pumping him for information in his final moments.

He jumps to his feet and backhands Alaina, keeping the gun trained on me the entire time. I grit my teeth and swallow all the rage threatening to explode.

"Don't fucking interrupt me again." He sits back down and stares at me for a moment. When I don't say anything else, he

317

nods. "Now, as I was saying. Alaina Gallagher was promised to me by my mother. Her name was Bethany Briggsby. And she had an affair with Conan Gallagher."

My eyebrows hit my hairline. Conan Gallagher is his da? Alaina's grandda?

"Good. I see you recognize the name." He stands in one quick movement and paces in front of us with his eyes on the ground in front of him. After a minute of silence, he stops abruptly and turns to face me. "Did you know that Aeron was the goddess of war?"

I raise my eyebrows at his sudden change in topic. He doesn't wait for an answer from me.

"'Course Ma thought she was having a girl at first. She told me that, ya know, said some fortune teller foretold some formidable ruler. Ha!" He barks the noise, less a laugh and more the beginning of a mental breakdown. "Aeron means strength too, but Ma—Ma couldn't get past the Welsh meaning. She set her sights on Gallagher Industries."

Benny spins to face Alaina, eyes wild. "I met you once. Do you remember that?"

"No, I don't remember ever meeting you." Her voice is strong despite the swelling around her eye and the blood dripping down the side of her face.

Trepidation slithers inside me as I watch the exchange. The stale air. Something in the air shifts, and the hair on the back of my neck rises.

Benny rounds on her, bending down so he's eye-level. "Stop lying, Alaina! You remember it. I know you do! Ma said you'd always remember me!" Spittle flies from his mouth, landing on her face. But my girl is strong, so much stronger than I ever thought, and she doesn't so much as flinch.

She looks him in the eye. "I've never met you before last year at O'Malley's."

Something about what she said flips Benny's switch, and he lunges at her, wrapping his hand around her neck. Fear pounds against my skin, and I can't still the struggle that surges through my veins. I have to protect her. I *have* to.

"Hey! Get your fucking hands off of her before I—"

He raises the gun and points it at me. "You, what?" He moves the gun so it's against Alaina's temple. "Hmm? What're you going to do, Sully?"

"You're hurting me, Aeron." Alaina's voice is thin.

"Don't call me that!" He squeezes her neck before letting go. He steps back from her, smoothing his hair away from his face and shaking his head like he's resetting himself. "I'm Benny, your friend."

Lainey nods, never taking her eyes off of him. "Okay, Benny. Tell me about the first time we met then."

Good girl, play into his delusions to buy us time.

He widens his mouth in a twisted semblance of a smile. "I was ten and you were five. Ma brought me to the Gallagher family picnic, and before we got kicked out, she pointed you out to me. You were wearing a yellow sundress with pigtails. You were nice to me, so I decided that I was going to keep you." He stares off to the side, his eyes unfocused and his smile almost wistful. "But then Ma started yelling at my da, and I didn't have time to take you with us. I had to make sure you remembered me though, to make sure that you knew I'd come back for you one day."

Chills skate down my spine as I realize the ramifications of what he's saying. And I'm not sure if I was more afraid in a sinking car or tied up in an empty building with my girl and her psychotic uncle who thinks she's meant to be with him.

36

ALAINA

MY WHOLE BODY stills for a moment. Then a lightbulb goes off, and a long-buried memory flashes before my eyes.

"Hey, can I play with you?" a little boy asks me from the drawbridge behind me. He's older than me with shaggy dark-blond hair and dark-brown eyes. He's wearing a baseball shirt, shorts, and red tennis shoes. The longer I look at him, the more my tummy hurts. "Well, can I?"

I bite my lip as I look from him to my parents. They're talking to my grandparents. I don't really know them well, but daddy told me to be on my best behavior, and mommy told me I should always be polite. I look back at the boy and shrug a shoulder. "Alright."

"Great. We're going to be best friends, Alaina Gallagher," the boy says with a smile.

"My cousins are my best friends. And I don't even know your name." I don't want to hurt his feelings, but Mary and Maddie are my best friends.

He opens his mouth, but before he says anything, a woman starts yelling. She waves her arms in the air before she picks up a plate of food and launches it at my grandparents. A gasp leaves me when I see mommy wipe something from her shirt. Oh no, she is going to be so mad about that.

"Bucky! Bucky, it's go-time, buddy! Just like we talked about!" the

woman yells as she runs toward the playground, arms in the air, hair flying behind her.

I jump and step back, my gaze flying to my daddy. Daddy always protects me.

"I'll be back for you." I feel two hands on my shoulders, and before I know it, I'm flying through the air. The ground rushes up to greet me, and I scream.

"It was you." I lift my head to look at the man in front of me with new eyes. "You pushed me off the top of the slide. I broke my arm that day, and I never went back to see my dad's family again."

Benny's face lights up. "I knew you'd remember."

I nod slowly, feeling faint like my face drained of color. "Why did she call you Bucky?"

"Don't," Benny grits the word out, stepping into my space. "That was a nickname my ma gave me. That's not a name for you."

I will my hands to keep their exploration of the rope behind my back. I feel like I'm close to getting out. I glance around the warehouse we're in, hoping for a flash of my other two men. Frustration pounds at my skin when I don't see anything. Just the same empty space surrounds us.

"I've been waiting for you for a long time, Alaina Murphy Gallagher. Now we don't have to wait for the loophole. Once we're married, your shares will automatically shift to me, so no one can challenge my paternity." The shift in Benny is startling. He moves to kneel in front of me, and I can feel my eyes widen. "Now we can finally be together. I got rid of all our obstacles. I did that for you—for us."

"What obstacles?"

"Don't play coy, Alaina. You know what you did. What messages you were sending me." The look on his face sends the hair on my arms up. He tilts his head to the side for a moment before standing up and walking to Sully. Raising the gun, he points it at Sully. "If you're worried about your little boyfriend, don't be. He won't be here much longer anyway. I mean, I wasn't going to kill him yet, but I guess I can be a little flexible." He shrugs his shoulders like I've seen athletes do before they compete.

My heart flies to my throat when he adjusts his grip on the gun. "Wait! Wait, Benny. Don't kill him yet. Please."

Benny narrows his eyes at me. "Are you asking because you're still pretending to love him? Or because you want to do the honors?"

I wet my lips and swallow, my fear nearly choking me. "I, uh, thought we could torture him first." I force the words out, and it takes everything inside of me to not flinch at the lie I just spewed.

His shoulders sag in relief. "Of course. I knew you'd remember." Benny's eyes light up as he stares at me. He reaches back and scratches his head. "I got a little worried, you know, when I saw that cocksucker show up at O'Malley's for the third week in a row. Two weeks could be a coincidence, but after three, I just knew something was going on. So, I took matters into my own hands."

"You joined the Brotherhood," Sully says, even-toned.

Benny cuts a glare his way, his eyes flashing with malice. "No, I tried to join, but you guys wouldn't just let me in! So, I had to prospect and *pay my dues*." He rolls his eyes before a manic smile covers his face, and his chest puffs out. "And did you ever suspect me, James Fitzgerald? Hmm? No, I don't think you did." Benny chuckles. "Ma said it was too risky to move there and play the game. Said I should just take her in one fell swoop."

My gut churns at all these . . . these delusions.

Benny steps in front of Sully, his gaze beseeching. "But I

wanted her to love me, y'know? Anyone can just take, but I wanted her to come to me willingly."

Sully nods, his eyes guarded as he watches the breakdown happening in front of us. Can someone break down if they're already broken?

My fingers twist, and I roll my wrist so I can widen the small amount of slack in the rope. My nails rake across the coarse material, and I feel one lift up. The bite of pain grounds me, and I refocus on Benny. I missed something he said, too busy focused on freeing my hands.

"And it was going so well. I would see her every Friday night, but it was taking too long. And I needed to give her a push. So, I hired some people to help me. People will do anything for the right price."

"So, you hired Liam Mason to kidnap her," Sully says.

Benny's back goes ramrod straight. "No. Ma said the best way to get her to love me would be to become her hero. So, I paid Liam to take her from O'Malley's. He wasn't supposed to hurt her. I"—he pounds his chest with his open hand—"I was the one who was supposed to save her. Me."

He starts to pace again, three quick steps to the left and three quick steps to the right. "But then Ma said I should just leave Alaina be. But I can't do that." He pulls at his hair with one hand, spinning to look at me. His eyes are wide, his pupils blown. "You were supposed to be mine! And then they fucked it all up."

I freeze when he sets his manic gaze on me. I'm so close to freeing one wrist—and that's all it takes. Ava taught me that I shouldn't waste energy focusing on freeing both wrists at first. Just one at a time. And sometimes, like this situation, I'm not actually tied to anything, so if I free one wrist, then it's all over.

Of course, once I'm free, I have another problem to face. Fear threatens to drown me, but I shove that down deep. One breath in and one breath out.

First. Free your hands.

Next. Get the gun.

Then. Untie Sully.

That's it. Those are the only three things that matter right now. I can do it. I know I can. I'm so close to slipping my hand free. I just need another minute. I just need to keep Benny talking for sixty more seconds, and then it'll be okay. It'll all be okay.

Benny extends his gun, pointing it at Sully's head. "You had to go and ruin everything. I was the one who was going to rescue her from the cabin! You and your brothers, who put their filthy lips on her. Now she's not perfect anymore!" Spittle flies in the air as he screams at us. He licks his lips and takes a deep breath as sweat beads on his brow. "That's okay. It's okay, I've got a plan to clean her up real good. But first, it's time to—"

At last, my hand slips free of the rope. Blood trickles down from two broken fingernails and my wrists are raw and bleeding, but I fucking did it. I don't wait, the element of surprise is my best asset right now. I let go of the lid on my rage and use it to my advantage.

I spring up from the chair and charge him. I go low, my shoulder colliding with his thighs. I don't pay attention to his surprised shout; I just focus on the moves that Sully taught me. With a guttural yell, I extend my legs, pushing up as hard and fast as I can. I feel his body weight pushing me back into the earth, but I funnel my rage and adrenaline into that super-human strength you hear about when mothers need to save their kids.

A cry rips from my soul as I fling him up and over my shoulder with everything inside of me. It wasn't a clean sweep, but it's enough for him to land awkwardly on the ground, half on his back.

My chest heaves and my eyes search for the gun. He must've dropped it, because it's on the ground next to his knee. I dive for it, and my fingers curl around the handle just as his knee collides with my temple.

"You fucking bitch! Now look what you made me do!" Benny roars as he sits up. He reaches for either me or the gun—I'm not really sure. I can't see very well with the stars dancing in my vision. Nausea soars up my throat and I fight the urge to vomit.

"Hey! Hey you shrimp-dick motherfucker! I bet you did fuck your mother, didn't you, you fucking piece of shit," Sully yells.

It's the perfect distraction. Benny switches his focus to him, and with a hand on the floor for balance, I gain a few precious seconds to beg the room to stop spinning.

I push to my feet, leaning to the right before shaking my head to clear some of the dizziness. Benny advances on Sully, and it feels like time slows down.

In a second, I see what my life would've been like had I not kissed Rush or met Wolf at Summer Knoll or reconnected with Sully. Or worse, what my life would've been if Benny succeeded.

"Stop!" I scream the word, splitting the air with the impact. Both men freeze, though Sully wasn't moving much anyway. "Turn around. Slowly."

Benny spins on his heel, raising his arms up, palms facing me. The look on his face spells murder. He takes a step toward me. "Give me the gun, Alaina. I'll take care of him."

I widen my stance and throw my shoulders back. "I said stop, Aeron."

I watch the fake polite mask fall away and the monster he is looks back at me. It's not the same kind of darkness that my men have—the kind that will bend and make room for me, the kind that has some boundaries even if they aren't conventional.

No, this is the kind of darkness that's solid, impenetrable. Oily and laced with poison so once you're ensnared, you'll never be able to leave. Benny will never be free of his darkness. It's been rotting him from the womb.

He tips his head down and looks at me from underneath his furrowed brow as he takes another step toward me, blocking my view of Sully. "I told you to call me Benny."

I don't back up, even if my instincts are screaming at me to move. "Why? Is it because calling you Aeron Briggsby reminds you that your father is my grandfather? Because 'Benny' makes you feel as normal as you can. But you're not normal, Aeron. You're a sick fuck."

The light above me buzzes before flaring and dying with a pop, plunging us into more darkness. I glance at the darkened area above my head and back to Benny, who's inching toward me. "I will shoot you if you don't stop moving."

Back-lit by the spotlight on the floor behind Sully, Benny slides toward me, his moves serpentine. He cocks his head to the side as he stares at me. "No, I don't think you wi—"

A crack fills the air, echoing off the metal walls around us. Bright red blooms on Benny's light-blue shirt on his chest. Surprise colors his face, his jaw slackening.

High-pitched ringing fills my ears, and everything feels like it's in half-time.

Benny stumbles back a few steps, dragging his hand to his chest. He presses against it as he stares at me with betrayal in his gaze.

"How could you, Alaina? You're mine." He stumbles another couple of steps to the side. "We were meant to be together."

I keep the gun trained on him as I try my best to ignore my quivering muscles.

Tattooed fingers cover my hand and gently push the gun down. I follow the familiar tattoos until I see the familiar espresso-brown eyes I love.

"Shh. It's alright, baby girl. You did good," he murmurs.

It's like his words unplug the dam, and I feel my body sigh, pitching to the left. He catches my stumble and wraps his arms around me. I bury my face in his chest and breath in his familiar sandalwood scent.

He takes the gun from me and clicks the safety on before tucking it in his pants. It's only then I see Rush cutting Sully's zip ties. Benny lies still on the concrete floor, his lifeblood slowly spreading out around him. I can't seem to tear my gaze from the widening red stain.

Sully runs to me and scoops me up into his arms. "Jesus Christ, princess. You nearly gave me a heart attack." He puts me back on my feet and runs his hands up and down my arms, his gaze scanning my body almost frantically. "You're okay?"

"I'll be okay. Are you hurt?"

He pulls me in for another bone-crushing hug and I squeeze him with my arms around his middle. "I'm fine. You did good, Lainey. I'm so proud of you."

Rush joins us with his phone to his ear, murmuring something too low for me to hear. My head pounds loud enough that it's drowning out a lot of other noise, making it hard for me to concentrate.

Rush tucks his phone into his pocket as he looks me over while Sully's arms are still wrapped around me. "Called in an order for donuts. Quinn owes me one."

My brow furrows. *Donuts?*

"Good. Let's get the fuck outta here. I'm ready to go home," Wolf grumbles, leading the way out of the warehouse.

"What about Gallagher Industries? What are we gonna do about that?" Sully asks.

Rush looks at me for a moment. "That's up to Alaina. But she doesn't have to make a decision now. I bought us some time."

"Another favor to Quinn?" Wolf asks.

"Nah. I set Roisin free on their servers. She's going to freeze everything until we're ready to make a decision. What's left of the legitimate board has already been informed of the change."

I nod, grateful for that. I don't know what I'm going to do with a company I didn't know existed until a few weeks ago. And I'm in no condition to make that kind of decision.

"Take me home, Rush."

He leans forward and brushes his lips against my head. "Let's go home."

37

ALAINA

three months later

THE SUMMER FLEW BY.

When we got back from Ireland, I spent three days recovering at their apartment. It mostly consisted of sleeping and eating and processing—and making good use of those luxury showers they all have.

A week after that, we spread my mother's ashes in the ocean per her request. We held a small gathering for just our family and mom's closest friends. I visited her headstone for the first time last week. It's in a nice cemetery overlooking some hills. And I had one made for my dad too.

I spent the rest of the summer enjoying the hell out of life. Time with Mary and Maddie—neither of which will spill any details on their summer flings. Time with the King sisters when they were around. I've learned so much from each of them, and we've all grown close over the last couple of months. And lots of time with my men. I spent every night with them at their apartment, and many, many hours in their beds. I think I convinced them to order a custom-made bed that will comfortably sleep all of us last night.

I truly went through a sort of sexual awakening, and it lit a fire in me that I don't ever see going out. Not while these three crazy-hot men are mine.

After Roisin froze everything with Gallagher Industries, and Rush helped me understand all the reports she gave us, I decided to dissolve the company. I didn't agree with the way they conducted business, and I don't want any part of a company that Aeron manipulated and used to terrorize me. I'm still in the process of everything, but I think after it's all said and done, I'm going to donate a healthy chunk to a local mental health charity.

Even though my craziness has calmed down considerably, things are still crazy but not in the I'm-getting-kidnapped kind of way. More like I-have-three-boyfriends-who-all-do-questionable-things way. And oh, I have three boyfriends.

That's something that's hard to believe sometimes. Every day I feel lucky that I get to call them mine, and that's only increased tenfold since we got back from Ireland.

"You're awfully quiet. Get that good dick last night?" Maddie asks as she waggles her brows at me.

"Jesus, Maddie!"

"What?" She shrugs. "You've got three super-hot boyfriends. You should be getting some every time you turn around." Her smile is mischievous as she seals another box closed.

"Are you speaking from experience?" I tease Maddie with a twist of my lips. "How are those Rossi boys these days?"

"*Men.*" Maddie sighs. "They're men, and they're—" She fans her face dramatically.

Mary scoffs. "Ever since the couple weeks you spent with Matteo, you've been different. More . . ."

"It's called a sexual awakening, Mary. I highly recommend it. Wouldn't you, Laincy?" Maddie looks at me with her eyebrow raised and her fist on her hip.

"I'm not getting in the middle of this," I say as I fold the top of the last box over and tape it closed.

I tune out my cousins' banter as I take in our dorm suite that we shared for the last six years. We'd planned to share it for college too, but I've decided to move into the apartment the guys share. A decision that was proposed by Rush, of course, but Wolf and Sully were both quickly onboard.

After spending most nights this summer with them, the thought of staying at my dorm room most nights sent a pang of anxiety through me.

I'll still attend classes here, so it's not like I'll never see them. Plus, the apartment isn't *that* far away. But it'll be weird not to live with them anymore. The university already assigned them another roommate, and today's the day she moves in, so I have to get the rest of my stuff out.

All that's left are these two boxes. Rush and Wolf already took the small rental trailer over, and Sully's here helping me pack up and move the last few boxes before we follow them.

The man in question pushes open the door with a finger, his dark-blond hair hanging over his forehead in that messy way that makes me a little crazy.

"Just these two, princess?"

"Yep. Last two. Careful though, that one's heavy. It's all my books," I tell him as he bends down to pick it up.

He flashes me a cocky grin. "I'll be back for the last one in a few minutes."

"Alright." Patting the top of the closed box, I turn to face my cousins. They're quiet now, both them facing me with matching expressions of sadness on their faces.

"We're going to miss you," they say at the same time.

A smile curves up the corners of my lips. "You guys know I love it when you do your twin mojo thing."

"We know," they answer together again. Maddie rolls her eyes with a smile.

"I'm just across the city. And we'll still see each other during the day for classes like usual."

Mary nods a few times, and my sinuses tingle, threatening tears. We look at each other for a moment before all three of us stride toward one another. We meet in the middle and throw our arms around one another for our favorite triangle-style hug.

A watery laugh breaks free from my lips. "I don't know why I'm upset. I'm happy, excited even, to move in with them. I just . . . I'm just going to miss living with you guys."

"Us too, Lainey. But you're right. We'll still see each other all the time," Maddie says with a sniff.

A knock on the open door breaks our moment up, and as one, we turn to face the doorway. A girl with long lavender hair stands in the doorway, a duffel thrown over her shoulder and a suitcase in her hand. But what captures my attention is the person behind her.

"Diesel? What are you doing here?"

"Hey, Alaina. This is Edie, my baby sister." He gestures to the girl in front of him.

Edie rolls her eyes and steps inside the suite with an outstretched hand. "Hey." Maddie's the first one to reach her, bypassing her hand and pulling her into a hug. "Okay then. So you're the hugging type."

Maddie pulls back with a grin. "Sure am. I'm Maddie, and this is my sister, Mary."

It's not until I turn my head and look at Mary that I notice all the color drained from her face. "Are you okay?"

"Hm? I'm fine."

"It's good to see you, Mary," Diesel says, his gaze roaming all over my cousin.

My brow raises and then I remember. "That's right. You two spent time together earlier this summer."

"Not really." Mary's reply is too quick, her voice high-pitched. "I, uh, forgot something." She turns on her heel and all but runs down the hallway to her room, slamming the door.

"Okay . . ." I drag out the word as I turn to look at Diesel. A smile twists his lips, but otherwise, he doesn't say anything.

Sully walks in then, breaking up this awkward moment. They do that guy greeting thing where they shake hands and half hug with chin lifts.

I turn toward Maddie and Edie. "Hey, I'm Alaina. It's nice to meet you."

"Oh, I know all about you, girl," Edie says with a teasing smile.

I tilt my head to the side. "Good things, I hope."

She steps closer to me and lowers her voice. "Is it true you have three boyfriends?"

Mirth dances in my veins as I answer, "Sure is."

Edie whistles. "Damn. Teach me your ways!"

"Ready, princess?" Sully asks from next to me. He's holding the last box, and I take a moment to admire his muscles stretching his Clash tee.

"No, really. Please teach me how to get that," Edie murmurs, her gaze going hazy as she stares at Sully.

I get it. He's a walking wet dream. It's probably good that she didn't come earlier when Wolf and Rush were here.

I laugh. "I think you'll fit in here just fine, Edie. And I'm sure we'll be seeing lots of each other.

"Count on it!"

I walk out of the place I called home for the last six years with a light heart and a bittersweet smile.

I'm ready for the next adventure life throws at me. I know with all three Fitzgerald boys at my side, it's going to be one amazing ride.

EPILOGUE

THREE YEARS LATER

"CONGRATULATIONS, graduating class! It's my absolute pleasure to be the first to wish you the best of luck in all your future endeavors. And may you use all your knowledge that you acquired to live a long and prosperous life."

I tune out the guest speaker's words. Honestly, I don't find them all that inspiring. These days, I have something else that inspires me.

I let my gaze wander the massive crowd as I discreetly wipe the bead of sweat rolling down the side of my face. These polyester caps are the worst, and when it's ninety degrees outside, it feels like I've got my head in an oven.

There, sitting off to the side, are the faces I was searching for. Mary and Maddie sit next to some familiar faces. I look forward to next year when our positions are switched, and they're roasting in these polyester saunas while I cheer them on from the stands. All those extra classes paid off, and I graduated early.

The Kings take up an entire section with their entourage. All five sisters insisted on receiving four tickets each, and somehow, they figured it out.

Wolf leans back against the bleacher seat behind him, spreading his legs wide. And Sully scowls at the people sitting down the bench from them, despite the wide berth surrounding all of them.

But Rush—Rush stares right back at me, a small smile playing around his lips, eyes twinkling.

I have a sneaky suspicion that he knows my secret, but he would never tell them before I'm ready.

The guest speaker asks everyone to rise and move our tassels from one side to the other to signify change.

And with a hand on my slightly rounded stomach, I move my tassel to the other side.

I'm ready to begin my next journey, and with Wolf, Rush, and Sully next to me, I know it's going to be the best thing I've ever experienced. A once-in-a-lifetime sort of cosmic love.

A NOTE TO READERS

I cried a little when I wrote the end at the end of this book, but I absolutely love how their story turned out, and I hope you do too! These characters will forever hold a special place in my heart, and I'm so grateful to each and every one of you for joining me on their journey.

I can't thank you enough for taking a chance on a new author and a new series. And I hope you stick around, because I already have the next series planned!

drumroll

Maddie's series is next! I left some breadcrumbs throughout Alaina's trilogy, so I'm sure you have an inkling who her love interests will be. It's *Gossip Girl* meets *Sopranos*, and it's available on Amazon! Turn the page to read an excerpt!

You can read Gilded Princess here: books2read.com/gilded-princess

As always, my DMs are always open if you need to slide in there and chat—or proverbially throw your kindle at me! ;)

I would be honored if you had the time to leave a brief review of this book! Reviews are the lifeblood of a book, and I would appreciate it so much.

xoxo
—pen

Stay in the loop!
Join my newsletter
Join my Facebook group, Penelope's Black Hearts
Follow me on Instagram @authorpenelopeblack

Continue reading for an excerpt from

Gilded Princess:
The Five Families book 1
Available now on Kindle Unlimited

PROLOGUE

MATTEO

SWEAT CLINGS to the back of my neck and underneath my arms, but I don't move to wipe it off. I'd rather suffer the persistent itch than incur the wrath of my father.

He's on a warpath tonight.

Earlier at dinner, he told me to lay out my Sunday best and be ready at midnight. It was time for me to step into my role as a member of our family. Ma started crying, and then Dad got mad, and they started arguing—per usual.

I don't understand why she's so upset. I'm old enough to help out the family now, and it'll be good for me to learn how to do more stuff and make Ma's life easier.

Plus, the more focus I keep on me, the less time my father has to terrorize anyone else.

So here I am, baking in my black suit I wear to church on Sundays in my father's office. The air feels heavy this time of year, but my father's office doesn't have any windows to open. It's all dark wood and dark rugs. Intimidating and lightless, just like him.

My uncle Abram and my cousin Nico sit in the chairs across from my dad, who's reclined behind his massive oak desk. He's smoking a cigar and staring at the two men in front of him, his posture deceptively calm. His shoulders are loose, and he's casually puffing on his cigar.

It's a demeanor I've seen all too often.

Tension simmers in the air, so thick I can almost see it. Dad asked me to stand behind him to the right and stay against the wall, no matter what. I'm not entirely sure what will happen tonight, but I can't imagine it's anything good.

Uncle Abram adjusts his tie and cranes his neck to the side to release the tension as the silence continues.

Without a word, Dad slides open his top desk drawer and pulls out a gun.

"Half-assed murder plots are for boys. In this family, you act like a man. So, let this be a lesson to you, son. If you want to be the king, you have to kill the king."

My eyes widen as I glance between the gun my father placed on the desk and my cousin. He's eight years older than me, so we didn't exactly grow up together, but I always looked up to him. My palms feel clammy, and I stifle the urge to wipe them off on my pants. I know he hates it when I fidget.

"Do you understand why this is necessary?" Dad looks over his shoulder at me, waiting for my answer.

I nod, even though I don't understand. The memory of Dad making me watch *The Godfather* years ago flashes before my eyes. He told me this is what I should expect from our family, and at the time, I thought he was being sarcastic.

I was wrong.

He turns toward Uncle Abram. "The choice is yours, brother. Either you or him."

If he's surprised, Uncle Abram doesn't show it. He stares back at Dad, unflinching. "You know my choice, Angelo." He turns toward Nico. "I love you, son. No matter what."

Dad nods twice before he picks up the gun and points it at Uncle Abram. He fires two shots. Uncle Abram's body jerks violently, tipping over the chair.

I jump with each crack of the gun, unable to stifle my shock.

He shifts his hold to point it at Nico. His eyes look like saucers, bloodshot and wide.

"Uncle Angelo, please. D-d-don't do this. My dad—"

A gunshot splits the air.

Nico's eyes shine with tears, disbelief slackening his jaw. He pushes a hand to his chest, and bright red blood oozes out between his fingers.

Another shot lands in between his eyes, Nico's head jerking back in a swift, violent motion.

"I don't give second chances." His words are slow and contemplative like he's wondering if there's rain in the forecast today.

I bite my lip hard enough to draw blood, desperate to keep my fear inside. Anything to keep my dad's focus off of me.

It's selfish. A coward's move. But at twelve, I know I can't win against him.

Not yet.

Continue reading book 1 in Maddie's story, Gilded Princess, here: books2read.com/gildedprincess

WHEN IT ENDS EXCERPT

When It Ends:
A Dark Apocalyptic Romance
Available now on Kindle Unlimited

What if the end is just their beginning?

They stole my heart at fourteen and broke it before we even graduated high school.

It's been five years since I've seen them, and only a twist of fate reunites us when the mountain falls. It's the first disaster in a predicted apocalypse—a string of natural disasters that could be catastrophic.

It's the beginning of the end of everything.

Finis omnibus.

Old feelings reignite and new feelings blossom as the four of us form an unbreakable bond. As the world starts to fall and society fractures, it's a race against time for survival.

Available now on Kindle Unlimited
bit.ly/WhenItEnds

CHAPTER ONE

AMELIA

"You come here often?"

I pause the maze I was creating with the condensation on my vintage tumbler. The drinkware is one of the only memorable things about this aging bar-casino on the outskirts of Las Vegas. The overused and uninspired pickup line is the cherry on top of my shitty-day sundae. I've had just enough alcohol and too little sleep in the last two days to reel in my annoyance.

"Do you have a small dick?" I ask over my shoulder without turning around to see the face that goes with such a terrible line.

It's not the first time I've thrown such a crude question at someone. And nine times out of ten, it gets the message across succinctly.

I'm not interested. Move along.

Much to my surprise, laughter greets my question instead of curses or insults. It's a carefree sort of sound, like he just heard a surprising joke. It's enough to pique my interest, and I swivel the barstool to the right and look over my shoulder.

He's tall enough that I have to tip my head back to take him in. Wavy dark blond hair, long enough to pull back. The blinking lights from the bank of slot machines behind us highlights his in flashes, but it's too dim in here to make out the exact color of his eyes. But they're dark, alluring even.

His laughter tapers off, leaving only dimples to wink at me as if to hint at his mischief. He mock-wipes a tear from underneath his eye as he slides his hands into his pockets, leaving his thumbs hooked over the top of his dark-wash jeans.

A charcoal gray tee stretches across his chest, the once-white logo faded. I idly wonder if he bought it purposely distressed or if it's worn from use. I'm not discreet about my perusal, but this mystery man only tips his head to the side. Patiently waiting until I've had my fill.

Heat warms my cheeks, but it's not from being caught. I like that he's giving me space to ogle him, it's oddly endearing. I pause when our gazes connect.

The low lights from the bar don't do either of us any favors, I'm sure. And the blinking lights from the machines to his right give his beard—a day or two past a five o'clock shadow—a tie-dye effect. On any other man, I'm sure it would take down his desirability factor, but he gets another point in his favor because it only heightens everything about him.

He nods and shoots me a secret sort of smile. I almost kick myself when my own lips curl up in response. He takes it as an invitation and slides onto the stool next to me.

My brows hit my hairline at his presumption, but I manage to check myself when I realize that it's one of the only available seats at this little bar. And I did just check him out for two solid minutes.

My new seatmate signals to the bartender with a finger and a friendly smile. I sip my drink, letting the harsh burn of rum and Coke—heavy on the rum—coat my throat as I watch him interact with one of the two men behind the bar of Tennessee Pete's.

You can tell a lot about a person by the way they interact with people in the service industry. I've seen firsthand the way people treat waitstaff and baristas and bartenders. It doesn't matter how attractive this guy is, I'm not going to sleep with him if he's rude.

Wait.

Where did that thought come from? I wasn't—I'm not going home with anyone tonight. I'm just here for a few drinks, maybe a burger and fries, and then I'm crashing for a few hours before I finish driving. I'm on the last leg of my cross-country trek home. Sleeping with some random man I meet in an old casino slash motel isn't on my to-do list for the day.

I suck my bottom lip as the man next to me orders a whiskey sour with a smile and some small talk, gesturing with his hands. He does have nice hands though, big palms with long fingers.

Sipping my drink, I tilt my head and study him. He reminds me of someone, but I can't quite put my finger on who. A celebrity, maybe.

He flashes those dimples at the bartender, and little tendrils of lust sit up and take notice.

I suppose having a little fun never hurt anyone.

He half turns his body toward me. "So, do you come here often?"

"Are we back to that so soon?" I counter quickly with an arched brow. "Should I repeat my question now too?"

He smiles at me and drags his teeth into his bottom lip. "Is that an invitation?"

My nose wrinkles as I stare at him for a moment, mentally chastising myself. Sure, he's good-looking. Okay, so maybe more than good-looking. He's downright hot. That kind of attractive that would make you throw your morals out the window.

Kind of like what I just mentally decided a moment ago.

I am going to be so disappointed if he turns out to be an asshole.

I sip my drink and eye him over the rim of my glass. "Does that line ever work for you—the come here often one."

The bartender, an older man with salt-and-pepper hair, smiles and slides his drink across the lacquered oak bar. The stranger next to me snatches it in a smooth movement, the veins in his forearms popping as he grips the glass. He accepts the drink with a murmured thanks. "I don't really hit on women often."

"Wow. I don't even know how to take that."

"Nah, it's not like that, Blondie. More like I don't really hang out in casinos or bars."

I roll my eyes at the nickname. Having naturally dark blonde hair seems like it would be great, right? Except it's this in between color—lighter and brighter in the summer and darker and moodier in the winter. Or if we're living in a city that actually has seasons like we have for the past couple years. "Blondie, huh? Because I haven't heard that one before."

He dips his chin. "Alright, what's your name then?"

I smirk with just a touch of incredulousness, but it gives me an idea. I've been in a deep '90s movie binge lately. "Cher."

"Damn. What are the odds, Cher? I'm Sonny." He holds out his hand, but since there's not much space between us, his finger-tips skim the fabric of my olive green tank top.

I can't help it. He's too charming for his own good. Or maybe mine. "What are the odds," I murmur as I slide my hand into his. His grip is firm but not overpowering, and he pumps our hands for a few seconds too long, his dark eyes twinkling as they hold my gaze.

* * *

"Wait, wait. You're telling me the most embarrassing thing

you've ever done is run around in the snow?" I arch a brow at him, my mouth pinched to the side in disbelief.

"Well, I was thirteen, remember? And they'd dared me to run around the house in my boxers. I still remember feeling that adrenaline rush of doing something dangerous and catching the eye of the hottest girl in the eighth grade. It was a win-win."

I laugh as I point a French fry smothered in cheese sauce at him. "That doesn't sound even remotely embarrassing!"

He grins and pops his own cheesy fry into his mouth. "Well, that's because you haven't heard the embarrassing part yet."

"You tripped! Lost your boxers! Shrinkage!" My voice increases in volume and glee with each guess, laughter tripping over my words.

Sonny shoots me a mischievous side-eye. "Where do you think this story is going?"

I lift a shoulder and swipe another fry through the addicting sauce. "Spill then."

He blows out a breath, his cheeks puffing out to the sides. There's an air of playfulness around him. It's a welcome respite from my usual type. He lowers his head and looks at me from underneath his long, dark lashes. "Well, you see, my granddad came home and nearly had a stroke seeing my lily-white ass running around the house—"

"Ha! You did lose your underwear then!"

He straightens with a smirk. "Did I mention I was thirteen? Jake Thompson bet Carl Hannoc twenty bucks that I wouldn't actually streak. So I doubled-down on both of them and walked out with eighty bucks. And an earful from Pops. He read me the riot act in front of everyone that night—before he let me put my clothes on."

The mental image of an eighth-grade Sonny running around and trying to impress his friends plants itself in my mind, and I can't stop the giggles before they're out. He chuckles along with me as he takes another fry.

We switched out cocktails for soda and greasy food an hour ago. For bar food, it's pretty good. The company helps too.

The cheese sauce drips down onto the edge of my hand. I'm not one for messy hands while I eat, but I'm having too much fun to care right now. I toss the fry in my mouth and halfheartedly wipe my hands on the crumpled up napkin next to me.

I shake my head a little. "I can't even remember anyone's name from eighth grade, let alone memories so clearly like that."

I guess that's not entirely true. There are a couple people I don't think I'll ever forget, no matter how old I am. I take a sip of my Cherry Coke, the bubbles fizzing on my tongue.

"So you were thirteen, and that was ... how long ago?" I squint with a tilt of my head.

"You fishing for my age, Cher?" He smirks. "I'm an open book, baby girl. All you have to do is ask."

I pause at the new nickname, my brows slanting low over my eyes. I don't know how long we've been chatting, but either it's long enough for him to read me—which seems unlikely—or it's a throwaway pet name. One of those things guys use all the time because they can't remember the girl they're on top of.

Disappointment threatens to prick my bubble of fun, but I shove it out of the way at the last second. Two baskets of fries and a handful of drinks doesn't mean anything more than exactly what it is. And I won't be here long enough to find out if he's a player or not, so no skin off my back.

Ready for more? Read When It Ends here!

THE WREN EXCERPT

Continue reading for an excerpt from
The Wren: A Dark Arranged Marriage WhyChoose Romance
Available now on Kindle Unlimited

As the firstborn King, I should be the heir of the Irish Syndicate.

Instead, my father wants to marry me off to the highest bidder to fund a war I don't believe in.

My carefully controlled life starts to unravel, spiraling out of control faster than I can stop it.

And then I meet them and everything stops for a moment.

Tall with perpetual smirks and covered in tattoos, they remind me what it feels like to live.

They remind me that I don't need someone to save me.

I'm a King. I can save myself.

CHAPTER ONE

NICO

"I've found your wife."

I stop in front of the wet bar on the side wall of my office in one of our nightclubs, Violet Oak. I don't bother responding to my father just yet. I need something to settle my nerves. I thought my fucking heart was going to explode out of my chest when my father walked in my club ten minutes ago.

My long-lost sister, Madison, and her men were scattered around the private level of our club and the dance floor. They were here on my assurances that they'd be safe.

Fucking hell—they wouldn't have even been in Las Vegas is I hadn't given my sister's husbands my word that our father was out of town on business. And then that asshole strolls in like he's owns the place, and I looked like a fucking fool.

There's little more in this life than I despise than looking like a fool.

And just when I was starting to build a relationship with her, too.

Fuck.

I exhale and resist the urge to stretch my neck from side to side to release the tension. We're in my office on the third floor of Violet Oak, and it's a sharp contrast to the dimly-lit levels of the club below.

Light gray walls with charcoal gray accents, wrought-iron up-light sconces make the room feel larger with their beams of white light. My desk sits to the right, with two safes behind it, and plush leather seats facing the front.

"Did you hear me, son? I said I've found your new wife."

I nod my head, an acknowledgement that I heard him and nothing more.

"Let's wait until Rome is here." I make sure to keep my voice even. I learned a long time ago it's best not to needle Dad when he's worked up like this. It never ends well for anyone.

I grab four old fashioned glasses from the shelf next to me and line them up. I splash three fingers of my favorite barrel-aged sixty-proof whiskey in all four glasses. I pinch the edges of two glasses between my fingers and thumbs and turn around, handing my father his drink first as a sign of respect.

I set my brother Tommy's glass in his open palm and leave our youngest brother Rome's drink on the edge of my desk. "Rome should be up here in a minute."

Dad sips his drink, but he's unable to wipe the excitement from his face. I haven't seen him this excited in a long time, so it must be something really good.

"And where is your brother, Romeo?"

Sneaking our sister and her men out of the back door.

"Probably fucking someone in one of the private rooms on the second floor," Tommy drawls.

Dad grins, his mouth stretched too wide. "I bet you make a killing on those private rooms, eh, son? This is the city of sin, after all."

I catch his innuendo, but I do my best to not think about my father using private rooms all over this city with his many, many mistresses.

"We do alright." I sip my drink and look out of the tinted window to the levels below. To everyone down there who happens to look up, all they see is an iridescent window.

Dad puffs out his chest, his chin tipped high. "So modest, my oldest son. It's why you're so successful."

I swipe the droplets of whiskey on my lower lip with my tongue, my eyes narrowing at my father. He's untrustworthy on the best of days, and I can count on one hand the times he's ever given me a compliment.

He's buttering me up for something.

Rome walks in, saving us from the silence. It was nearly reaching uncomfortable territory.

"Ah, perfect timing as always, son," Dad says.

Rome closes the door and beelines for the drink on the edge of the desk. "What did I miss?"

"Now we can begin. I came home early to tell you the great news: I've found Nico's wife." He pauses and stares at us with a smile.

My father's face turns redder the longer the silence stretches, but I genuinely don't know what to say. I lean my hip against the wall and watch the anger play out over my father's face.

Maybe I've been a bit overserved tonight, not that I would admit that to anyone, because I'm not nearly as concerned with him right now. Or more likely, Tommy told the bartenders to pour with a heavy hand tonight to celebrate.

"What the fuck does that mean?" Tommy finally asks what the three of us are all thinking.

I'm still stuck on the fact that Dad cut his business trip short by five days. Guilt gnaws at my frayed nerve endings. I would've never forgiven myself if Dad ambushed our sister tonight.

Dad hates being questioned, and Tommy's tone was laden with derision. He glares at my brother as he sinks his one hand in his pants pocket and cradles his drink to his abdomen with his other. He strolls around my office, pausing next to me by the window and perusing the club-goers shedding their inhibitions on the dance floor.

It's all a ruse.

He doesn't care about the people, and he doesn't care about the club. We own and run it ourselves, one of the few legitimate business ventures we have. And he's always taken it as a personal offense, as if we should desire to be under our father's thumb forever.

"It means that I've secured an alliance for us. One that's going to expand our operations tenfold," he says with his back to us, his gaze still out the window.

Now I know that I've had too much to drink, because it takes me longer than it should to connect the dots.

"An arranged marriage. That's what you meant about a wife." It's not a question.

Dad spins on his heel, his face lighting up with genuine glee. About the prospect of *more*—as if we need more money or men or territory or fucking stress in our lives. We have enough wealth to last us several generations over.

But Vito Santorini is a selfish, greedy man. And the boss of the west coast Syndicate. It's a deadly combination.

"Yes, son. Think of all we can achieve together once we cement this alliance." His eyes dance with excitement, and I can't recall the last time I saw him this excited. Not even when he recently saw our sister—his daughter—for the first time in fifteen years.

"You've never pushed this before. Why now?" Tommy asks.

Dad clenches his jaw and glares at Tommy before switching

his gaze to me. "Arranged marriage isn't uncommon in our life, you know that."

I nod a few times. "Aye, I do. But Tommy's right. Why now? What else is going on?"

His greed and desire to grow the family business? Sure, that I buy. But this sudden arranged marriage proposal that isn't needed to grow? I'm not buying it.

He waves a hand around the air in front of him, batting our questions away like they're gnats. "As I was saying, negotiations went exceptionally well, and in two months' time, our two families will be joined. Then, my son, we'll be one step closer to unstoppable."

Rome sits forward in his chair. "Which family?"

"Is there a contract?" I ask at the same time.

Uneasiness churns in my lower gut. The idea of Dad brokering some deal with someone that involves my life has me feeling a little murderous. It's an unexpected feeling.

"Of course. But before you ask, no, you don't get to see it."

I tense. "Why?" I can't think of one good reason why he'd keep the contract—the name of my soon-to-be wife—from me.

"Eager to find your bride?" He leers at me, and that earlier feeling of apprehension rises.

So I do what I always do and play along.

I force my expression into something closer to his and lift a shoulder. "You know me, Dad."

He claps me on the shoulder. "All in due time, son."

The Wren now available on Kindle Unlimited
bit.ly/theWren

ACKNOWLEDGMENTS

Thank you to my readers! Thank you for hanging in there with me on all those cliffs too, sending all of you air hugs for that!

To all the bookstagrammers and bloggers and readers that send me messages and create beautiful edits for my books—I'm still in awe. Thank you so, so much. On my most insecure days, I pull up your edits and kind words and never fails to reignite my spark.

Thank you to my husband who's always the first one to champion me. I don't know what I'd do without you! And I love that you're always shouting, "My wife's a romance author!" with pride to anyone you pass on the street. I'm so grateful for you— and your delicious food!

To my tiny humans: I love you both more than all the stars in the sky. And you have to wait until you're older to read Mommy's books.

To my wonderful family who's encouraged and supported me —thank you, thank you! And thank you to each and every one of you who read my books—I'm lookin' at you, Grandma + Grandpa!

Thank you to the amazing babes on my ARC team! I'm so grateful to have you in my corner!

To my amazing beta readers Claire, Tracey, and Savy. I'm so thankful for each of you. Your kindness and support means the world to me.

To Savy—I'd be lost without you, girl. One day, I'm going to hop on a plane and then tackle-hug you.

And finally, I want to thank each and every author who has been so kind and wonderful while I asked a million questions. There are far too many of you to thank, and for that alone, I'm forever grateful. There are a lot of wonderful people in this community, and I'm so glad to be apart of it.

ALSO BY PENELOPE BLACK

THE BROTHERHOOD SERIES

Wolf

Rush

Sully

THE FIVE FAMILIES SERIES

Gilded Princess

Twisted Queen

Vicious Reign

Fractured Dynasty

THE BLUE KNIGHTS MC SERIES

Coming Spring 2023!

STANDALONES

When It Ends:

A Dark Apocalyptic Romance

THE KING SISTERS WORLD

The Wren

The Wild

Made in the USA
Monee, IL
27 November 2024

71459350R00225